## Two-Timin'

A tall, skinny hombre walked out and turned toward the Prairie Queen Saloon.

That was bad timing, but it could have been worse, Longarm supposed. He pulled back from the whore as she continued to kneel in front of him, patted her on the shoulder, and said, "Thank you very kindly, darlin', but I got to go now—"

She lunged toward him again, her hand reaching under his slicker, but she wasn't making a grab for his manhood this time. Instead, she snagged the butt of his Colt, dragged it out of the holster, and flung herself to the side.

"I got it, Fred!" she screamed. "I got his gun! Kill the son of a bitch!"

Cussing the woman for her treachery would have been a waste of time, breath, and energy. So Longarm just jumped after her instead, for a couple of reasons. He wanted his gun back, and he hoped that Gaunt might hesitate for a second if he saw that the woman was in the line of fire.

He should have known better about the second thought. Gaunt had already stopped, spun around, and slapped leather. Colt flame bloomed in the rainy darkness as the man started shooting.

# TABOR EVANS

# LONGARM

## AND THE GOLDEN EAGLE SHOOT-OUT

JOVE BOOKS, NEW YORK

**THE BERKLEY PUBLISHING GROUP**
**Published by the Penguin Group**
**Penguin Group (USA) Inc.**
**375 Hudson Street, New York, New York 10014, USA**
Penguin Group (Canada), 90 Eglinton Avenue East, Suite 700, Toronto, Ontario M4P 2Y3, Canada
(a division of Pearson Penguin Canada Inc.)
Penguin Books Ltd., 80 Strand, London WC2R 0RL, England
Penguin Group Ireland, 25 St. Stephen's Green, Dublin 2, Ireland (a division of Penguin Books Ltd.)
Penguin Group (Australia), 250 Camberwell Road, Camberwell, Victoria 3124, Australia
(a division of Pearson Australia Group Pty. Ltd.)
Penguin Books India Pvt. Ltd., 11 Community Centre, Panchsheel Park, New Delhi—110 017, India
Penguin Group (NZ), 67 Apollo Drive, Rosedale, North Shore 0745, Auckland, New Zealand
(a division of Pearson New Zealand Ltd.)
Penguin Books (South Africa) (Pty.) Ltd., 24 Sturdee Avenue, Rosebank, Johannesburg 2196,
South Africa

Penguin Books Ltd., Registered Offices: 80 Strand, London WC2R 0RL, England

This is a work of fiction. Names, characters, places, and incidents either are the product of the author's
imagination or are used fictitiously, and any resemblance to actual persons, living or dead, business
establishments, events, or locales is entirely coincidental.

LONGARM AND THE GOLDEN EAGLE SHOOT-OUT

A Jove Book / published by arrangement with the author

PRINTING HISTORY
Jove edition / October 2007

Copyright © 2007 by The Berkley Publishing Group.
Cover illustration by Miro Sinovcic.

ISBN: 978-0-515-14358-4

JOVE®
Jove Books are published by The Berkley Publishing Group,
a division of Penguin Group (USA) Inc.,
375 Hudson Street, New York, New York 10014.
JOVE is a registered trademark of Penguin Group (USA) Inc.
The "J" design is a trademark belonging to Penguin Group (USA) Inc.

PRINTED IN THE UNITED STATES OF AMERICA

10  9  8  7  6  5  4  3  2  1

# Chapter 1

A cold rain was falling in Wichita.

Longarm huddled in a doorway, cussing under his breath as he watched the building across the street. Water dripped from the brim of his flat-crowned, snuff-brown Stetson. Even though he was wearing a slicker, water got under it, too, and wormed frigid trails along his skin.

A fella couldn't keep a smoke going in weather like this, so he chewed on the end of an unlit three-for-a-nickel cheroot until it got soggy like everything else. He spit it out in disgust.

Longarm hoped the bartender he had talked to earlier in the evening had been right. He hoped that Felix Gaunt was in that building over there with a whore. And he sure as hell hoped that Gaunt hadn't paid the soiled dove for the whole night. In that case, Longarm was going to get mighty cold, wet, and tired before morning.

He crossed his arms over his chest, glared at the place he was watching, and considered walking over there and kicking down all the doors until he either found or didn't find the man he was looking for. Sure, that would irritate

1

some folks—nobody liked to be interrupted in the middle of a good poke, or even a mediocre one, for that matter—but that wasn't Longarm's lookout. All that mattered to him was corraling a killer.

Felix Gaunt had come to the attention of the United States government when he tried to sell some diseased beef cattle to an Indian agency in Wyoming Territory. If the agent in charge there had been dumb enough not to notice, or corrupt enough not to care, both of which were distinct possibilities, Gaunt could have gotten away with it.

But the Indian agent, a man named Roger Carlson, was not only good at his job, he was conscientious, too. When he realized what Gaunt was trying to pull, Carlson called him on it and threatened to report him to the army. As it turned out, the cattle were not just diseased. They were stolen, too, and Gaunt didn't want to be linked to them.

So he had lost his head for a minute, pulled his gun, and shot Carlson dead, landing himself smack-dab in more trouble than he would have been otherwise, because now he was wanted for the murder of a federal employee.

Billy Vail had explained all this to Longarm a week earlier in Vail's office in Denver, as well as handing over the information his clerk, Henry, had gathered on Felix Gaunt.

"It's no surprise that Gaunt tried to solve his problems with a gun," Vail had said. "He's been doing that for a long time. Killed his first man when he was just a kid, and he's gotten himself quite a reputation as a fast gun since then."

"Sometimes a rep like that don't have much to do with the truth," Longarm had said as he blew a smoke ring toward the banjo clock on the wall of Vail's office. "Things get blowed up all out o' proportion."

"If you'll read those reports, you'll see that Gaunt deserves his notoriety. He's killed more than a dozen men in gunfights and is suspected of involvement in all sorts of shady deals. Nothing that involved federal offenses, though, until he gunned down that Indian agent, Carlson."

"So now you're sending me after him?" Longarm had said.

Vail hadn't answered directly. He hadn't needed to. "Gaunt was last spotted in Hays, Kansas, a couple of days ago. Hustle over there and pick up his trail, Custis."

Longarm had hustled, but Gaunt was gone from Hays by the time he got there. Not particularly surprised by that, Longarm had asked around until he found out that Gaunt had boarded an eastbound train a couple of days earlier. By now he could be back East somewhere.

Gaunt had lived in the West all his life, though, so Longarm thought it doubtful he had lit a shuck for Philadelphia or New York or Boston. Even if he had, Longarm was charged with tracking him down, so the big lawman had headed east, too, checking at each stop to make sure Gaunt hadn't gotten off the train there.

The fact that Gaunt lived up to his name was a stroke of luck. Tall and skinny almost to the point of looking like a corpse, he was the sort of fella folks tended to remember once they saw him. A porter at the depot in Wichita recalled seeing him get off the train. In fact, Gaunt had asked the man for the name of a good but not too expensive hotel. In return for four bits, the porter had given Longarm the name of the same hotel.

After that it was just a matter of showing his badge and bona fides to a clerk at the Morrison Hotel and describing Gaunt. The clerk had admitted readily enough that a man matching Gaunt's description was staying there, but he had registered under the name Fred Garvey. For all Longarm knew, that was Gaunt's real moniker. Names were a sort of fluid thing for hombres on the wrong side of the law.

"Fred Garvey" did his drinking at a saloon down the street from the hotel. Before setting out for it, Longarm took a room in the same hotel and pulled his rolled-up slicker from his warbag, since it had been starting to rain when he came in. On his way out, he admonished the clerk not to say anything to Garvey about somebody looking for him, if he happened to see him before Longarm caught up to him. Doing so would put the clerk in Dutch with the law,

3

Longarm pointed out, and got an emphatic promise that the clerk would do no such thing, honest to God.

Longarm hadn't flashed his credentials in the Prairie Queen Saloon, since it was the sort of place where doing so could backfire on a fella. But in return for a couple of dollars that would go on the expense account for Henry to fuss about, along with all the other such bribes Longarm had handed out since leaving Denver, the drink juggler had admitted that a man matching Gaunt's description had left the place a short time earlier with a whore named Betsy. Betsy's crib was in a nearby building known for such activities, and for another dollar the bartender had told Longarm where to find it.

The rain had settled in good by now, and there was no place Longarm could get out of it and still keep an eye on the door of the building where Gaunt and Betsy had gone. So he stood there and let the rain drip on him and got more peeved by the minute.

The place probably had a back door, but Longarm couldn't be in two places at once, and besides, he figured it was likely Gaunt would return to the Prairie Queen for another drink once he got through screwing Betsy, before he returned to the hotel for the night. Anyway, if he lost Gaunt's trail, he could pick it up again at the saloon or the hotel.

"Hello, cowboy."

The rain made enough racket so that Longarm hadn't heard anybody approaching him. He had left one of the slicker's buttons undone so he could reach in and grab the Colt from the cross-draw rig on his left hip, and his hand started in that direction as he turned his head to see who had spoken to him. He stopped the draw when he realized it was a woman. She wore a rain cape and a hat with a feather on it that looked a mite bedraggled because of the rain.

Longarm couldn't see her face very well because there wasn't much light in the street on this rainy night, but she seemed reasonably young and pretty. Her hair under the feathered hat was fair, he could tell that much for sure.

4

He gave the brim of his hat a polite tug, spilling a few drops of rain that had collected there. "Ma'am," he said. "Not a very good night for a lady to be out."

"Or a gentleman," she said. "I have rooms across the street, if you'd care to get out of this dreadful weather for a while."

The offer came as no surprise. Longarm had already figured out she was a whore. Unless there were extraordinary circumstances, a respectable woman wouldn't be out this late on a night like this.

For some reason she hadn't found anybody to come back to her room with her, so she must have thought it was good fortune for her to find a man waiting right across the street from the place where she lived and worked. Longarm was sorely tempted to take her up on the offer. At least it would be dry in there, and the woman probably had something to drink, too.

But he was working, and after spending the time and money to get this close to Felix Gaunt, he didn't want the varmint to slip away from him. So he shook his head and said, "Sorry, ma'am. I'd best stay right here."

"Oh, that's a shame. I was looking forward to getting to know you." She paused. "If you'd like, I can stay here and converse with you for a while."

She was offering to let him do her standing up, right there in the doorway. Longarm heard an edge of desperation in her voice. He slipped a hand inside his slicker and found a coin in his vest pocket. Pressing it into her hand, he said, "I'm glad to help out, ma'am, but you should get in out of the rain. You don't have to stay here."

"You don't want my company?"

"It ain't that."

The coin disappeared inside a little purse. "I have to do *something* for you." She put a hand on his chest. "Lean back against the wall there."

He started to argue with her and insist that she didn't need to do him any favors, but he figured it might hurt her pride if he did. Anyway, he thought as she got down on her knees in front of him, he could still see the door across the street from here, no matter what she was doing.

She undid a couple more buttons on his slicker and sort of tented it over herself as she leaned in close to him. Her skilled hands unfastened the buttons on his fly, hauled out his by now semierect manhood, and brought him to full hardness in a few strokes.

"My lands!" she said. "There's no way I can get all of that in my mouth!"

She tried, though, Longarm had to give her that. Opening her lips wide, she enveloped the head of his shaft. On a cold, dank night like this, the warmth of her mouth felt even better than it would have under other conditions.

Longarm's eyes narrowed. If he hadn't been watching for Gaunt, he would have closed them and given himself over to enjoying what she was doing to him. As it was, though, he had to keep watch, so he forced his eyes to stay open a little.

She was mighty good at it, no doubt about that. Her tongue swirled around the head, her lips applied just the right amount of suction, her hand stole inside his trousers and long underwear to cup his balls. She had him ready to explode in a matter of minutes.

Longarm drew in a deep breath and let go, emptying himself into her mouth. He felt her swallowing. She had more than earned that coin he gave her. Longarm wondered if he could slip it past Henry as a legitimate expense, then pushed the idea aside. Having some sport with the four-eyed young clerk was one thing, but cheating Uncle Sam was another. Longarm decided that he could still pay for French lessons his own self, thank you very much.

That's what he was thinking as the whore squeezed the last drops out of him and the front door of the building across the street opened. A tall, skinny hombre walked out and turned toward the Prairie Queen Saloon.

That was bad timing, but it could have been worse, Longarm supposed. He pulled back from the whore as she continued to kneel in front of him, patted her on the shoulder, and said, "Thank you very kindly, darlin', but I got to go now—"

She lunged toward him again, her hand reaching under his slicker, but she wasn't making a grab for his manhood this time. Instead, she snagged the butt of his Colt, dragged it out of the holster, and flung herself to the side.

"I got it, Fred!" she screamed. "I got his gun! Kill the son of a bitch!"

# Chapter 2

Cussing the woman for her treachery would have been a waste of time, breath, and energy. So Longarm just jumped after her instead, for a couple of reasons. He wanted his gun back, and he hoped that Gaunt might hesitate for a second if he saw that the woman was in the line of fire.

He should have known better about that second thought. Gaunt had already stopped, spun around, and slapped leather. Colt flame bloomed in the rainy darkness as the man started shooting.

Longarm reached to shove the woman down, but she brought his Colt up and fired. The muzzle flash half blinded him, and the roar of the shot pounded against his ears. He went diving to the street, knowing that her hurried shot had missed. The next one might not, though.

And he still had Gaunt throwing lead at him, too. A slug whined off the pavement near him. Wichita had paved its main streets not long before, so that bullets ricocheted from them now instead of burying themselves in the dirt. That was progress for you.

Longarm rolled and came up on his feet. He tore his

slicker open, not caring that he popped some buttons. Another bullet whistled past his head as he darted behind a parked wagon. He didn't know if the shot had come from Gaunt or the whore, whom he assumed was Betsy, the one Gaunt had brought here from the Prairie Queen.

Gaunt had spotted him somehow, Longarm thought, and sent Betsy out the back door to circle around and find out what he was doing lurking across the street. When he reacted like he did to Gaunt leaving the building, Betsy had been certain he was a lawman and acted accordingly, grabbing his gun and disarming him.

Or so she thought. Longarm reached inside his coat and closed his hand around the watch chain that looped across his chest from one vest pocket to the other. A big gold turnip watch was attached to one end of that chain, but at the other end was welded a two-shot, .41-caliber derringer. The hideout gun had saved Longarm's bacon more times than he liked to remember. Maybe it would again.

Gaunt would have to get closer, first, though. When it came to accuracy, Longarm could spit farther than the derringer's effective range.

He crouched behind the wagon and heard the impacts as several more slugs thudded into it. A glance along the street told him that Betsy had disappeared. He didn't know if she had retreated to leave him to Gaunt, or if she was trying to work her way behind him.

He got his answer a minute later when she sprang back into view from the mouth of an alley and started emptying the Colt at him from a distance of about eight feet. She held the gun in both hands, but even so, the recoil of the heavy revolver was too much for her. The barrel rode up as she fired.

Staying low, Longarm went into her in a diving tackle, taking her around the waist and driving her back into the alley. Both of them sprawled on the ground. He got a hand on one of her arms and slid his fingers along it until he came to her wrist. She had the gun in that hand. He plucked it free of her grip.

Unfortunately, it was empty, so the derringer was still the only firepower he had. And Gaunt was charging across the street now, spraying flame and lead through the rain.

Longarm rolled away from Betsy and snapped a shot at Gaunt. The .41-caliber slug didn't hit the killer, but it came close enough to make him break off his attack and duck to one side. That was all Longarm intended to accomplish with the shot. He came up on his knees, pressed his back against the wall of a building, and stood up. At the same time, his fingers took fresh cartridges from his pocket and began thumbing them into the Colt's cylinder.

As soon as the gun was loaded, Longarm burst out of the alley and triggered a couple of shots at Gaunt, who threw himself behind a water barrel. Before Longarm could fire again, something hit his legs from behind and toppled him off his feet. He put his left hand down to catch himself and scraped it on the rough pavement.

Betsy scrambled on top of him, flailing at him with her fists. Longarm knew she was the one who had tackled him, and he was angry with himself for being brought down by such a little bit of a woman. She must have been really fond of Gaunt, though, because she whaled away at Longarm with hysterical strength.

Longarm swept an arm around and flung her to the side, then rolled over and came up on his knees, lifting the Colt. He couldn't see anything to shoot at, because Gaunt was gone.

The sound of rapid footsteps that faded away into the rainy night told Longarm that his quarry had cut and run. In the rabbit's warren of buildings, streets, and alleyways that downtown Wichita had become, the chances of finding him again were slim. Longarm was about to try anyway, when he heard a groan behind him.

He glanced over his shoulder and saw Betsy still lying on her back where he had thrown her. Longarm didn't think he had flung her aside hard enough to hurt her, but maybe she had made an awkward landing and broken a leg or arm or something. He grimaced as he pondered his options—go after Felix Gaunt, or check to see how badly Betsy was hurt.

Muttering a curse under his breath, he turned toward the woman. He couldn't just walk away and leave her to her fate, whatever that might be. Devotion to his job was one thing, but he still wanted to be able to sleep at night.

Dropping to a knee beside her—but not too close, in case she was shamming and wanted to make another grab for his gun—he asked, "How bad are you hurt, ma'am?"

She didn't say anything, but he could hear her breathing now. It had a raspy, bubbly sound to it that he didn't like. Frowning, he dug a lucifer from his pocket and shielded it with his other hand while he snapped it to life with his thumbnail. The match flared for only a few seconds before the dampness extinguished it despite Longarm's sheltering hand, but that was long enough for him to see the dark stain on the front of her dress.

"Damn it," Longarm said.

He couldn't hear Gaunt's running footsteps at all anymore. The man was gone. Longarm holstered his gun, leaned forward, and ripped Betsy's dress open. His fingers explored her body and found the bullet hole in her right breast. From the sound of her breathing, the slug had gone on through her lung.

Longarm cast his mind back over the past few hectic minutes. To the best of his recollection, he hadn't fired any shots in Betsy's direction. That meant the bullet that had struck her had come from Gaunt's gun. Like most owl-hoots, Gaunt didn't give a damn about what happened to anybody else. He had blazed away at Longarm despite the threat that stray bullets represented to the woman. And Gaunt was the one who had sent her into harm's way to start with, damn what passed for his soul.

Longarm knew the woman was hit bad enough that she couldn't last very long, even if she got medical attention. He leaned over her and said in a low, urgent voice, "Betsy! Betsy, can you hear me?"

Her face was wet from the rain falling on it. Droplets

clung to her eyelashes. Her eyelids fluttered and then opened. He could see that much, although the light was so bad he couldn't tell if she had really heard him.

He took one of her hands in both of his. Her skin was cold and clammy. "Betsy," Longarm said, "Gaunt shot you. Tell me where he was going, and I'll even the score for you."

He didn't hold out much hope that she would spill any useful information. She had to be really fond of Gaunt, because she had tackled Longarm even after she'd been shot, the depth of her emotions overcoming for a short period of time the damage that had been done by the bullet.

"F-Fred . . ." she whispered. "Fred, you got away from . . . that bastard . . ."

Longarm knew he was the bastard in question. She had mistaken him for "Fred Garvey." And he felt like a bastard as he leaned still closer and said, "That's right, honey, I got away, thanks to you. You really helped me out. When I leave Wichita, I'll take you with me if you want to go."

"You . . . you'll take me to . . . Texas?"

"Damn right," Longarm told her. "We'll go to Texas. We'll go to . . ." He let his voice trail off, hoping she would supply a more specific location.

Instead she said, "You'll w-win. I know you . . . will."

Win? Win what?

Longarm was about to ask her when her hand clutched tighter at his and she husked, "Is it . . . morning already? The sun's out . . ."

The night was as dark and rainy as ever, but as a last long sigh came from Betsy's lips, Longarm knew she had seen the sun again. He hoped it was a good morning for her.

He laid her hand on her breast, over the bullet hole, and stood up. The street was still deserted. Folks in this part of town probably didn't get too excited when they heard gunshots. The law might show up to investigate sooner or later, but on a cold, wet night like this, it was going to take a while.

Longarm couldn't just leave her lying in the street. He picked her up and placed her body in the back of the open

12

wagon he had used for cover a short time earlier. At least that way the dogs couldn't get to her.

With grim lines etched into his face, he stalked back to the Morrison Hotel. The clerk gave him a nervous look as he strode into the lobby, so Longarm walked right across the threadbare carpet to the desk, reached over it, and got hold of the clerk's shirt and tie. The gent let out a frightened squeak as Longarm hauled him halfway across the desk.

"Garvey came hurrying in here a little while ago, didn't he?"

"I . . . I didn't see—"

"Said he'd come back and kill you if you told anybody you'd seen him, didn't he?"

Longarm saw the truth in the clerk's wide, frightened eyes, and a shake got it out of him.

"Yes, he . . . he was here! He said if anybody came looking for him, I . . . I was to lie!"

"Did you tell him about me being here earlier?" Longarm wanted to know.

"I didn't, Marshal! I swear I didn't!"

If the clerk was telling the truth—and Longarm thought he was too spineless not to—then Gaunt might not know that there was a deputy United States marshal on his trail. He probably had Longarm pegged as a lawman, or maybe a bounty hunter or a Pinkerton, but he might not realize that Longarm would follow him all the way to Texas if necessary. A small advantage at best, but Longarm wouldn't turn it down.

He relaxed his grip on the clerk's shirt. The fella's collar had been twisted so tight he was starting to turn a mite blue in the face, so he was grateful when Longarm let go.

"Take me up to his room."

The clerk was rubbing his throat. "I'm really not supposed to—"

A glare from Longarm shut him up and made him reach for a passkey.

A couple of minutes later they were upstairs in the

13

second-floor room that "Fred Garvey" had rented. Longarm didn't know what, if anything, he would find there, but he wanted to take a look around anyway. The wardrobe was empty, and so was the trash can. Gaunt hadn't left anything on the bedside table except a few pinched-out butts of the quirlies he had smoked. Longarm looked around, sighed, and shook his head in disgust. Texas was a mighty big state, and he had been hoping for something that would point him in the direction Gaunt intended to go.

He was turning away when he spotted something sticking out just slightly from under the bed. He bent over, grasped it, and pulled it out. In his hand he held a folded newspaper. When he opened it, he saw that it was a two-day-old copy of the Wichita *Herald*. Gaunt had probably dropped it on the floor and kicked it under the bed by accident, then forgotten it was there.

Longarm didn't figure the paper would do him any good and was about to toss it back on the bed when a story on the bottom half of the front page caught his eye. The headline read *SHOOTING CONTEST IN TEXAS*.

Before dying, when she thought she was talking to Gaunt, the whore called Betsy had said she knew he would win. As Longarm scanned the story, he felt his pulse quicken. This might be what he was looking for after all.

The story was about a competition scheduled to take place on a ranch belonging to somebody named Edmund Corrigan. Longarm had never heard of Corrigan, but he gathered the hombre was as rich as Midas, because in addition to having a huge ranch in West Texas, he also owned a railroad. He liked to throw his money around, too, because he was sponsoring this contest, which was intended to find the fastest draw and best shot in the West. As a prize, the big winner would receive a life-sized statue of an eagle.

That didn't sound like much of a prize at first, but then the story went on to explain that the eagle statue was going to be coated with a thick layer of gold, making it worth a small fortune, maybe as much as a hundred thousand dollars or even more.

14

Longarm smiled. Felix Gaunt had a reputation as a fast gun, and he had to be a good shot, or he wouldn't have survived for as long as he had. A man like that would have a hard time resisting the lure of such a prize.

Longarm tossed the newspaper on the bed, turned to the still-nervous clerk, and asked, "You happen to know when the next train to Texas leaves?"

# Chapter 3

The sound of the hammer striking the anvil was like music to the big man's ears. He had been working at this blacksmith business for a couple of years now and hadn't grown tired of it. Sure, it was hard physical labor, what with stoking the forge, working the bellows, and swinging the hammer, but he had never minded that. It beat shooting people, and getting shot at.

And too much of the time, that was exactly what Raider's job as a Pinkerton had consisted of.

So one day he had up and quit, sending off a telegram to William Wagner, Allan Pinkerton's second-in-command in Chicago, saying that he was done. He had quit before, but this time it took. Raider had gotten dragged back into one case after his resignation, but since then he had been here in Arkansas, living near some of his relatives and plying an honest trade. Turned out he was a pretty darned good blacksmith, too. Folks came from miles around to get him to do jobs for them.

The only thing that hadn't worked out so far was his desire to find some gal to marry up with. His dream of living a quiet, peaceful life included a wife and some young'uns. He had courted some of the eligible women in the area, but none of those courtships had worked out. Too many mamas were anxious to find husbands for their old-maid daughters, so that even a battle-scarred old hellraiser like Raider looked acceptable after a while.

Take Chastity Doolittle, who was surely misnamed. "Chastity" was a condition with which she hadn't been familiar in a good many years, and when it came to messing around with men, she didn't do little; she did a lot. Pretty much anything they asked her to do, in fact. As a result, she had attained twenty years of age without a husband, which her mother deemed a shameful state of affairs. Most of the boys in the county had already had ol' Chastity, though, so while they were quick enough to slip over to her folks' place and rattle some gravel against her window as a signal for her to come out and have a good time with them, none of them wanted to stand up in church with her and promise to cleave to her for the rest of their natural-born days. She'd done cleaved too much for that.

Raider liked Chastity just fine. She had a wild mane of red hair, an eager, athletic body, and a bawdy laugh that made a man's soul feel good. She was a mite young in years, but she liked to say that she had an old spirit, and Raider agreed with that. He considered her a good friend and enjoyed romping with her, be it in a barn or on a nice grassy hillside under some pine trees, but she just didn't fit into the vision that had prompted him to leave the Pinkertons.

Raider took the horseshoe he had been shaping from the anvil and used the tongs he gripped it with to plunge it into a barrel of cool water. The hot iron hissed, and several tendrils of steam rose from the water.

The sound of hoofbeats made him look up from the barrel. Three men on horseback were reining their mounts to a halt in front of the blacksmith shop. They rode ugly, raw-boned mules, and they themselves weren't any prettier than the mules were.

As the men dismounted, Raider saw that one of them

was short and wide, with massive shoulders and dangling arms like an ape. His jaw was covered with a bristly black beard, and a thatch of black hair stuck out from under a battered old hat crammed on his head.

The second man was a head taller, a scrawny sort of fella with long, greasy blond hair and an Adam's apple so prominent it stuck out from his neck like a tent pole. The third hombre was the most normal-looking of the bunch, until you took a gander at his eyes and saw how small and close-set they were. He looked like the sort of gent who giggles all the time for no good reason, Raider thought.

He didn't know any of the men, but he didn't have to know them to dislike them. Some might say he was jumping to conclusions and forming an impression based solely on appearances; he thought of it as being a shrewd judge of character based on his years of experience as a detective. Also, he knew a damn crazy hillbilly when he saw one, having been accused of being of that persuasion his own self from time to time.

Raider took the horseshoe from the water and set it aside to finish cooling. Then he put the tongs down and walked toward the front of the blacksmith shop, calling through the open door, "Can I help you boys?"

The fat one said, "We're lookin' for a son of a bitch called Raider."

"He ain't here right now," Raider said. "Something I can do for you?"

"When'll he be back?"

Raider shrugged his shoulders. "With that shiftless scoundrel, who knows? I swear, if he didn't have me to hold down the fort, this here blacksmith shop would go under in a month's time. I'll be glad to give him a message for you, though, when he comes draggin' in."

The tall, scrawny blond one leaned over and whispered something into the fat one's ear. Raider caught a few of the words—"supposed to be," "black hair," "mustache," "big fella," and "like him." The one with the close-set eyes didn't

pay any attention to the conversation. He stood there holding the reins of all three mules and giggled, pretty much
like Raider expected.

The fat one glared at Raider and said, "My brother
Theodore informs me that you match the description of the
son of a bitch we're lookin' for. Are you sure you ain't this
fella Raider?"

"I been mistook for him in the past," Raider said, "but I
ain't him." He started backing up slowly, toward the hammer he had left lying next to the anvil.

"You know who we are?"

"Can't say as I've had the pleasure."

"I am Roscoe Burkett, and this is my brother Theodore
and my other brother Varney. We are the Burkett brothers."

Raider nodded and said, "Pleased to make your acquaintance, boys," even though that was a bald-faced lie. He
didn't think there was anything pleasant about getting to
know the Burkett brothers.

Roscoe Burkett went on, "I am also the betrothen of
Miss Chastity Doolittle. You know her?"

"I've heard the name," Raider hedged. He tried to keep
the surprise off his rugged face. He hadn't heard anything
about Chastity being engaged to anybody, much less to a
repulsive varmint like Roscoe Burkett, who had about a
month's worth of dirt on his face and smelled worse than
the mule he'd ridden in on. He wondered how Chastity's
mama felt about that. There was desperate, and then there
was *desperate*.

"Thing of it is," Roscoe continued, "when I told Chastity
her and me was gettin' hitched up, she said she couldn't
marry me. Said she was in love with a fella name of Raider,
who had a blacksmith shop over here."

Now that really was a surprise. Raider had had no idea
Chastity was in love with him. But she probably wasn't,
not really, he decided. She had just thrown out the first
name she could think of to try to convince Roscoe Burkett
she couldn't marry him.

"So I come over here to find this son of a bitch Raider and kill him," Roscoe said, "and that way Chastity won't have no reason not to marry me."

*Other than gagging every time you get within five feet of her,* Raider thought. He said, "I don't think you have to worry about Raider. I know him pretty well, and I don't think he's got any plans to marry this gal Chastity."

"When it comes to gettin' hitched, it don't matter about the fella's plans, only the gal's," Roscoe said.

Which was sure enough true, Raider thought, and proof positive that philosophy could come from the strangest damned places, like the mouth of Roscoe Burkett. He'd have to have a talk with Chastity and find out just what her true intentions were, assuming that he lived through this encounter with the Burkett brothers, of course.

"Well, I got work to do," Raider said as he reached for his hammer. "If you want, I won't say nothin' to Raider about you fellas comin' by lookin' for him—"

"It's him, I tell you," Theodore burst out, grabbing Roscoe's shoulder and giving it a shake for emphasis. "That's Raider! I seen him at a barn dance once! I remember now!"

Roscoe's piggish eyes narrowed as he took a step forward. "Is my brother right?" he demanded. "Are you Raider, mister?"

"Would I tell you if I was," Raider said, "since you already told me you plan on killin' him?"

Roscoe and Theodore looked at each other. "He's got a point," Roscoe said.

Varney laughed and suggested, "Kill him anyway. If he ain't Raider, we ain't lost nothin' but a little time."

Roscoe and Theodore nodded. "I always said you was the smart one in the family, Varney," Roscoe said. "And if this fella *ain't* Raider and we kill him anyway, maybe it'll scare Raider out o' this part o' the country."

"Damn right," Theodore said.

None of them were carrying guns as far as Raider could see, but each of the brothers had an Arkansas Toothpick sheathed at his waist. They reached for the big knives at the

20

same time, with the clear intention of carving Raider into little pieces.

Raider snatched up the hammer and backed off some more. "First one of you boys gets within arm's length is gonna get his head stoved in," Raider threatened.

"Get 'im, Varney!" Roscoe said.

Varney giggled and rushed at Raider, slashing his Arkansas Toothpick back and forth in front of him.

Raider ducked under the blade and swung the hammer, aiming at Varney's knee. Despite the threat he'd made, he didn't really want to kill these peckerwoods. He had put enough men in the ground in his life. He didn't have any compunction, though, about busting the hell out of Varney's knee and putting him out of the fight. The young idiot might limp for the rest of his life, but at least he'd be drawing breath.

Varney was fast physically, if not mentally. He dodged the hammer blow and lunged at Raider. The point of the Arkansas Toothpick snagged the thick blacksmith's apron that Raider wore. That turned aside the knife enough to spare Raider more than a foot of cold steel in the guts, but it didn't keep the Toothpick from raking a fiery trail across the big man's side.

Raider roared in pain and anger and swung the hammer again. It cracked hard against Varney's left shoulder. Varney screamed and stumbled backward, dropping the knife.

Roscoe and Theodore spread out, putting several feet between them. If they came at Raider like that, he wouldn't be able to stop both of them. As Varney collapsed and curled up in a whimpering ball, clutching at his shattered shoulder, his brothers advanced across the blacksmith shop toward Raider.

"Aw, hell," Raider mumbled. He dropped the hammer, being careful not to let it drop on his toes. Then he lifted his hands to shoulder level and started backing away. "Don't kill me, boys," he pleaded. "I'm sorry I hurt poor Varney. Please don't kill me."

"Got to, now," Roscoe said. "You hurt one Burkett, you hurt 'em all."

Raider's back bumped against the rear wall. Nowhere else for him to go now.

So he reached under the coat that was hanging there on a nail and pulled a revolver from the holster that hung behind the coat. He leveled the gun at a point between Roscoe's eyes and asked, "Does that mean if I blow your brains out, I got to shoot all your kinfolks, too?"

# Chapter 4

Raider had meant the vow he had made not to kill again when he left the Pinkertons. Circumstances had forced him to break that vow a couple of times, and he was afraid this might work out that way, too.

But it would take a mighty devout Quaker to stand there without fighting back and let a couple of lunatic hillbillies chop him up, and Raider had never claimed to be a member of that particular sect or any other that believed in non-violence under all circumstances. There were a few crazy assholes in the world who needed to be shot, and even though Raider would have preferred that somebody else be the one to oblige them, he was ready to take up the challenge if need be.

Roscoe swallowed hard and said, "Easy on that trigger, hoss. That hogleg's liable to go off."

"Damn right it will," Raider said, "if you don't gather up your brothers and get the hell out of here right now."

Roscoe squinted at him. "You're him, ain't you? You're Raider."

"I am for a fact," Raider said.

"You're the fella what Chastity's in love with."

"I wouldn't know about that."

"You been screwin' her!" Roscoe accused.

Raider snorted in disgust. "Hell, so have half the fellas in the Ozarks. Maybe more'n that, for all I know."

"Yeah, but you're the one she likes the best. She told my cousin Drusilla that there ain't nobody who diddles her as good as you do."

Raider hadn't been aware that Chastity felt that way, even though he recalled now that she had jumped around and moaned quite a bit while he was plowing her field. He made one more attempt to get the brothers to be reasonable, although he doubted that was possible with Varney still lying on the ground whimpering from the busted shoulder.

"Look," Raider said, "I don't have any intention of gettin' hitched with Chastity Doolittle. You're welcome to her if she'll have you, Roscoe. You can even tell her I said so."

That made Roscoe even madder. "Hell, if I tell her that, it'll hurt her feelin's. She's got her cap set for you."

Raider shook his head and said, "I'm sorry. But that's the way it is. I'm sorry your brother made me whack his shoulder with that hammer, too. Now, you boys best put those pigstickers up and take poor Varney to the doc. Your business here is done."

"Not hardly," Roscoe said. But he slid his Arkansas Toothpick back in its sheath and motioned for Theodore to do likewise. Theodore looked like he didn't care for it, but he did as he was told.

"He hurt Varney," the tall, skinny hillbilly said.

"I know, and we'll get even with him for that," Roscoe said. "If we don't get out o' here, though, he's gonna shoot us."

"You got that right," Raider said.

Muttering and cursing, the two uninjured Burkett brothers lifted Varney onto his feet, setting off a fresh round of screaming as the movement caused broken bones in his shoulder to grate together. "Get him on his mule," Roscoe told Theodore, then turned back to Raider. "I'll see you again, big man. Until then, you stay the hell away from Chastity."

"Stop runnin' your mouth and git while the gittin's good," Raider said, emphasizing the words with a jerk of the Colt's barrel.

Roscoe left the blacksmith shop, with a scowl on his face that was as dark as the thunderheads that sometimes built up over the mountains. Theodore had lifted Varney onto one of the mules. The process had prompted lots of yelling and carrying on from the youngest Burkett brother. Roscoe and Theodore mounted up, too, and rode out, with Theodore leading Varney's mule. Raider could still hear the racket Varney was making even when the three men were out of sight.

He didn't holster the Colt until he couldn't see nor hear any sign of them. Then he sat down on a barrel and sighed, wondering why it was that trouble seemed to like cropping up in his life. It wasn't like he went hunting for it anymore. He had stopped doing that when he resigned from the Pinkertons.

He had more horseshoes to make, so he got back to work. But his heart and mind were both heavy as the afternoon passed.

Raider lived in a cabin a short distance down the creek from the farm that belonged to his uncle Jess and aunt Hannah. When he'd first returned to the Ozarks, he had stayed with his uncle and aunt while he built the cabin, then moved in thinking that soon he would have a wife to bring there. Things hadn't worked out that way, but Raider tried not to brood about it. He often took his meals with Jess and Hannah, and he went there that night since they were expecting him.

Their son, Johnny, Raider's cousin, came to supper, too, along with Johnny's wife, Joanie, whose belly was starting to get round with their second child. Their first one, a boy named Enos, was a little over a year old and a real handful. Raider was fond of the tyke, though. It was good for an old bachelor like him to be around kids once in a while. He enjoyed the warmth of the farmhouse, the smell of food cooking, and the friendly talk and laughter that filled the air along with the delicious aromas.

Raider waited until after supper to say anything about the visit that the Burkett brothers had paid him. He hadn't wanted to ruin the meal. Once he and Jess and Johnny were sitting in rocking chairs on the front porch, though, with their pipes going and little Enos playing in the yard in the slanting rectangle of lamplight that came through the open front door of the farmhouse, Raider told his uncle and cousin about what had happened.

"I know them damn Burketts," Jess said when Raider was finished. "No-account, the whole bunch of 'em."

"I remember bein' in school with that Varney," Johnny said. "He ain't right in the head. Didn't go to school but a couple o' years, and the teacher was glad to see him go, let me tell you." Johnny was proud, and rightly so, that he'd had six whole years of schooling, the most of anybody in the family.

"You best watch your back, Ray," Jess added. "I wouldn't put it past them sorry Burketts to try to ambush you."

Raider nodded. "I plan to be careful. It's sort of a habit, still."

Johnny grinned and asked, "What about Chastity Doolittle? You gonna stay away from her?"

"Maybe. Maybe not." Raider didn't like being told what to do, which was one reason for his frequent clashes with Allan Pinkerton and William Wagner. Knowing that Roscoe Burkett didn't want him having anything to do with Chastity didn't sit well with Raider's contrary nature. Maybe he *would* ask her to marry him, he thought. From the sound of what Roscoe had said, Chastity would probably say yes to a proposal. Raider supposed he could live with the knowledge that his wife had had more men than a dog has fleas, as long as she wasn't doing it anymore.

Hannah stepped out on the porch, drying her hands on the apron she wore. She and Joanie had been washing up the dishes after supper. Joanie followed her onto the porch as Hannah asked, "What's that you're sayin' about Chastity Doolittle?"

Hannah was friends with Chastity's mama, so the menfolk tended to be a mite circumspect in their discussions of the hot-blooded redhead whenever Hannah was around. "Oh, nothin'," Jess said now. "We was just wonderin' if she was ever gonna get hitched, and to who."

"That's none of your business," Hannah said in a scolding tone. "I swear, you men like to talk about how women gossip, but you're as bad or worse about it your own selves!"

"Now, Ma," Jess began, "we wasn't gossipin'—"

"I don't care what you call it. And I ain't your ma." Hannah sniffed. "I'm sure Chastity will settle down when the right fella comes along."

She gave Raider a hard look that made the big man a mite uncomfortable.

He was saved from any further discussion along those lines by Joanie, who moved to the top of the porch steps and said to her son, "Enos, put that down, whatever it is! Don't you dare put it in your mouth!" Raider thought she looked mighty pretty, her body rounded a little with child, her blond hair shining in the lamplight from the house.

The toddler grinned at her and stuck his fist in his mouth, along with whatever it was he had picked up off the ground. Joanie said, "Oh!" and hurried down the steps. She pulled Enos's hand out of his mouth, then picked him up and gave him a swat on the bottom that made him squirm and whimper a little. She looked at Johnny and said, "I thought you were watching him."

"Aw, it was just a bug or a dirt clod or somethin'," Johnny protested. "It wouldn't't'a hurt him. Shoot, I ate stuff I found on the ground for years."

"And look how you turned out."

"Good enough for you to marry, thank you kindly."

"Let me see the boy," Raider said. "He can sit on his uncle's lap for a spell."

"You ain't his uncle," Johnny pointed out. "You're his second cousin."

"Yeah, well, but I'm so much older it seems more like he's my nephew." Raider stood up and reached for the youngster.

As he did, he heard the sharp crack of a rifle shot and felt a disturbance in the air next to his ear. He knew it was the wind-rip of a bullet, but the knowledge barely had time to register on his brain before it was followed by a cry of pain. Joanie's knees unhinged and she fell to the floor of the porch, dropping Enos as she did so.

Raider's instincts took over. He lunged forward and grabbed the boy in midair, pulling him close and turning so that his body shielded Enos. He knew the shot that had missed him had struck Joanie, but he didn't have any idea how badly she was hit.

"Inside!" he bellowed. "Everybody inside!"

Jess was already up out of his rocker and had grabbed Hannah's arm. He shoved her through the open door and was right behind her. Johnny leaped up as well and threw himself down beside his wife. "Joanie!" he cried in a choked, frightened voice.

Another shot blasted from the darkness. This one chewed splinters from the porch railing. One of them stung Raider as he hurried through the door into the house, carrying Enos. He thrust the toddler into Hannah's arms as he said, "Hunt some cover! Keep the boy safe!"

He swung around toward the porch and saw that Johnny tried to pick up Joanie and get her inside. A third bullet smacked into the planks. Raider surged through the doorway, bent over, and gathered Joanie into his arms. Straightening, he dived back into the house just as another slug knocked a chunk out of the doorjamb.

Johnny piled into the house behind Raider and kicked the door shut. Only a handful of seconds had elapsed since the first shot rang out. In that time, four bullets had come

28

whistling out of the night, but only one had done any damage. The family was lucky Roscoe and Theodore Burkett were such piss-poor shots.

Raider had no doubt the Burkett brothers were behind this attack. The varmints had it in for him, and they were low-down enough not to care that their quest for vengeance might hurt innocent folks, like Joanie. As Raider laid her down on the divan, he saw a red streak on the side of her head, above her left ear. The crimson of blood stood out starkly in the fair hair. But it didn't look too bad, he decided. The bullet must have barely grazed her.

"Somebody blow out that lamp!" he called as he straightened.

Jess leaped to comply. Darkness fell over the room as he puffed out the flame. Enos cried in fear, a thin, wailing sound in the gloom.

"Hush, little fella," Raider said as he made his way toward one of the windows. "Your ma's gonna be all right."

"Are you sure, Ray?" Johnny asked. "I couldn't tell how bad she was hurt."

"Slug just nicked her. Stunned her for a minute. She'll come around in a little while and be fine except for a headache. I've seen grazes like that a hundred times." He had been kissed by bullets like that himself on numerous occasions.

"Burketts," Jess spat. "Got to be. By God, I ain't gonna stand for this. It's a feud, boys, a good old-fashioned feud!"

And in these mountains, Raider thought, that meant bloodshed. It meant death, and plenty of it, before things would finally be settled.

He couldn't allow that to happen because of him. There had to be a way to put a stop to the feud before it got started good.

He had worn his gunbelt over from the blacksmith shop, but he'd hung it up on a peg when he came into the house. He went to it now, finding the gun with unerring instincts even in the dark, and slipped the heavy revolver from the holster.

"Everybody stay put," he said. "Take care of Joanie and Enos."

"Where are you going?" Jess asked.

"Out there," Raider said. "I got me some business with the Burketts."

# Chapter 5

Spring was late in coming to Boston this year. A cold rain mixed with occasional spats of sleet tapped against the window of the office in which Doc Weatherbee worked late. Everyone else in the bank had gone home for the night, but Doc was still going through the welter of papers spread out on his desk, trying to solve a particularly irksome mystery.

During his years as a Pinkerton agent, often partnered with the big man from Arkansas called Raider, Doc had solved many mysteries. Few of them had involved him on a personal level, however. His detective work had been done on behalf of the Pinkerton Agency's clients.

Tonight's problem was vexing because it involved Doc's family.

The Weatherbees had been involved with the financial industry in Boston for many years, going all the way back to colonial days. Doc's brother, Aaron, was currently the president of one of the largest banks in the city, the bank in which Doc had gone to work after leaving the Pinkertons.

Because of that, Doc had a personal as well as a professional stake in finding out which of the bank's employees had been steadily embezzling money over the past year or so, to the tune of nearly eighty thousand dollars so far.

A gust of wind briefly rattled the window pane and made Doc look up from the documents that held the secret he was looking for. His mind strayed for a moment to his home. On a cold, damp night like this one, a man ought to be nestled in the bosom of his family, as the old saying went. Doc thought about his wife, Rebecca, and his son, Timothy, and how much more pleasant it would have been to be spending the evening with them in front of a roaring fire. But he had promised his brother that he would discover the culprit's identity, and he intended to keep his word.

The sooner he figured out this puzzle, the sooner he could go home, he told himself. With a sigh, he returned his attention to the sheets of facts and figures, and soon he was lost in them once more.

Doc wasn't sure how much time had passed when he finally stabbed his pencil against one of the papers and said, "That's it! It has to be him."

Doggedly, Doc had tracked the embezzler through the maze of numbers, following the trail that was there even though the man had tried to obscure it, and now he had a name to go with the incriminating evidence: Ned Montayne. Doc knew that Montayne was an assistant cashier in the bank, a handsome young man who set the hearts of some female customers aflutter. He was also good at concealing his crimes—but not quite good enough.

Montayne had one other quality that made him well-known to Doc: The young man was fascinated with the West. An avid reader of dime novels, when Montayne found that one of the vice presidents of the bank had actually lived and worked in the West as a Pinkerton agent, he had sought Doc out and asked him all sorts of questions about his experiences. Doc wasn't ashamed of his former profession, but he didn't want to dwell on it, either. Trying to be polite about it, he had turned aside most of Montayne's inquiries.

Now, Doc thought as he straightened up the papers and got ready to leave, Montayne would get to experience first-hand what it was like to have a Pinkerton agent on his trail . . . although Doc was no longer a Pink, of course.

Doc put all the important documents in a folder and placed it in the center drawer of his desk. He pulled up his tie, which he had loosened earlier, put on his suit coat, and went to the hat rack beside the door to retrieve his pearl-gray derby. Before he could put it on, he heard a thudding sound from somewhere else in the bank. A watchman was on duty, so Doc supposed the man had made the noise and didn't think anything else about it.

Until a moment later, when he heard a groan and then another thud that abruptly silenced it.

Old instincts made alarm bells go off in Doc's brain. He wasn't armed—the days when he had carried a gun as a matter of habit were long gone—but a heavy walking stick leaned against the wall in one corner of the office. It was there more for ornamentation than anything else, but in a pinch it was long enough and heavy enough to serve as a cudgel. Doc snatched it up and blew out the lamp on his desk, plunging the office into darkness.

He eased the door open, being careful not to make a sound, and listened. Soft footsteps whispered across the floor. The high-ceilinged main room of the bank created echoes but also had a muffling effect on sound and made it difficult to tell where the steps were coming from. Doc slipped out of the office, the walking stick grasped in both hands.

As he moved to one side, away from the door, he realized that the intruder was coming toward him. Doc had no doubt now that there *was* an intruder in the bank. Those thuds he had heard were the watchman being knocked out. Doc felt a cold wind against his face, confirming his suspicions. A door had been left open somewhere, probably to facilitate a fast getaway.

The vault was secure; only a few people knew the combination to it, and Doc, who was one of them, trusted all the others. The intruder might not be aware that he couldn't get to any of the money, though.

Doc held his breath. He heard a door open. The man was going into *his* office. A moment later a match scraped to life, and Doc heard the clink of glass as the lamp on his desk was lit and the chimney adjusted. A yellow glow spilled through the door the intruder had left open.

Moving into the doorway, Doc saw the figure of a tall, well-built man leaning over his desk. The man muttered to himself as he pawed through some of the papers Doc had left there.

"You won't find the evidence against you there, Ned," Doc said in a loud, clear voice. As the intruder gasped and wheeled around, Doc went on, "I've put it all in a safe place so that I can turn it over to the authorities and have you arrested for embezzlement . . . although now I suppose assault can be added to that charge. I hope you didn't kill that poor watchman when you knocked him out."

Ned Montayne glared at Doc for a second. His normally handsome face—under thick, wavy blond hair—was twisted with anger and hatred. That reaction lasted only a heartbeat, however, before Montayne controlled it. Putting a startled but otherwise bland expression on his face, he said, "Mr. Weatherbee! You gave me quite a fright, sir. I didn't expect you to still be here."

"Obviously, or you wouldn't have come skulking into my office like this. How did you figure out that I was onto you, Ned?"

"Onto me, sir?" Montayne shook his head. "I'm afraid I don't know what you're talking about."

"Oh? Then why are you here, if not to search for the evidence I've assembled against you?"

Montayne didn't say anything, because he couldn't. He had been caught red-handed, and no explanation he could come up with would convince anyone of his innocence, especially when the evidence against him became public.

A skunk always left a trail, as Raider might have said.

Doc backed toward the open door, saying, "Come on,

Ned. I want to check on that watchman, and then we'll find the nearest policeman."

Montayne shook his head. "I don't think so, sir."

"Let's don't make this any uglier than it already—"

Doc stopped short as he felt the cold, hard ring of a gun barrel press against the back of his neck. Montayne had a partner, damn it!

"It's about to get a lot uglier, Weatherbee," Montayne said as a smirk appeared on his face. "Drop that walking stick, or my associate will be forced to blow a hole through you."

Doc's heart pounded. He thought about his wife and son and how much he loved them. He loved his brother, too, and felt a strong sense of duty to both Aaron and the bank. But money paled next to his family, and with a sigh he said, "All right, just take it easy. I'll do what you say."

However, he had no intention of doing what Montayne had commanded. If Doc surrendered, either Montayne or the other man would kill him. Montayne couldn't afford to leave him alive, knowing that Doc was aware of his crimes.

So Doc held the walking stick in front of him in one hand and leaned forward a little, as if he intended to place it on the floor, but as he did he suddenly dove and twisted, whipping around and lashing out with the stick to knock the legs of Montayne's partner out from under him.

He was shocked to see that Montayne's partner was a woman, rather than a man. She cried out as Doc hit her legs and she crumpled to the floor. She wore a dark traveling outfit with a hat that included a veil, so he couldn't get a good look at her features.

There wasn't time for that anyway, because with a rush of footsteps, Montayne charged him. He grabbed the walking stick and tried to wrestle it out of Doc's hands.

Doc drove the stick's heavy handle into Montayne's belly, causing the embezzler to grunt in pain and double over. Montayne had the strength of desperation, though, and the next second he tore the stick out of Doc's grasp and slashed at him with it. The ferrule struck Doc a glancing blow on the temple and staggered him.

As Doc bumped against the desk and used it to catch his balance, Montayne dropped the walking stick and scooped up the gun that the woman had dropped when Doc dumped her on her derriere so unceremoniously. Doc dived behind the desk as Montayne snapped a shot at him. The bullet missed and thudded into the bookshelves behind the desk.

Doc might not have had a weapon on his person, but there was a pistol in the bottom desk drawer. He jerked it open, grabbed the gun, and fired at Montayne, missing. He couldn't risk another shot, because the woman was on her feet again and took hold of Montayne's arm, tugging on him.

"Come on, Ned," she pleaded. "Let's get out of here!"

A shock went through Doc as he realized that the woman's voice was familiar, but he couldn't place it right away. Montayne started to shove her away, then evidently thought better of it and decided she was right. Flight was their best chance now. He threw two fast shots that made Doc duck behind the desk again, then turned and fled from the office, clutching the woman's arm as he did so.

Doc ran after them, pursuing them into the main room of the bank. Montayne twisted and fired again, forcing Doc to veer to one side. As Doc angled across the floor, his foot struck something and he fell, toppling forward to land heavily on the tile floor.

He heard the slam of the door and a moan at the same time. The door slamming meant that Montayne and his partner had reached the exit they had left open.

The moan had to have come from the injured guard.

Doc grimaced as he scrambled to his feet. One of his knees throbbed where he had hit it against the floor when he fell. In the light that came from his office, he saw the shape on the floor—the unconscious watchman.

The police could pick up Montayne, Doc decided. Now that his complicity in the embezzlement was known, it was only a matter of time until the law caught up with him. And he certainly wouldn't have the chance to steal any more.

Anyway, Doc couldn't just leave the watchman lying there. His name was Carl Dunwoody, and he had worked for the bank for at least fifteen years. Doc had to check on him and see how badly he was hurt.

Dropping to a knee beside the injured man, Doc felt over his head and body for wounds but found only a good-sized lump on Dunwoody's head. The watchman would have quite a headache when he woke up, Doc thought with relief, but he ought to be all right other than that.

Doc hurried back into his office. In addition to the pistol that had come in so handy, the bottom drawer of his desk also contained a fifth of fine Scotch. A jolt of that would brace up Dunwoody until he could receive some actual medical attention.

Doc was about to start out of the office, when something on the floor caught his attention. He bent to pick it up. It was a locket, and as he stared at it lying in his palm, he knew that the woman who was Montayne's partner must have lost it when she fell. The thin gold chain attached to it had broken.

The worst part about it was that Doc recognized that locket, just as he had recognized the woman's voice. He opened the locket to make sure he wasn't mistaken, and bit back a curse as he saw the faces of his brother and sister-in-law looking up at him from the tiny cameos mounted inside the locket.

The previous Christmas, the locket had been a present from Aaron and his wife to their eighteen-year-old daughter, Katherine. Katie, she was called.

Katie, Doc's own niece, had put a gun to his head and then fled from the bank in the company of an unscrupulous bastard who had embezzled eighty thousand dollars.

Doc had been eager to tell Aaron what he had discovered about Montayne, but he wasn't eager to break this bit of news. He wasn't looking forward to that conversation at all.

# Chapter 6

"You're insane! Damn it, you've lost your mind!"

Doc looked into his brother's shocked face and held out his hand with the locket lying in it. "I almost wish I *were* crazy, Aaron," he said. "But there's no mistake about it. I recognized Katie's voice, and this is her locket."

Aaron stared in horror at the piece of jewelry, as if Doc were offering him a diamondback rattlesnake or a venomous spider. Slowly, and without taking the locket, he began to shake his head. "It can't be," he said. "It simply can't."

A step sounded on the staircase that curved down to the Beacon Hill mansion's foyer from the second floor, and a woman's voice asked, "What can't be, dear?"

Doc and Aaron both turned toward the stairs, jumping a little as if they had been caught doing something they were ashamed of. The woman coming down the stairs was serenely beautiful, with fair hair that was pulled back into a large bun.

"Nothing, Victoria—" Aaron began, but Doc stopped him with a hand on his arm.

"You can't keep the truth from her," Doc told his brother in a low voice.

Aaron turned his head to glare at him. "Damn it—"

Once again he was interrupted, this time by his wife. "If something's wrong, Aaron, I'd appreciate it if you would tell me. I know that you feel you have to protect me from everything that's bad in the world, but you don't. You really don't. I won't break, you know. I'm not made of glass."

Aaron took a deep breath, glanced at Doc again, then went to the bottom of the staircase to meet his wife. He took her hands.

"Oh, my," Victoria said with a frown. "It really *is* something bad, isn't it?"

"It's Katie," Aaron said. "She's . . . gone."

Victoria took a sudden step to one side, as if she were trying to avoid a blow. Her shoulders hunched. "Katie?" she whispered. "Katie's dead? That can't be—"

"Dead? God, no!" Aaron moved his hands up his wife's arms and gripped them. "Listen to me, Victoria. I shouldn't have said it like that. What I meant was, Katie is gone from the house. Perhaps gone from the city by now. She's run away . . . with a man."

Victoria stared at him, clearly relieved to learn that her daughter was still alive, but still confused and frightened. "That's not possible. She's upstairs in her room. I spoke to her earlier this evening."

"Maybe she should take a look," Doc suggested.

Victoria looked at him. "Does this have something to do with *you?*"

Knowing that she was upset, Doc didn't take offense at the tone of her voice. He had always gotten along fairly well with his sister-in-law, and his wife, Rebecca, was friendly with Victoria. But at the same time, Victoria had never been anywhere close to poor a day in her life, and she had never been able to grasp the concept of someone working for a living, especially by choice, as Doc had done, and especially in such a dangerous, sordid profession as detective work. Unfailingly polite most of the time, deep down she considered him as alien as if he had come from another planet.

"Let's just go upstairs," Doc said, "and make sure Katie's not in her room."

Aaron let go of Victoria, and she turned to start up the stairs. "You'll see," she said over her shoulder. "You'll see."

She hurried along the second floor hallway, almost breaking into a run. When she reached the door of her daughter's room, she rapped a delicate fist against it, calling, "Katie? Katie, dear? I hate to disturb you, but your father and I need to talk to you."

Aaron and Doc had followed Victoria up the stairs and along the corridor. In a low voice, Doc asked his brother, "Sort of early for an eighteen-year-old girl to have turned in for the night, isn't it?"

"Katie tends to retire early," Aaron said. He sounded shaken, and Doc made a shrewd guess as to what he was thinking.

Had Katie been going to bed early . . . or had she been sneaking out of the house most nights to see Ned Montayne?

Victoria knocked again and said, "Katie?" She reached down and tried the doorknob. It was locked, but that didn't stop Victoria from rattling it. "Katie!"

Aaron came up behind her, put his hands on her shoulders, and gently moved her away from the door. "Let me try," he said.

"I don't understand this. I just don't understand . . ."

Aaron knocked on the door. The raps and his voice were forceful as he said, "Katie, if you're in there, open up this door immediately. Your mother and I have to speak to you."

No response came from the other side of the panel.

Aaron looked over his shoulder at Victoria. His bushy eyebrows were drawn down so far in a frown they seemed like they were trying to reach out and touch his side whiskers. "Where's the key to this door?"

"I . . . I'll fetch it."

Victoria hurried away. While she was gone, Aaron began to pace back and forth. He tapped his right fist in his left palm in time with his steps. "Montayne," he said. "I can't believe it. He's always been a good employee. To think that he stole all that money, and . . . and . . ."

*And stole Katie, too.* Aaron couldn't finish putting that thought into words, but Doc knew it was in his brother's brain.

Victoria came back with a key. She tried to slip it into the keyhole, but her hand was trembling and she missed. Aaron took it from her, not roughly, and managed to unlock the door. When he swung it back, Doc already knew what they were going to find inside.

Katie wasn't there, and her bed hadn't been slept in. Victoria went to the wardrobe, opened it, and said in a choked voice, "Some of her things are . . . are gone." She pressed her fingers to her mouth. "Oh, Aaron, what are we going to do?"

Aaron put his arms around her and drew her against him. He was a lot larger than she, but at this moment they seemed both of a size, shrunken by what had happened.

"We'll find her," he said. "We'll bring her home safely, don't you worry."

"Aaron's right," Doc said. His own voice was brisk and businesslike now. He felt the past two years falling away, as if he had never spent those long months sitting in a quiet office and shuffling papers. Something inside him seemed to be growing sharper by the second, as if this trouble were honing all his old instincts.

The banker was disappearing, being replaced by the manhunter that Doc had once been—and would be again.

"I'll find Katie," he went on, "and I'll find Montayne, too."

Victoria blinked at him in confusion. "Montayne?" she repeated. "Ned Montayne, that nice young man who works at the bank? The one who wants to be a cowboy? What does he have to do with this?"

"Katie's run away with him, dear," Aaron said. "And he stole eighty thousand dollars of the bank's money, too. He's a criminal."

She began to sob.

"Don't worry," Doc said. "Montayne is my business now."

As Montayne's employer, Aaron had the man's address. Montayne lived in a rooming house not far from the Charles River, with a view of Cambridge across the way. The landlady didn't want to let Doc look around Montayne's room at first, but when he told her in a flinty voice that it was police business, she got a worried look on her face and relented. Doc didn't actually identify himself as a policeman, but if she wanted to think he was, that was none of his affair. It was an old Pinkerton ploy.

There was nothing to find in Montayne's room, however. It had been cleaned out without the landlady knowing anything about it. Doc searched it from top to bottom without finding anything that would tell him where Montayne had gone.

Doc turned to questioning the woman. "Do you recall Montayne ever saying anything about where he would go if he ever left Boston?"

She shook her head and said, "Only that he talked about going west, you know. He always had his nose in one of those lurid little yellowbacks, Deadwood Dick and that sort of thing."

Doc nodded. He was well aware of Montayne's fondness for dime novels and the outlandish yarns their authors spun about the West. Many of those fictioneers had no idea what the frontier was really like and had never even been west of the Mississippi, but that didn't matter to their readers.

"He didn't act any different recently, as if he were worried about something or eager about something?"

"Not around me, he didn't." The woman looked disconsolate. "I can't believe he's gone. He was always so handsome and charming, such a joy to have around the house."

"Did you ever see him with a young woman, about eighteen years old, very attractive, with blond hair?"

42

The landlady sniffed. "He knew not to bring chippies around here. I wouldn't allow it. I run a respectable house."

Doc suppressed the annoyance he felt at hearing his niece referred to as a chippie. He didn't want to waste time explaining who Katie was, and anyway, Aaron and Victoria wanted this whole thing kept as quiet as possible. If it was simply a matter of going after an embezzler, Aaron would have called in the police and sent them after Montayne with all the power they could muster. Katie's involvement changed everything, though. Now the situation called for discretion.

It still bothered Doc that Katie had put a gun to his head. She must really be in love with Montayne, he thought, or at least believe that she was, for her to have done such a thing. She had just been trying to frighten him, he told himself. She wouldn't have pulled the trigger.

He wanted to believe that, anyway.

"Is there *anything* you can tell me about Montayne?" he asked the landlady.

"No, I'm sorry." She shook her head. "I almost wish now that I had asked him to leave when I saw that gun."

"What gun?" Doc asked.

"He had a . . . a pistol of some sort, a big, heavy pistol. Sometimes when he was in his room, he wore a belt with some sort of sheath attached to it. I came in once when he wasn't expecting me, and I found him standing in front of the mirror, sort of crouching, you know." The woman bent over and held her right arm out away from her body in a bizarre approximation of what she was describing. "He would reach down and pull the gun out of the holster, then put it back and do it again. He did that two or three times before he realized I was there. I think he was embarrassed when he realized I'd been watching him."

Practicing his fast draw, Doc thought. Maybe Montayne fancied himself a gunman.

Now he was on the run with eighty grand in stolen loot and an infatuated, beautiful young woman. Doc might not know Montayne's precise destination, but he had a pretty good idea in which direction the fugitive had fled.

West.

The frontier was a big place, still vast and sometimes wild despite the advancing tide of civilization. Doc would need help tracking down Montayne.

Fortunately, he knew where to get it.

# Chapter 7

By the time Longarm got to the depot in Wichita, the last southbound train of the night had pulled out, and he didn't doubt for a second that Felix Gaunt was on it. The next train headed for Texas wouldn't leave until eight o'clock the next morning.

By that time, Longarm thought in disgust, Gaunt would be in Fort Worth, where, according to the article in the newspaper he had found in Gaunt's hotel room, the contestants for the shooting competition would be gathering before setting out for Edmund Corrigan's ranch in West Texas.

He could have rented a horse or tried to find a stagecoach line that would take him to Texas, but both of those options would be considerably slower in the long run than just waiting for the next train. Longarm knew that, but the delay chafed at him anyway. He trudged back to the hotel in the rain, stopping only to buy himself a bottle of Maryland rye and stock up on cheroots. He would spend the night commiserating with ol' Tom Moore about his bad luck.

But he was a lot luckier than the whore called Betsy had been, and he knew it. At least he was still alive.

A mite fuzzy-headed from the booze but fortified by a pot of black coffee and a big breakfast, Longarm arrived at the depot the next morning carrying his warbag, his saddle, and his Winchester. He showed his badge and bona fides to the conductor, stowed his gear in the baggage car, and found a seat. The rain had moved on, leaving a blue, cloudless sky over Wichita, although the downpour had continued long enough after midnight so that the streets were still wet. The warmth of the sun would dry them before much longer. It was a beautiful spring day.

Longarm might have appreciated it more if he'd felt better, and if he weren't on the trail of a killer. And if he hadn't been haunted by the memory of the dying woman's face as the rain dripped on it. He took out a cheroot, clamped his teeth hard on one end of it, and lit the other with a lucifer he snapped into life with his thumbnail.

A deputy U.S. marshal had to be good with his fists, reasonably fast and accurate with a gun, and smart enough, or cunning enough, to figure out what moves a lawbreaker might make. He also had to have the ability to shove aside unpleasant memories, because one thing was for sure in that line of work—there would be plenty of unpleasant memories.

So Longarm put Betsy out of his mind. Her death could be laid right at the feet of Felix Gaunt. One more mark against the son of a bitch when the time came for settlin' up.

Longarm dozed as the train rolled south. The day warmed up and so did the car in which he rode, which made him even more drowsy. The train was crossing Indian Territory when he became aware that someone had sat down beside him. Earlier, he had tipped his hat down over his eyes. Now he straightened up and thumbed the Stetson back into its normal position.

"Oh," the woman sitting beside him said. "Did I wake you? My apologies, sir."

"No apology necessary, ma'am," Longarm told her. She was a pretty strawberry blonde in her mid-twenties, wearing

46

a relatively expensive traveling outfit. Out of habit, Longarm checked her ring finger. No wedding band.

"I hope you don't mind me sitting here," she went on. "To tell you the truth, a man has been bothering me, so I thought that if perhaps you and I could pretend to be acquainted, he might leave me alone."

Longarm nodded. "Sure thing. I'm always glad to oblige a lady."

She slipped her arm through his in a companionable gesture and said, "Thank you so much. Traveling alone can be rather intimidating for a woman."

Longarm had his doubts about just how intimidated she really was. The way he saw it, there were only three real possibilities here: she had seen him, liked his looks, and wanted to spend some time with him, maybe have a little no-strings railroad romance; she was working the old badger game, trying to lure him into the proverbial compromising position so that her partner could bust in and claim to be her husband or brother or some such; or she was telling the truth and some lecherous hombre really had spooked her. Longarm didn't really care which of those was true. He wasn't in the mood right now for playing slap-and-tickle, even with a good-looking strawberry blonde, so she wasn't going to lure him into anything, innocent or not. And if some gent really was making a pest of himself, he would regret crossing the path of a lawman who felt rather bearlike, as Longarm did at the moment.

"I'm Hannah Wilbanks," the woman introduced herself.

"Custis Long," he said, without adding the deputy U.S. marshal part in front of it.

"I'm certainly glad I made your acquaintance, Mr. Long."

"The feeling's mutual, Miss Wilbanks. Or is it Missus?"

"No, I'm not married."

Longarm nodded. Asking the question had been another instance of habit kicking in. He had found out her marital status even though he told himself he wasn't interested in any sort of fooling around with her.

"Where are you going?" she asked.

"Fort Worth."

"Business or pleasure?" Before he could answer, she gave a little laugh and added, "I hope you don't think I'm being too inquisitive. I've been here in the West long enough to know that curiosity is sometimes frowned upon."

"No, that's all right," Longarm assured her. "It's strictly business."

"What line of work are you in?"

"Freight," Longarm said. It wasn't a total lie. Most times his job consisted of finding some desperado and hauling him back to face justice. Or if not that, then often he had to haul back some owlhoot's carcass to show that the varmint was beyond the reach of man's law.

"That sounds fascinating," Hannah said.

The lie made Longarm even more suspicious of her. There was nothing fascinating about the freight business. It was difficult, vital, but often deadly dull work. He shrugged in response to her comment but didn't say anything.

"I'll bet you have all sorts of interesting stories to tell," she went on.

"Not particularly." Longarm looked around. "Where's this fella who was bothering you? Maybe I ought to have a talk with him and tell him to leave you alone."

"Oh, I'm sure that won't be necessary. When he sees the two of us together, he'll get the idea."

The promptness of her answer convinced Longarm that she was up to no good. If she had really been scared, she would have been more than happy to have some big, strong-looking galoot like him step in and run off whomever had been pestering her. More out of idle curiosity and to keep his brain occupied than anything else, he decided to play along with her.

"All right, but the fella done me a favor without ever meaning to," he said.

"How's that?"

Longarm grinned at Hannah. "He got the prettiest girl on the train to sit down here and talk to me."

She laughed and her face reddened, and the blush was quite becoming. He figured she'd had a lot of practice at it. "Now *you're* being forward, Custis. But I don't mind it coming from you. It's all right if I call you Custis, isn't it?"

"Sure thing."

They talked for the next hour as the train continued its southward journey, with Hannah carrying most of the conversation. She laughed and squeezed his arm a lot, too, and after a while she slid her hand down and clasped his hand so that their fingers intertwined.

"I think I could use some fresh air," she said.

"Well, you won't find much of it on a train," Longarm said.

Hannah laughed again. "Silly. Let's go for a walk and maybe stand out on one of the platforms for a while."

Longarm pretended to hesitate, then nodded and said, "Sure, why not?"

He got to his feet first and helped her up, being very gentlemanly about it. Arm in arm, they walked to the back of the car. Hannah had abandoned any pretense of being worried about an unwelcome admirer. She kept up the bright chatter as they went through the car's rear vestibule and stepped out onto the platform.

"It's beautiful, isn't it?" Hannah asked as she paused and looked at the Indian Territory countryside sweeping past along the train tracks.

To Longarm it just looked like stubby hills covered with sparse grass. The wildflowers weren't up yet. In another couple of weeks or so, the scenery would be a lot prettier.

But he said, "It sure is," playing along with her.

She turned toward him and rested a hand on his arm. "Custis, would you think it was terribly bold of me if I . . . if I asked you to kiss me?"

He couldn't resist saying, "I thought you were worried about strange hombres bothering you."

49

"But you're not strange! I mean . . . I like you, Custis."

Her lips were full and red and succulent, moist and inviting. Longarm said the hell with it and bent his head to hers. Her mouth tasted as good as it looked, sweet and hot and almost intoxicating. He slipped his arms around her and tugged her closer. She pressed her body to his.

When they broke the kiss, she whispered, "Now I *am* going to be bold, Custis. I have a private compartment in the next car. Would you . . . care to join me in it?"

"I think that'd be mighty nice," Longarm murmured.

She held his hand and led him into the next car, which consisted of nicely appointed private compartments that ran along one side, with a corridor next to the windows on the other side. These were the most expensive accommodations on the train, and the fact that Hannah had one of the compartments put the lie to the story she had told Longarm earlier. If she'd really been worried about someone bothering her, she could have simply retreated into her compartment and snapped the latch on the door. She was counting on him being too overcome with desire for her to think things through to that extent, however.

She opened a compartment door and stepped inside. Longarm followed her. Without appearing to do so, he noticed that she closed the door behind him but didn't fasten the latch.

That was the last bit of evidence he needed. Up until now, it had still been possible that she was just feeling randy and looking for a middle-of-the-day romp with a stranger she'd never see again after the train reached Fort Worth. The fact that she had left the door fixed so that somebody could come in behind them made Longarm certain he was dealing with a badger game. He wasn't surprised when she came right into his arms and started kissing him again, with even more passion and fervor this time.

"I . . . I don't know what's come over me, Custis," she panted when she pulled her mouth away from his after a long moment. "I swear, I've never done anything like this before! You're just so nice and handsome, and I . . . I . . . Oh, my goodness, is it getting hot in here?"

With that, she started taking her clothes off, unfastening the jacket of her traveling outfit and practically ripping her blouse open, so that the slopes of her full breasts mounded enticingly in the low-cut chemise she wore. She reached for Longarm again.

At that moment, he heard the click of the door opening and put his left hand between those plump breasts. Instead of caressing them, though, he gave her a shove that made her cry out in surprise as she flew backward. The back of her legs hit the edge of the compartment's bunk, and she fell over onto the mattress.

Meanwhile, Longarm had whirled around and swung a looping right at the jaw of the big, black-bearded gent who had just bulled into the compartment. The man wore a derby hat and a tweed suit and might have been a drummer of some sort, but no traveling salesman had such hard, brutal features. He had figured to take his victim by surprise, but that had backfired on him. Longarm's fist slammed into his jaw and sent him crashing back against the door.

Instincts honed by long years spent in a dangerous business warned the big lawman. He looked over his shoulder to see Hannah on her feet and pawing a derringer out of a pocket in her skirt. She held the little gun in both hands as she tried to lift it toward him.

Longarm's hand closed around one of her wrists and shoved her hands up as she jerked the trigger. The derringer spat, but the bullet went into the ceiling of the compartment. Longarm twisted Hannah's wrist. She cried out in pain and dropped the derringer before she could fire its second barrel.

The scrape of boot leather told Longarm he was again under attack by Hannah's partner in crime. He wheeled around, maintaining his hold on Hannah's wrist so that she came with him. She collided with the bearded man, who had lost his derby. Their legs tangled up and they both went down. Longarm saw the man trying to pull a knife from under his coat and kicked the fella in the head. The man groaned and dropped the knife.

Longarm stepped back and picked up the knife and the derringer. He wasn't wearing his Colt—the shell belt was coiled around the holster and tucked away inside his warbag—so he opened the compartment's window, tossed the knife out, and then trained the derringer on the two grifters, who still lay tangled up on the floor.

"You folks picked the wrong fella to try that old dodge on," he told them. "I'm a deputy United States marshal."

Hannah groaned in despair. The man glared at her and said, "A lawman! All the men on this train, and who do you go for? A damned lawman! You stupid bitch!"

"Careful," Longarm said. "I don't like you, old son, and I could be persuaded to kick you in the head again, harder this time."

"What are you going to do with us?"

"Turn you over to the conductor. He can deal with you however he wants to."

"If you'll let us go," Hannah said, "I'll make it worth your while."

Thinking about Betsy and what had happened in Wichita, Longarm shook his head and said, "I don't think so, darlin'."

Maybe he ought to just swear off women for a while, he told himself. Seemed like every gal he got mixed up with these days tried to shoot him sooner or later.

# Chapter 8

The conductor kept Hannah and her partner, who claimed his name was Doakes, locked up in the caboose with a fireman standing guard over them until the train reached its next stop. There the conductor booted the two grifters off, with the warning that if he ever caught either of them on one of his trains again, they would have to get off before the train reached a stop—and without it slowing down, either.

That was fine with Longarm. He didn't hold grudges. If he let himself brood about everybody who had tried to rob him or kill him over the years, he wouldn't have time to do anything else.

The rest of the trip passed without any trouble, and the train reached Fort Worth that evening, rolling through the sprawling stockyards on the north side and across two forks of the Trinity River before hissing to a stop on the southern edge of the downtown area, a couple of blocks from the wild and woolly region known as Hell's Half Acre.

Longarm had no interest in the saloons, gambling dens, and whorehouses of the Acre. His quarry would be in one of the nicer sections of town. He had torn the story about

53

the shooting competition out of the newspaper and brought it with him. Unfortunately, the story didn't say where the competitors were gathering. And for all Longarm knew, they might have left Fort Worth by now and were already heading for Corrigan's ranch, a couple of hundred miles west of there.

Luckily there was a cigar stand in the depot lobby, run by an elderly black man. Longarm bought a current copy of the Fort Worth *Telegram* from him and asked, "Say, do you know anything about a rancher, name of Corrigan, and that shooting contest he's putting on?"

"Mister, I know all about it," the man replied. "Folks ain't been talkin' about much else here lately. Mist' Corrigan, he's one of the richest men in Texas, got the biggest spread this side o' the XIT or the King Ranch."

"Funny I never heard of him before," Longarm commented.

"That's because he ain't been out here for long. Come out from somewheres back East, he did, and bought up two or three ranches, then shoved 'em together to make one big spread. If'n you was to ask me, I'd say this here shootin' contest is just so's folks'll know his name from here on out, if you know what I mean."

Longarm nodded, understanding what the cigar stand owner was getting at. Edmund Corrigan wanted to be as well-known a cattleman as Charlie Goodnight or Captain King. The competition, and the Golden Eagle that would go to the winner, would put Corrigan on the map.

Scanning the front page of the newspaper, Longarm found a prominent story about the contest. It told him that the competitors were still in town, staying at the Palace Hotel along with Corrigan himself and the cattleman's wife. From the sound of it, there was a continuous party going on while the group waited for all the contestants to arrive. Longarm found out something else he hadn't known until now: each entrant in the competition had to put up a two-thousand-dollar entry fee. That wasn't enough to pay for the cost of the Golden Eagle, but it would help Corrigan throw one hell of a fandango, which was evidently the idea behind the whole thing.

"Where's the Palace Hotel?"

"You go outside and head north on Main Street. When you come to Seventh, the hotel be there on the corner."

"I'm much obliged, old-timer." Longarm started to turn away, then paused. "While I'm here, let me have three of those cheroots."

"That be a nickel," the proprietor said with a dry grin. "You a big spender, mister."

Longarm returned the grin. "I've got to be careful with my money," he said. "I may need it. I'm thinking about entering that shooting contest to see if I can win me a Golden Eagle."

He wasn't really interested in the prize, although he supposed that a statue of an eagle covered with solid gold would be a nice enough dingus to have. He had made the comment about entering the contest on impulse, but as he thought about it while he walked up Main Street toward the Palace Hotel, he realized that it might not be a bad idea.

Gaunt couldn't have gotten a good look at his face during that rainy shoot-out in Wichita the night before. By pretending to enter the competition, Longarm would have a perfect excuse to stay close to Gaunt and wait for the right moment to arrest him. He didn't want to try to take Gaunt when there were innocent bystanders around who might get hit by flying lead.

Gaunt had already proven in Wichita that he wouldn't allow himself to be arrested peacefully.

Of course, Longarm would have to let Corrigan in on what he was doing, otherwise he'd really have to come up with the two-thousand-dollar entry fee. Longarm had to grin as he thought about what Billy Vail's reaction would be if he wired the chief marshal and asked him to send that much money down to Texas. Might be worth it, though, to make Henry foam at the mouth a mite.

Longarm came to the hotel, a solid-looking brick structure that was several stories tall. Buildings like that seemed to be sprouting in all the cities these days, with each new one taller than the one before, like they were engaged in their own competition to see which one could rise closest to the heavens. Skyscrapers, some folks called them.

Longarm went into the Palace, which was as opulently appointed as its name indicated. Fancy tile floors, big potted palms, gilt trim around the walls of the lobby . . . To say it was a nice place would be an understatement.

He crossed to the desk, where a slick-haired gent in a suit and a flashy vest held court. The man looked at Longarm and seemed to be making an effort not to sniff in contempt. The big lawman wore a suit and vest of his own, but the duds were a little wrinkled from traveling.

"May I help you?"

"Are Mr. Corrigan and his guests still here?" Longarm asked.

"I'm afraid I can't divulge any information about our guests. It's against the hotel's policy."

Longarm thought about hauling out his badge and forcing the snooty hombre to answer, but he discarded the idea right away, recalling that he was trying to be discreet about this. Instead, he growled, "Corrigan'll want to see me. I'm gonna win that shooting contest he's setting up."

"Is that so?" The clerk didn't look or sound impressed. He had to know that the contest required a two-thousand-dollar entry fee, and it was clear he didn't think Longarm had that sort of money.

Longarm slid a cheroot from his vest pocket and put it in his mouth, leaving it there unlit. "Charlie Goodnight ever stay here when he comes to Fort Worth?" he asked around the cheroot.

The clerk frowned. "Mr. Goodnight has stayed with us, yes."

"I'm surprised," Longarm said.

"Surprised? Why?"

"Oh, I just am."

The clerk's frown deepened. "See here. Are you saying this hotel isn't good enough—"

"Not saying anything. Reckon I'll be going."

The clerk held up a hand. "Wait just a moment."

Longarm knew what the clerk had to be thinking. The implication that Longarm was acquainted with Charles Goodnight had to have made an impression, although the clerk couldn't be sure that he wasn't running a bluff. If he had been in the hotel business very long, though, he had to be aware that some of the richest men west of the Mississippi didn't dress or act like they had a fortune. Goodnight was that way, a frontier cattleman at heart despite his wealth.

And as a matter of fact, Longarm *did* know Goodnight and had given him a hand on more than one occasion, although always in conjunction with some case of his own. If Goodnight had been there, he would have vouched for Longarm.

Untroubled, Longarm stood for a moment until the clerk made up his mind. The man nodded and said, "Yes, Mr. Corrigan is still here. If you'd like, I can send a message up to him and ask if he'd be willing to see you."

"I'd be obliged," Longarm said with a nod. "My name is Custis Parker." It was an alias he had used in the past.

The clerk summoned over a bellboy, scribbled something on a piece of paper, and sent the boy upstairs with the note. Longarm lit his cheroot and smoked patiently while he waited.

The bellboy reappeared a few minutes later and handed what looked like the same piece of paper back to the clerk. The man looked at what was written on it and nodded. He turned to Longarm and said, "Mr. Corrigan has agreed to see you, Mr. Parker. I caution you, though: Your visit had better be in earnest."

"Don't worry about that," Longarm said. "I'm about as earnest as you can get."

"Mr. Corrigan is in Suite Four-C. The boy will take you up."

Longarm nodded his thanks. He didn't much care for

the idea of the bellboy riding herd on him, but he had expected it and would tolerate it.

Longarm followed the bellboy up the broad staircase. The youngster wore a tight jacket and a little round hat that made him look like an organ grinder's monkey. Making conversation, Longarm asked, "You like working here, son?"

The bellboy looked around to make sure they were alone on the stairs, then said, "Hell, no, mister. Would you like wearing a getup like this all the time?"

Longarm had to grin. "Can't say as I would."

"I had me a ridin' job on a ranch south of here, but I had a horse fall on me and got stove up for a while. I'm better now, but my old spread don't need any hands. Couldn't sign on anywhere else, neither, so I drifted up here to Fort Worth and took whatever chore I could find." The bellboy shook his head. "I reckon this is better'n clerkin' in a store or workin' as a fry cook, but not much." He sized up Longarm. "Suit or no suit, you look like you done some cowboyin'. No offense."

"None taken," Longarm returned, still smiling. "I rode drag on a few trail herds, about fifteen years ago."

The boy let out a low whistle. "Those must have been some of the first cattle drives."

Longarm nodded. "Yeah, and they were enough to convince me I didn't want to eat dust the rest of my borned days, so I started looking around for another line of work."

He didn't offer any details about that line of work, and the boy didn't ask, which pushed him up another notch in Longarm's estimation.

As they turned at the third-floor landing and started on up to the fourth, the bellboy said, "Mister, I hope I ain't bein' too bold here, but . . . you're goin' to see Mr. Edmund Corrigan, right?"

"That's right," Longarm said.

"I'd sure admire to work on the Box C. That's his spread. If you and him are, uh, doin' business, do you think you might put in a good word for me?"

"I don't know that he'd listen to me. I never met the man. But if things work out that way, sure, I reckon I could do that. What's your name?"

"Riley," the bellboy said. "Riley Hutchins. And I sure am obliged to you, Mr. Parker."

"Don't thank me yet. Might not anything come of it."

"Yeah, but I'm grateful just for the chance."

They reached the fourth floor, and Riley led Longarm to a large, elaborately worked door. The bellboy rapped on the thick panel. "I talked to Mr. Corrigan's secretary," Riley said over his shoulder. "He's a nice enough fella, but I reckon you'll have to speak to him before you see Mr. Corrigan himself."

It wasn't a secretary who opened the door, however. A woman stood there who was so beautiful she made Riley gawp, and when she smiled at Longarm he felt the heat that came from her all the way down to his toes.

# Chapter 9

Raider went out the back of the farmhouse, slipping through a window rather than the door. He crouched there for a moment, then moved to the corner of the house as two more shots rang out. He hoped his loved ones were keeping their heads down inside.

A fierce blaze of anger heated up his insides. It was one thing for those damned Burketts to come after him over a grudge, real or imagined, but when they endangered his family, they crossed a line.

They were going to be damned sorry for doing it, too.

The trees came up close to the house in back. Raider moved into the thick shadows underneath them. The darkness seemed to swallow him whole. He circled the house, using the continuing sporadic gunshots to guide him as he closed in on the bushwhackers. Shots came from the house, too, as Jess and Johnny put up a fight.

Raider could see the muzzle flashes in the woods in front of the house now. There were two riflemen out there, and he had no doubt they were Roscoe and Theodore Burkett. He supposed it was possible somebody else was trying to kill him—he had made plenty of enemies during his years as a Pinkerton, after all, and not all of them had wound up in the cold, cold ground—but the timing of the attack made it much more likely the Burkett brothers were responsible.

Moving through the woods without making any sound was next to impossible, but Raider came pretty damn close. Not only had he grown up in the Ozarks and been able to stalk game when he was only a kid, but the time he had spent on the frontier hunting killers and other owlhoots had also sharpened his skills. The bushwhackers seemed to have no idea that he was behind them.

He was close to one of them now, only about a dozen feet behind the rifleman. He could have stood up from his crouch, blazed away at the son of a bitch, and likely ventilated him in fatal fashion. As mad as Raider was, though, he still wanted to end this without any killing if that was possible. He drew a deep breath in through his nose, then rushed forward, no longer caring if he made any noise.

The bushwhacker heard him coming and tried to whirl around to meet the threat, but Raider was too fast. His keen eyes picked out the darker, man-shaped patch of shadows, and he swung his Colt at the varmint's head.

"Roscoe!" the man yelped in alarm just before Raider's heavy revolver thudded against his skull and dropped him in a senseless heap. The name he had called out meant that this was Theodore Burkett.

That left the apelike Roscoe as the other bushwhacker. Sure enough, it was Roscoe's rumbling voice that called out, "Theodore! Theodore, you all right? Answer me, damn it!"

Theodore couldn't answer, though, because he was out cold, and Raider didn't make a sound as he crouched there beside Theodore's unconscious form. The silence would eat at Roscoe and make him want to find out what had happened to his brother. That was Raider's plan, anyway.

Sure enough, after a few long, tense moments, Raider heard Roscoe moving through the woods toward him. Roscoe wasn't able to attain the same level of stealth as Raider. Brush crackled and branches snapped under his feet.

Since the guns of the bushwhackers in the woods had fallen silent, the defenders in the house had stopped shooting, too. Raider was glad of that. He would have hated to get killed by a stray bullet fired by his uncle or cousin—not that he would have been any deader for that.

Taking shallow breaths, Raider waited. Roscoe came blundering up and hissed, "Theodore! Blast your mangy hide, where are you?"

Raider moved behind Roscoe and pressed the barrel of his gun against the burly hillbilly's back. "Theodore can't hear you, Roscoe," he said.

Roscoe jerked in surprise but didn't try to spin around and bat Raider's gun aside. Raider would have pulled the trigger if he had. Instead, Roscoe asked in a ragged voice, "Is he dead?"

"Nope," Raider said. "I've been tryin' to get it through your thick skull that I don't want to kill you boys. I just want you to leave me and mine alone."

"Might as well shoot me, you bastard, 'cause I can't do that. You tried to steal my gal, and if that wasn't bad enough, you done broke Varney's shoulder. He won't never be the same, damn you."

Raider seethed with impatience and frustration. "I told you, I never tried to steal Chastity Doolittle from you. I couldn't, anyway, since you never had her. And Varney didn't give me no choice. He's lucky I didn't bust his head wide open with that hammer."

Roscoe didn't even seem to hear. "You hurt one Burkett, you hurt us all. You got to pay, you and all them that stand with you."

For a second, Raider thought about pulling the trigger. He didn't do it, not only because he didn't want any more blood on his hands, but also because he knew it wouldn't really end anything. He could kill Roscoe and Theodore both, and as soon as Varney healed up enough to tote a gun, the youngest Burkett brother would come after him. Probably the other males of the Burkett brood would, too.

"I'll make you a deal," Raider said as he thought about

Uncle Jess and Aunt Hannah. About Johnny and Joanie and little Enos and the babe that was on the way. He said, "I'll leave."

Roscoe sounded surprised. "What?"

"I said I'll leave this part o' the country. Put that rifle down and give me your word that neither you nor your kin will harm any of my kin, and I'll pack up and take off for the tall and uncut."

The thought of leaving his family, of abandoning the blacksmith shop he had built with his own hands, gnawed at Raider's guts. But that wouldn't be as bad as losing one or more of his loved ones to a senseless feud. Sure, the Burketts were the ones in the wrong here, but they were too dumb and too stubborn to ever be reasonable about things. Somebody had to put an end to this before innocent blood was spilled, and as far as Raider could see, he was the only candidate.

"You'd do that?" Roscoe said.

"That's right. You'll have a clear field with Chastity." *Just you and every other able-bodied hombre in the county over the age of sixteen,* he added silently.

"Well, I reckon that might be—" Roscoe stopped short and gave his head a shake like an angry old bull might have. "Damn it, no! We still got to have vengeance for what you did to Varney!"

"Well, if you think I'm gonna stand still and let you bust my shoulder with a hammer just to even things up, you're dumber'n you look, Roscoe. Better think again. This is the best chance you'll get to end this thing 'fore somebody gets hurt really bad."

"Don't want to end it, big man. Not 'til you're dead."

Roscoe didn't try to spin around. He dropped straight to the ground instead. Raider cursed and lashed out, trying to wallop the stubborn son of a bitch with the Colt, but the blow missed. Roscoe rolled backward and crashed into Raider's legs, knocking them out from under him.

Raider felt himself falling and lashed out with a foot, aiming the kick in Roscoe's general direction. The heel of his boot sank into soft flesh. Roscoe grunted in pain. Raider landed on his butt and rolled to one side as fast as he could. That was a good thing, too, because despite the kick Raider had landed on him, Roscoe lunged forward and crashed down where Raider had been a second earlier.

It was too dark to see if Roscoe still had his rifle or one of those Arkansas Toothpicks. Raider had managed to hang on to his revolver despite the rough-and-tumble. He came up in a crouch, with the Colt thrust out in front of him. He listened for the telltale sounds that would divulge that Roscoe was about to launch another attack.

Instead, he heard his cousin Johnny's voice calling from somewhere nearby, "Raider! Ray, you out here? You all right?"

"Johnny!" Raider bellowed. "Get down!"

It was too late. Flame gouted from the muzzle of Roscoe Burkett's rifle, but the shot wasn't aimed at Raider. He heard Johnny cry out in pain.

Raider guessed that the silence from the woods had been too much for the folks in the farmhouse to stand. Fearing for Raider's safety, Johnny had come out to check on him and walked right into a bullet instead. With the location of Roscoe's muzzle flash imprinted in his mind, Raider brought the Colt up and began to fire. The revolver bucked against his palm as shot after shot rolled out of it.

The gun blasts echoed through the woods. They were slow in dying away when Raider finally ceased fire. He had aimed just to one side and above the muzzle flash. Instinct had taken over and directed his shots, and now as silence fell once again, he listened for the sounds of movement or breathing and didn't hear either one.

A soft moan came from his right, though. That was Johnny.

Raider ignored Roscoe for the moment and headed for his cousin. He followed the sounds of pain and found Johnny lying at the edge of the trees. Dropping to a knee beside the young man, Raider said, "Blast it, Johnny, ain't you got the sense God gave a goose? You shoulda laid low in the house until I told you it was clear."

Raider didn't know if Johnny was conscious enough to hear and understand the words. His response showed that he was. Through teeth gritted against the pain, he said, "We was afraid . . . them damn Burketts . . . got you, Ray. Are you . . . hit?"

"No, but you sure are." Raider ran his free hand over his cousin's body and found a wet spot on Johnny's upper left arm. "He just wing you?"

"Yeah, but . . . it hurts like blazes."

"Good," Raider snapped. Now that he knew Johnny hadn't suffered a life-threatening wound, he gave in to the anger he felt. "Maybe that'll learn you to do what I say from now on."

"What about . . . the Burketts?"

Before Raider could answer, a howl came from the woods, a cry like that of an animal in pain. "Roscoe!" Theodore Burkett shouted. "Damn it, Roscoe, you can't be dead!"

Raider picked up the rifle Johnny had dropped when he had been shot and stood up, turning toward the trees. He had emptied his Colt at Roscoe, and he didn't have any more cartridges on him. Johnny's rifle was an old Henry, but it was well cared for, and Raider could make it sing and dance when he wanted to. He followed the sound of Theodore's sobbing and found both Burkett brothers about twenty feet into the trees. Roscoe was sprawled backward over a good-sized log. Theodore knelt beside him.

Roscoe wasn't moving. Raider figured that at least one of his shots had found the burly hillbilly. He covered both of them and said, "Don't try nothin', Theodore. I don't want to kill you, too."

Raider's stomach had a ball of sickness rolling around inside it. Despite all his good intentions, he had taken another man's life. Maybe he had been wrong to ever swear that vow, he thought. Maybe he had been wrong to come back here to the Ozarks, to his family. It was starting to look like killing was his destiny, like dealing out death was in his blood. He ought to go far away from civilized folks.

He became aware of the fact that it was getting lighter in the shadows under the trees. A yellow, wavering glow grew up around him as somebody approached, carrying a lantern. Since Theodore seemed too shaken up over Roscoe's death to try anything, Raider risked a glance over his shoulder and saw Uncle Jess coming toward him, rifle in one hand, lantern in the other. Johnny stumbled along behind him, clutching his wounded left arm with his right hand.

Raider glanced back at Theodore and Roscoe and got a shock. Now that he could see better, he saw the reason Roscoe was lying like that, bent backward over the log. The jagged end of a broken branch stuck out from the middle of Roscoe's broad chest. The branch was red with blood. From the looks of it, it had gone all the way through Roscoe's body.

"What the hell!" Uncle Jess muttered when he saw the same thing Raider did.

Raider's eyes were searching Roscoe's body for signs of any other wounds, but he didn't see any. The only thing he could figure out was that all of his shots had missed, but in scurrying to avoid the barrage of bullets, Roscoe had tripped and fallen—and landed right on that broken branch. His weight had driven the jagged tip of the gnarled wooden shaft into his body. Pure bad luck had kept the branch from breaking off. It had gone through Roscoe like a spear instead.

Roscoe's eyes were wide open, staring sightlessly into the night.

Theodore turned to look at Raider and said, "You kilt him, you bastard! You kilt my brother!"

"He killed himself," Raider said in a hard voice. He was in no mood to offer sympathy. "It was stubbornness and bad luck that did Roscoe in, not me."

"No, it was all your fault," Theodore accused in a cold,

bitter voice. "You ruint Varney, and you kilt Roscoe. I won't never rest until you're dead, you son of a bitch."

"Why don't you go ahead and shoot him now?" Johnny suggested in a voice that was thin and strained from the pain he was in. "No sense in waiting."

Raider shook his head. Providence has decreed that Roscoe Burkett hadn't died directly at his hand after all. He wasn't going to turn his back on that reprieve. "The killing's over," he said.

But the look on Roscoe's dead face was like a voice from across the divide, proclaiming that it would never be over, not as long as anybody on either side drew breath.

# Chapter 10

Raider found the Burkett brothers' mules hidden deeper in the trees. After Jess helped Johnny back to the house so that Hannah could tend to his wounded arm, he stood guard while Raider helped Theodore get Roscoe's body draped over the back of a mule and lashed down so it couldn't go anywhere. Neither Raider nor Jess trusted Theodore not to try anything, despite his grief.

Even though Raider knew it wouldn't do any good, once Theodore was mounted up he said, "Let it end here, Theodore. No good'll come from anybody else dyin'."

Theodore just regarded him with a stony stare and didn't say anything. He turned away and rode off into the night, leading the other mule with its grisly burden.

Raider returned to the house. When he went inside, he was relieved to see that Joanie was up and around, with a bandage tied around her head where the bushwhacker's bullet had creased her. She was holding Enos and watching with an anxious expression on her face as Hannah cleaned the wound in Johnny's arm.

Raider went over to Joanie, put a hand under her chin,

and looked into her eyes. He grunted in satisfaction as he saw that they were clear. "I imagine your head hurts, don't it, girl?" he asked.

Joanie nodded. "It sure does, but I'll be all right."

"You remember what day it is, and you're not seein' double or anything?"

"I'm fine," she said. "Don't worry about me, Raider." Her voice took on a more scathing tone. "Worry about what's going to happen when the Burketts try to settle the score again."

"Joanie!" her husband said. "You got no call to talk to Ray that way. None of this was his fault."

"Oh, I know that." She sighed and shook her head. "I'm just scared, that's all. Johnny and me got hit this time. Might be Enos next time."

"Nope," Raider said. "Ain't gonna be a next time."

Uncle Jess stared at him in disbelief. "How can you say that? You don't know them Burketts like I do, Ray. They's all crazy as loons."

"Crazy's one thing, stupid's another." Raider set Johnny's rifle on the table. "I almost made a deal out there with Roscoe, before he changed his mind and started fightin' again."

"Deal?" Jess repeated. "What sort o' deal?"

"I told him I'd get out of this part of the country if him and his kin would leave the rest of you folks alone."

"No!" Johnny burst out. "Damn it, Ray, you can't do that. We're family, and family sticks together, through good times and bad, no matter what."

Raider shrugged. "That's easy to say, but don't forget I was away from here for a lot o' years, lookin' after myself and not givin' the home folks a bit of thought. I don't deserve to have any of y'all gettin' yourselves killed on my account."

"That just ain't true," Johnny insisted. "You come back and helped us when we really needed you, more'n once. Remember that business with the Arkansas Hellrider?"

Raider remembered, all right, and when he glanced at Joanie and saw the look of shame cross her face, he knew that she remembered, too. He had risked his hide to help her during that mess, and none of them had forgotten it, least of all her.

"I was glad to lend a hand back then," Raider said, "and I know that any of you would do the same for me, without ever askin' any questions. But it don't change the fact that it's me the Burketts want. If I'm gone, they'll leave you alone."

"You can't be sure about that," Jess pointed out. "They might come after us just to draw you back here."

Raider shook his head. "Nope, because I'm gonna arrange things so that don't happen. I'm gonna go see whoever runs that family and make a deal with him."

The others all stared at him, even Enos, who couldn't understand a word yet except maybe "no" and "mama."

"You can't do that," Jess finally said. "Old Asa Burkett is the, what do you call it, patriarch o' that clan, and he's the craziest one in the whole bunch! The meanest, too. I'm talkin' rattlesnake mean, Raider. You ride up to his place and he's liable to have his boys tie you down so's he can peel the skin right off you, one strip at a time!"

Raider didn't like the sound of that, but he said, "Reckon I'll have to take that chance."

"Damn it, Ray," Johnny said, ignoring the glare of disapproval his wife gave him for cussing like that in front of the baby, "you're so worried about the chance of us gettin' hurt because of you, and you ain't even thinkin' about the fact that you might get your own self killed because of us!"

"Stop it!" Joanie said, directing her anger at all of them. "Just stop it! You're all so quick to take the blame. Well, the one who's really to blame was Roscoe Burkett! He's the one who got it in his head the reason Chastity Doolittle wouldn't marry him was because of Raider! He's the one who made it a killin' matter!"

"Well," Raider said, "if you want to get right down to it, ol' Roscoe never even asked Chastity to marry up with him. He just figured she wouldn't get hitched because he'd heard that she liked me."

"You see?" Joanie said. "It's all . . ." She hunted for the word she wanted. "Irrational!"

Raider couldn't argue with that. The whole thing was plumb senseless. But that didn't make the danger to his family any less real.

"Uncle Jess, can you tell me where to find this Asa Burkett?"

Jess frowned and scratched at his beard. "Reckon I can, but I ain't sure I oughta."

"I think I can hunt him up if I have to. I spent a lot of years findin' folks who didn't always want to be found."

Jess sighed. "Yeah, that's true enough. We can't talk you outta doin' this?"

Raider shook his head and said, "Nope."

"Well, then, you ain't goin' up there by your lonesome. Me an' Johnny will be goin' with you."

"That's right," Johnny said. Hannah had finished bandaging his wounded arm. He got to his feet and went to stand beside Jess. "If you're bound an' determined, then me and Pa will be ridin' with you."

"Dadgummit!" Raider said. "I'm tryin' to keep you two knuckleheads out o' danger—"

"Ain't no sense in arguin' with us," Jess said. "Our minds are made up."

Raider looked at Hannah and Joanie, hoping they would talk some sense into their menfolks, but he saw the same stubbornness in their eyes as he saw on the faces of Jess and Johnny. That came as no surprise to him. They were mountain women, after all, and no strangers to trouble.

"All right," he said. "You can come with me. We'll go see Asa Burkett and settle this, once and for all."


There were Burketts scattered all over this part of the country, but the main enclave of them could be found on the thickly wooded slopes of a good-sized hill known locally as Polecat Mountain. It was only a somewhat appropriate

71

name, Raider thought, because while the air was laden with various stenches, none of them really smelled like skunk.

Instead, the odors were mostly decaying vegetation, rotting meat, multiple kinds of animal shit, and a strong dose of unwashed human flesh. Raider knew he didn't smell like a daisy, but he still couldn't help but wrinkle his nose a little as he reined his horse to a stop in front of the cabin where Asa Burkett lived. It was the morning after Roscoe and Theodore had opened fire on Uncle Jess's house.

The cabin was a sprawling log structure that leaned every which way. It had been added onto numerous times as the Burkett family grew. According to Uncle Jess, Asa Burkett and his wife, Beulah, had seven sons and five daughters, and more than half of them were married with broods of their own, most of them living right there at the cabin. The ones who didn't had cabins nearby. Roscoe, Theodore, and Varney were the youngest of the boys. Varney, in fact, was the baby of the family.

Jess and Johnny rode right behind Raider and were mounted on sturdy saddle mules. All three men were heavily armed. Each carried a pistol, Raider and Jess had rifles, and Johnny had a shotgun across the saddle in front of him.

Riding up to the Burkett place like this amounted pretty much to bearding the lion in his own den, and Raider knew they might not come back alive. But they would give a mighty good account of themselves before they died, if it came to that, and they'd send a good number of Burketts to hell ahead of them.

Several hounds came from under the porch and bayed at the visitors. The sound was loud and mournful, but Raider knew the dogs weren't telling the Burketts anything they didn't already know. He was sure they had been spotted as soon as they started up Polecat Mountain.

No humans were in sight, only the rib-gaunt hounds. Raider leaned forward in the saddle with his hands on the Winchester that rested across the pommel. "Burkett!" he called. "Asa Burkett! I need to have words with you!"

When there was no response, Raider added, "You hear me, Burkett?"

"I hear you, you murderin' bastard." The rough, gravelly voice came from inside the cabin. The door was open, and so were the windows, and Raider felt confident that quite a few weapons were trained on him and Jess and Johnny at that moment. "I got nothin' to say to you," Burkett went on, "except that you're one dumb bastard for comin' up here."

"I won't argue about the dumb bastard part, but I ain't no murderer."

"You kilt my boy Roscoe!"

"Roscoe tripped and fell and stuck a broken tree branch through him," Raider pointed out. "That was *after* him and Theodore bushwhacked my family and came within a hair o' killin' my cousin's wife, who never did nothin' bad to you or your'n."

"That don't matter. This is a blood feud. Ever'body's fair game."

Raider tamped down the anger he felt rising in him. "There ain't no need for it to be that way. Come on out, so we can talk about it. Face to face, man to man."

"You know there be a dozen guns pointed at you right now, don't you?"

"Figured as much," Raider said.

"So if you try anything funny, you won't live long enough to see how it works out."

"Not plannin' on anything funny," Raider said. "Just talk, that's all."

The warped boards of the ramshackle porch in front of the cabin squealed and groaned in protest as the bearded, heavyset form of Asa Burkett appeared in the doorway and stepped forward. He held an old muzzle-loader that could have belonged to Daniel Boone, but Raider had no doubt the rifle was in prime working condition.

"Say what you got to say before you die," Burkett growled.

"First of all, I had nothin' against your boys before they

73

showed up at my blacksmith shop," Raider began. "I didn't even know who they were."

"Didn't stop you from bustin' up Varney."

"I'm gettin' to that. Roscoe started in on me about Chastity Doolittle, about how she wouldn't marry him because o' me, and I told him time and again that wasn't true. I ain't gettin' hitched up to Chastity. Got no intentions of it."

"Then how come Roscoe—"

"Roscoe got an idea in his head and couldn't let go of it," Raider said. "I couldn't talk sense to him. Look, he was your boy. You ought to know how he was."

Burkett frowned. "Roscoe always had a mind o' his own, true enough."

"I told him he ought to go talk to Chastity and tell her how he felt. Hell, I would've gone to her and spoken up for Roscoe myself if he'd given me the chance."

That might be stretching the truth a little, but Raider figured he could get away with it.

"But he just wouldn't listen to reason, wouldn't give me a chance. Varney came at me with a pigsticker, and I fought back. Hell, you got to admit, Burkett, a man's got the right to defend himself."

Burkett's glare was as dark as a thunderstorm, but he rumbled, "Keep talkin'."

"I admit I busted Varney's shoulder. But I could've stove in his head and killed him. I didn't do that. And I would've let it go at that if Roscoe and Theodore had left me and my family alone. But they started shootin' at us with no warning last night. One of the bullets grazed Joanie on the head and came that close to killin' her. Another ventilated Johnny's arm."

"You ain't hurt," Burkett said.

"No, but it wasn't for lack o' trying. I'll admit I walloped Theodore on the head and threw some lead at Roscoe—"

"Snuck up on 'em like a damned Injun, I heard."

Raider shrugged. "They came a-skulkin' first. Anyway, if you saw Roscoe's body, you know there weren't any bullet holes in it. His death was an accident, Burkett, and that's the God's honest truth."

"Maybe you didn't shoot him," the patriarch of the mountain clan admitted, "but like you said, it weren't for lack o' tryin'."

"You shoot at a man, you got to expect him to shoot back."

For a long moment, Burkett stood there glowering at Raider. Then he said, "How come you're rehashin' all this? We both know what happened . . . and what's gonna happen."

"I just want it all clear in our minds, so I know you'll give what I have to say fair consideration."

"You ain't said nothin' yet."

"I'm sayin' it now: I'm ready to leave the mountains."

Burkett's hands tightened on the old flintlock. "Onliest way you're leavin' is in a pine box."

Raider held up a hand. "Hear me out. I'm sorry for what happened. I ain't sayin' it was my fault, but I wish things hadn't played out the way they did. And to prove it, I'm willin' to leave my family and the business I got built up and go somewhere else. You promise to leave my kinfolks alone, and I'll never set foot in the Ozarks again."

Burkett frowned. "That ain't blood. Blood's got to pay for blood."

"You think it won't hurt me to ride away like that?" Raider's voice roughened with genuine emotion. "I was fiddlefooted for a lot of years, Burkett. I drifted around, whorin' and drinkin' and killin' for the Pinkertons, until most o' the skin wore off my soul from livin' like that. I tried to quit, but every time I got dragged back in . . . until the last time. I came home, Burkett. Home. I reckon you can understand that."

Burkett still frowned, but he didn't say anything.

"These past two years I had things I never had before. A place to call my own, and folks who cared about me. *That's* what I'm offerin' to give up, even though this whole mess wasn't my fault. And I got to tell you, there's a big part o' me would rather shoot it out with you and your'n, right here and now, than do what I'm offerin' to do."

"You'd do that just to keep your kinfolks safe?"

"Damn right."

Raider could tell that Burkett was thinking about it, but the old man hadn't made up his mind yet. Raider let himself hope that Burkett would come to the right decision.

"It's a deal," Burkett said finally, but then he tempered Raider's hopes by going on, "on one condition."

"What's that?"

"You fight my boy Cleavon first. You live through that, I reckon you can go, with your word that you'll never come back to this part o' the country."

Raider grunted. "And your word that my kinfolks won't come to no harm?"

"Not at the hands o' the Burketts or any of our kin. My word on it."

"Good enough for me," Raider said with a nod, even though from the corner of his eye he saw the warning look on Uncle Jess's face.

Burkett turned his head and bellowed, "Cleavon!"

A moment later, Raider saw why Uncle Jess looked so worried. The porch shook and swayed like it was about to collapse as Cleavon Burkett stepped out of the cabin on it.

He was smaller than Polecat Mountain. A mite smaller.

# Chapter 11

The woman who stood in the doorway of Edmund Corrigan's suite had hair black as a raven's wing. It was pulled back and gathered into a thick braid that hung well down her back. Her lips were full and red, her eyes a deep brown. She wasn't overly tall. The curves of her body were opulent without being too lush, and they were displayed to fine effect in the low-cut gown she wore. Smiling, she said, "You must be the gentleman Edmund mentioned. Won't you come in, please?"

She stepped back and held the door open. The familiar way she had referred to Corrigan told Longarm that she was close to the cattleman, and he doubted that she was his daughter if she called him Edmund. That left his wife. As Longarm stepped past Riley Hutchins and entered the room, he took his hat off, nodded politely, and said, "Ma'am."

Remembering Riley—which wasn't easy to do with such a good-looking woman standing there smiling at him—Longarm turned back for a second and tossed a coin to the young man. Riley caught it, grinned, and said, "See you later, Mr. Parker."

The woman closed the door and said, "I'm Anita Corrigan, Edmund's wife." That confirmed Longarm's guess.

"Custis Parker, ma'am," he introduced himself, "and it's an honor to make your acquaintance."

"Edmund will be right out." She swept a slender, graceful hand around the luxuriously furnished sitting room. "In the meantime, please make yourself comfortable. Would you like a drink?"

"Much obliged. Maryland rye, if you've got it."

She laughed, a merry, musical sound. "Of course we have it. The bar is well stocked."

She wasn't joshing about that, he saw as she went over to a bar that sat on one side of the room and poured the drink for him. Judging from the number of bottles, they had every sort of who-hit-John under the sun.

Anita Corrigan brought him the drink and took his hat, hanging it on a brass hat tree next to the door of the suite. The door on the other side of the sitting room opened, and a man came in with his hand extended. Since Longarm was still standing, he turned and clasped the man's hand as Anita said, "Edmund, dear, this is Mr. Parker."

Corrigan was a big man, almost as tall and broad-shouldered as Longarm. He was around fifty, with a full head of graying red hair. His face was beginning to show the signs of heavy drinking and hard living, but he was still handsome in a rough-hewn, dignified way. His grip was strong.

"Glad to meet you, Parker," he said. "That bellboy tells me you want to enter the contest I'm putting on to find the fastest draw and best shot in the West."

"That's right," Longarm said. "I don't know how I'll stack up, but I'm eager to find out."

Corrigan let go of Longarm's hand and went over to the bar to pour himself a shot of whiskey. Anita moved closer to him and murmured, "Not too much, dear. You know what Dr. Phillips said—"

"Dr. Phillips is full of horseshit, pardon my French," Corrigan snapped. He threw back the drink. "I know what I can take and what I can't." Turning back to Longarm, the

78

cattleman went on, "The entry fee is two thousand bucks. Have you got that much, Parker?"

Longarm tried not to frown. He had planned to tell Corrigan who he really was and why he was here, so that he wouldn't have to come up with the two grand. But Mrs. Corrigan was standing right there, and he didn't know how trustworthy she was. Beauty and trustworthiness didn't always go hand in hand. But then, neither did ugly, he reminded himself.

He felt an instinctive dislike of Corrigan, though, and suddenly he was hesitant to reveal his real identity and purpose. Men who liked their booze too much sometimes said things they shouldn't, things that could get a lawman working undercover into a lot of trouble. Maybe it would be better for the time being to remain plain ol' Custis Parker, rather than Deputy United States Marshal Custis Long.

"I've got it," he said, trying not to smile as he thought about the reaction in Billy Vail's office when his telegram arrived asking for two thousand dollars to be sent to him. "I reckon cash will be all right?"

Corrigan grunted. "Cash will be fine. You have it on you?"

"No, I just got in to Fort Worth a little while ago. I'll have to arrange for the money, but that won't take long. Soon as the banks open in the morning be all right?"

"Of course." Corrigan reached for the bottle and poured himself another drink, ignoring the look that his wife sent in his direction. Longarm thought that it would be mighty difficult to ignore Anita Corrigan, even when she was put out at you. Corrigan downed the whiskey and went on, "There's one more thing . . ."

"What's that?" Longarm asked.

"You've got to prove you deserve to be in the sort of contest I'm putting on. You can't just buy your way in. There's going to be an exhibition—tomorrow, in fact— where all the contestants demonstrate their skill. You got here just in time, Parker. We'll all be leaving for my ranch tomorrow evening."

79

Longarm didn't much like the sound of that exhibition, but he didn't figure he could do anything about it. Corrigan was making the rules, and Longarm would just have to go along with them.

And hope that none of the other contestants recognized him as a lawman. That was a concern, too.

"Sounds fine to me," he said. "I never mind a chance to get in a little practice." He turned to the hat tree to reclaim his Stetson. "Now, if you folks will excuse me, I need to see about finding a place to stay tonight—"

"You have a room here in the hotel," Corrigan broke in. "I reserved the entire sixth floor for that purpose, and there are still a few empty rooms. Tell the clerk downstairs that you're my guest, and that he's to put you in one of the rooms on the sixth floor."

"You sure about that?"

"Of course."

"Well, then," Longarm said, "I'm much obliged to you."

"Don't mention it. Just bring me that two grand in the morning."

Longarm nodded. "I sure will." He looked at Anita. "Mrs. Corrigan, it was a real pleasure to meet you."

"I'm sure we'll be seeing a lot of each other on the ranch, Mr. Parker," she said with a smile. Longarm thought he saw a flash of something in those brown eyes of hers, but he couldn't be sure.

He would have to watch his step around her, he told himself. She had the sort of sensual beauty that greatly appealed to him. He was a professional, though. He wouldn't risk fouling up his capture of Felix Gaunt by messing around with the wife of a rich, powerful rancher. He wasn't afraid of Edmund Corrigan, but he didn't believe in unnecessary complications, either.

Longarm nodded good night to both of them and left the suite. When he reached the lobby downstairs, he caught the eye of Riley Hutchins, who was standing almost at attention beside one of the potted palms, waiting to see if there was any chore he needed to do for a guest. He hurried over to Longarm, who said, "I'm going to be staying here, Riley. I left my warbag, saddle, and Winchester down at the train station. Reckon you could fetch 'em for me?"

"I'd be glad to, Mr. Parker. And you don't have to pay me nothin' else, either. You already gave me a good tip."

Riley hurried out on that errand while Longarm spoke to the clerk at the desk, passing along what Corrigan had said about giving him a room on the sixth floor.

"Of course, Mr. Parker. Mr. Corrigan has quite a few guests staying with us. I assume you'll be taking part in his great shooting competition?"

"That's the plan," Longarm said. "I already sent the boy to fetch my gear from the depot. Now I need to know where the nearest telegraph office is."

"Two blocks west of here on Seventh Street."

"Will it be open this late?"

"The Western Union office stays open all night," the clerk said.

Longarm had figured as much. He nodded his thanks, collected his key, and nodded again when the clerk told him he would have Riley put Longarm's things in the room when he got back. Longarm left the hotel and walked straight to the telegraph office.

He printed his message on the yellow flimsy, short and to the point: WIRE TWO THOUSAND CASH CARE OF PALACE HOTEL SOONEST STOP VERY IMPORTANT STOP CUSTIS. Most key-pounders were trustworthy, but in case this one wasn't, there was nothing in the message to give away his true identity or mission.

With that taken care of, he went back to the hotel and turned in, sleeping the sleep of an honest man.


Give Billy Vail credit. He sometimes blustered and raised holy hell over Longarm's habits, but he knew that Longarm was devoted to his job. If Longarm asked for two grand and said it was very important, then it was really very important.

But that hadn't stopped Vail from adding a BE CAREFUL to his return telegram, which a different bellboy delivered to Longarm in the hotel dining room the next morning. Longarm didn't know whether Billy meant for him to be careful with his own hide, or with the money. Chances were, Vail was talking about a little bit of both.

But either way, Vail's telegram also said that Longarm would find the cash waiting for him at the First National Bank in Fort Worth as soon as it opened.

When he finished eating, he left the dining room and started through the lobby toward the front door. He was surprised when a young cowboy in chaps and a curled-brim Stetson stood up from one of the chairs and stepped in front of him. It took Longarm a second to recognize the waddy as Riley Hutchins.

"Mornin', Mr. Parker," Riley greeted him. "Did you get a chance to ask Mr. Corrigan about me ridin' for his spread?"

Longarm frowned. "Hold on a minute, son. What say we eat that apple one bite a time? The subject of your employment didn't come up last night."

"Oh." Riley's face fell. "It's just that I know Mr. Corrigan and his guests are leavin' tonight . . ."

"I'll say something to him today," Longarm promised. "You didn't up and quit your job here at the hotel, did you?"

"Not yet. But I will if you say so."

"Hold off on that," Longarm advised the youngster. "We'll see what happens later today. You got a horse?"

Riley nodded. "Yes, sir."

"Then you can always ride on out to the Box C later if you need to."

Riley agreed, although he didn't look too happy about it.

"In the meantime," Longarm said, "you can show me how to find the First National Bank."

They left the hotel together, Riley chattering excitedly as they walked down the street. "The fastest guns in Texas are gonna be at that contest," he said. "That means the fastest guns anywhere."

"Everything's always bigger and better in Texas, eh?" Longarm asked with a grin.

"Well, ain't it?"

Longarm chuckled and didn't waste his breath arguing. Instead, he said, "I reckon you've seen most of Mr. Corrigan's guests, there in the hotel."

"Sure have. I've run errands for most of 'em, in fact."

"Do you recollect seeing a tall, skinny galoot amongst 'em? Dark hair, lantern jaw, not what you'd call a handsome fella?"

Riley frowned in thought. "That sounds a little like Mr. Gordon."

"He got a first name?"

"Frank. Frank Gordon."

Longarm nodded, satisfied that Frank Gordon and Felix Gaunt were one and the same. Gaunt liked to pick aliases with the same initials as his own name. That was common practice among owlhoots, many of whom weren't all that bright, or they wouldn't be criminals to start with.

Preferring to err on the side of discretion, Billy Vail had wired the money to him under his own name, but without any mention of him being a deputy U.S. marshal. Longarm proved who he was to the president of the bank and collected the cash, a nice packet of twenty one-hundred-dollar bills. Longarm put them in an envelope the banker provided and stashed them in an inside coat pocket, then shook hands with the man and left the bank.

Riley was waiting on the sidewalk outside. "Anything else I can do for you, Mr. Parker?"

"Nope, can't think of a thing, unless you can tell me where Corrigan intends to stage that shooting exhibition he mentioned to me last night."

"I've heard about that. It's supposed to be at the Livestock Exchange Building, in the stockyards north of the river."

Longarm nodded his thanks. "Why don't you come to that, and we'll see if I've gotten you that job with Corrigan by then?"

"Thanks, Mr. Parker. I can't tell you what it'll mean to me to have a job I can do from horseback again."

Longarm knew what the young fella meant. He hadn't stayed with the cowboy life himself, but he knew how it could get into an hombre's blood, especially if that hombre was young.

He parted company with Riley at the hotel and went up to the fourth floor to give the two thousand dollars to Corrigan. He would get it back when the contest was over. At least he hoped that Corrigan wouldn't be stubborn about returning it once Gaunt was either dead or under arrest and the truth had come out. Longarm doubted that the rancher would want to get the federal government mad at him by hanging on to the money.

Corrigan wasn't the one who answered Longarm's knock on the door, however. Anita was, and she looked even more stunning than she had the night before, in a silk dressing gown that clung enticingly to the curves of her body. Her midnight-black hair was loose now, hanging around her shoulders, and the smile she gave Longarm rocked him down to the toes of his boots.

"My husband isn't here right now, Mr. Parker," she said. "But won't you come in anyway? I'm sure Edmund wouldn't mind if you waited for him."

Longarm thought about it, but only for a second. Then he said, "Why, thank you, ma'am. I don't mind if I do."

# Chapter 12

He knew he should have taken off for the tall and uncut, but he wasn't in the habit of running from either trouble or good-looking women—which were often one and the same, he reflected as he took off his hat and stepped into the hotel suite.

Anita Corrigan closed the door behind him. "Would you like some coffee?"

"That would be just fine, thanks."

"Have a seat. I'll bring it to you."

The remains of a late breakfast were scattered on a table, including a coffeepot and a couple of extra cups. Anita picked up the pot and poured coffee into one of the cups.

"How do you take it?" she asked.

"Black as sin and strong enough to run around on its own hind legs."

She laughed, set the cup on a saucer, and brought it over to the well-upholstered armchair where he had taken a seat. She was pretty well-upholstered herself, he saw when she bent over to hand him the cup and saucer and her dressing gown fell open a little, revealing the creamy upper swells of her breasts. She either didn't notice the glance he gave them or didn't mind that he was looking. Longarm would have been willing to bet on the latter.

She poured some coffee for herself and took a seat in another armchair opposite him. Longarm waited for her to cross her legs and let the robe fall away from them, but she wasn't *that* blatant about it. Instead she just smiled over her cup at him and said, "I suppose you've come to give Edmund that money for the entry fee."

"Yes, ma'am."

"Please, call me Anita. And you're Custis, isn't that right?"

He nodded. "Yes, ma'am . . . I mean, Anita. Yeah, I've got the two thousand now."

"I'm not sure why Edmund even insisted on an entry fee. It's not as if he needs the money."

"Well-to-do, is he?"

"Look around this suite." She smiled. "Look at *me*. What do you think?"

"I think your husband can afford the best," Longarm said, half expecting the bluntness of his reply to offend her.

Instead, she laughed. "And you'd be absolutely right." She paused. "Are you surprised by my candor, Custis?"

"Not particularly. You struck me last night as a woman who likes to speak her mind . . . even if your husband doesn't always listen to you."

She sipped her coffee. "Edmund is accustomed to dealing with tough, hard men, because he is one, himself. He worked for his fortune, back East in the steel mills, starting out, and then in other industries."

"So he's used to making the rules and getting what he wants."

"Exactly."

Longarm shrugged. "That's fine with me. I'm just here to win me a Golden Eagle, not to do any other business with him."

Anita smiled and said, "Confident in your abilities, are you?"

"I'm pretty good with a gun," Longarm said.

"And modest, too." She set her cup aside on a spindly legged table. "What else are you good at, Custis?"

"Just about anything I set my mind to."

"And what about this? Would you like to set your mind to this?"

She stood up, undoing the knot in the belt of her dressing gown with a deft touch. The gown fell all the way open this time, and she spread it even more with her hands, revealing that she wore nothing under it.

Longarm's jaw tightened. The impact of Anita Corrigan's nudity was like a punch in the belly. He felt himself growing hard right away as he looked openly at her magnificent, coral-tipped breasts, soft stomach, and rounded hips and thighs that flowed into an inviting triangle of fine-spun raven hair. Longarm thought it was crazy that folks had gone to war over women in olden times, but if ol' Helen of Troy looked anything like Anita Corrigan, he could sort of understand it.

Longarm's voice was taut with the strain he was under as he said, "You'd best put that gown back on, ma'am."

"I thought you were going to call me Anita. And don't you like what you see?"

"I like it just fine. Too much, as a matter of fact. And since your husband's liable to waltz in here any minute now, I reckon I better go back to calling you ma'am."

Her tone had an edge to it as she said, "Am I to understand that you're turning me down?"

"As much as it pains me to say it, Mrs. Corrigan, I reckon I am." Until Felix Gaunt was in custody or hell, Longarm couldn't allow anything to interfere with his job.

Anita pulled the gown closed and retied the belt with curt, angry motions. "Very well. But don't think this offer will be repeated once we get to the ranch. You had your chance. Only one to a—"

She stopped short and flushed, and Longarm knew she had been about to say "customer." He wondered for a second where the whorehouse was where Corrigan had found her. New Orleans, he decided. She had the look of a New Orleans whore about her.

A heavy footstep sounded in the hall outside the suite. Anita turned and went through the door into the other room, closing it a little harder than was necessary.

When Corrigan came into the room a moment later, he found Longarm sitting there, right ankle cocked on his left knee, Stetson on his lap, taking calm sips from the cup of coffee. The cattleman said, "Mr. Parker. I didn't know you were here."

"Your wife let me in," Longarm said as he set the cup aside and stood up. He reached into his coat and took out the envelope of cash. "Two thousand dollars, as agreed."

Corrigan took the envelope from him, glanced inside it for a second, and nodded. "Welcome to the contest, Parker. Assuming you pass the test at the exhibition this afternoon."

"I plan on it. In the meantime, there's something else I need to talk to you about."

Corrigan frowned. "What might that be?"

"There's a young fella who works here in the hotel as a bellboy, but he's really a cowhand who's been down on his luck. He'd sure admire to have a riding job again, but none of the spreads around here are hiring right now."

"You want me to hire him?"

"I reckon he'd make a good hand. He's a hard worker, that's for sure."

Corrigan waved a hand, and Longarm noticed the knuckles were big and scarred. "My foreman handles the hiring of the crew on the Box C. But if this youngster wants to come out there, I'll tell Jeff to give him a chance. No guarantees, though."

Longarm nodded. "That's fine. I'm obliged."

"I have buggies engaged to take everyone to the Livestock Exchange Building this afternoon. That's where the exhibition will take place. Be in the lobby of the hotel at one thirty."

Corrigan was definitely used to giving orders. That

rubbed Longarm the wrong way, but he nodded anyway and said, "I'll be there."

He would play the hand as Corrigan dealt it—for now.

The Livestock Exchange was a huge building with white-washed walls, a red tile roof in the Spanish style, and a large grassy area in front of it. The meatpacking companies that operated in the nearby stockyards had their offices in the building, and there was also an attached corral where cattle could be driven in, inspected, and bought and sold.

Not surprisingly, the smell of manure was strong in the air. Having worked around cattle many times, though, Longarm barely noticed it, and he suspected the same was true for most of the folks who lived and worked around there. Only when it rained would the aroma get really ripe.

More than two dozen men had entered the shooting competition. Longarm had ridden up Main Street in a buggy with two of them, neither of whom he recognized.

One of the men had long golden curls like Wild Bill Hickok or Commodore Perry Owens. He was dressed fancy, too, in a fringed buckskin jacket, tight cream-colored trousers, and a matching hat with a high crown and broad brim. The pair of Colts he wore in black holsters had ivory handles and were nickel-plated. He put out his hand to shake and said, "Hello, I'm Kid Montana."

Longarm thought he was about the silliest-looking gent he'd ever laid eyes on. But he shook and howdied anyway, just to be polite about it.

The other hombre was a lot more sober-looking, in a dusty black suit and hat. He had a long, dark brown face that was creased and weathered by the elements. "Name's Sale," he said, not volunteering any more information about himself.

Longarm provided his own name, or rather, the one he was using, and the three men sat back to enjoy the ride. When they got to the Livestock Exchange, they found that quite a crowd was waiting for them. The local newspaper had played up the shooting exhibition, and people had turned out to have a look for themselves.

Back at the hotel, and now here at the Livestock Exchange, Longarm had searched for Felix Gaunt without seeing any sign of him. He was beginning to worry that he had misjudged Gaunt's intentions and wasted the government's money, despite what Riley had said about seeing a man at the hotel matching Gaunt's description, when he suddenly spotted a tall, lanky figure that struck him as familiar. The only time he had seen Gaunt in person was during that shoot-out in Wichita, and he hadn't gotten any better look at the outlaw than Gaunt had gotten at him. He had seen Gaunt's picture on reward dodgers, though, and there was no mistaking the lantern jaw and the deep-set eyes. Longarm had found the man he was looking for.

Gaunt was talking to Edmund Corrigan at the moment, though, so Longarm couldn't just walk up and arrest him. He knew Gaunt would put up a fight, and there was too big a crowd around to risk that. Innocent folks were bound to get hurt if the bullets started to fly.

The time was coming, though. Longarm could afford to wait until the moment was right. Now that he had Gaunt in his sights, he was confident that the killer wouldn't get away from him again.

A few minutes later, Corrigan walked up to the long, shaded porch in front of the Livestock Exchange Building and picked up a megaphone. "Ladies and gentlemen!" he said into it, and the crowd began to quiet down. "Ladies and gentlemen!" he repeated. "Welcome to an exhibition of some of the finest shooting you'll ever see! I'm sure you've all heard about the contest I'm staging to find the fastest draw and best shot in the West. This is not that contest, but merely an exhibition so that the contestants can show off their skills for an appreciative audience! The actual contest will take place on my ranch, the Box C! Now, give these sterling pistoleers a hand!"

He gestured at the contestants, who had gathered on the porch with him. Longarm was about fifteen feet from

Gaunt, who hadn't paid any attention to him so far. Kid Montana was still next to Longarm, chattering away in excitement.

Something was fishy about the Kid's accent. He was trying to talk like a Westerner, Longarm thought, but he couldn't quite pull it off. Longarm decided he was from back East somewhere. Couldn't hold that against the Kid. Longarm himself had been born and bred a long way on the other side of the Mississippi, in the hills of West-by-God Virginia, and hadn't drifted out to the frontier until after the Late Unpleasantness that had pitted North against South.

"There's my girl," Kid Montana said, pointing to a pretty blonde about nineteen or twenty years old. She smiled and waved at him. "I'm a mite nervous," the Kid went on. "This'll be the first time I've shot like this in front of her."

"You'll do fine," Longarm told him. "Just think about what you're shooting at, not who's watching."

The Kid nodded. "Yeah, that's what I'll try to do."

Corrigan turned to the contestants and said, "Gentlemen, take your places. It's time to get this show started."

# Chapter 13

"Good Lord," Uncle Jess said when Cleavon Burkett appeared on the cabin's porch.

"You can't fight him, Ray," Johnny added in alarm. "He's as big as a damn mountain!"

Raider nodded. "Then I reckon I'll have to climb up him to wallop him in the face. Got to be done, otherwise the old man won't agree to leave you folks alone once I'm gone."

Jess said, "But he'll kill you!"

"Maybe not."

Raider wished he felt as confident as he sounded, which wasn't really all that confident to start with. He handed his Winchester to Uncle Jess, then swung down from the saddle. He took off his black Stetson and hung it on the horn.

Up on the porch, Cleavon was grinning an idiot's grin, and old Asa Burkett was chuckling in anticipation. Other faces appeared in the windows of the cabin, as the Burketts and their kin inside jockeyed for good places to watch the whipping that Raider was about to take. Raider knew that none of them figured he could beat Cleavon. He'd be lucky just to survive the tussle.

"No guns, right?" Raider asked Burkett.

The old man nodded and licked his lips. "That's right, no guns."

Raider unbuckled his shell belt and draped it over his saddle. "And neither you nor any o' your kin will take a hand, no matter what happens?"

"You got my word on it. This here fight's betwixt you and Cleavon."

"All right," Raider said as he stepped away from his horse. "Let's get to it."

With a roar, Cleavon charged down from the porch, not bothering with the steps, just leaping to the ground. He came at Raider like a maddened bull, with arms like the trunks of young trees, outstretched to pull his opponent into a bear hug that would crush the life out of him.

Raider didn't let the giant hillbilly get those arms around him. He sidestepped at the last second, and Cleavon had enough momentum built up that he couldn't stop. As he stumbled on by, Raider clubbed his hands together and smashed them against the back of Cleavon's neck. He had to reach up to strike the blow.

Cleavon didn't even seem to feel it. He caught himself after a couple more steps and wheeled around, swinging a backhand at Raider as he did so. It was no slow, easily avoided punch, either. Raider had all he could do just ducking in time before Cleavon's hamlike fist could take his head off.

He darted in and jabbed a couple of short, swift punches to Cleavon's belly. Even the biggest man had a weakness. Sometimes it was a glass jaw, others a tender gut.

Hitting Cleavon in the belly was like punching thick pine planks, though. Again, he didn't even seem to feel the impact of Raider's fists.

Raider danced back as Cleavon swept another tree-trunk-like arm at him. The other Burketts were coming out onto the porch now to shout encouragement to the giant. From horseback, Uncle Jess and Johnny shouted warnings to Raider, warnings that he didn't really need, because Cleavon was so big it was impossible to miss what he was doing.

He came at Raider again and launched a roundhouse punch, but this time it was a feint, the former Pinkerton discovered to his dismay when he weaved aside to avoid it and found his shoulder caught in the viselike grip of Cleavon's other hand. He yelped in surprise and pain as Cleavon jerked him up completely off the ground.

Since his feet were already in the air, Raider decided he might as well make use of them. He drew his knees up and then straightened his legs in a powerful kick that drove the heels of both boots into Cleavon's chest.

For the first time, one of Raider's moves had an effect on the monster. Cleavon stumbled backward a couple of steps, and his grip on Raider's shoulder loosened. Raider tore free and fell on the ground, sprawling there.

"Stomp him, Cleavon!" Asa Burkett shouted. "Stomp the guts out of him!"

Cleavon tried to follow his father's advice. He charged forward and lifted a foot so that he could bring it down on Raider's face.

Raider didn't wait for that to happen, though. He kicked again, this time straight up into Cleavon's balls.

Cleavon staggered back, howling in pain as he clapped his hands to the injured area and clutched it. He doubled over but somehow stayed on his feet.

"You dirty sumbitch!" Burkett yelled as Raider scrambled to his feet. "You hit him below the belt!"

"Nobody said nothin' about . . . no damn belt," Raider replied as he struggled to catch his breath. He laced his fingers together again and swung both hands at Cleavon's jaw, pivoting so that all the considerable strength of his body was behind the blow.

Several of the Burketts screeched warnings, but Cleavon must have been in too much pain to hear them. Bent over like he was, his jaw was in perfect position for

Raider's clubbed hands to smash into it with stunning force. Cleavon's head was jerked to the side by the impact, and his chin slewed over into an unnatural position as the jawbone shattered. He pitched forward onto his face.

Raider had swung the punch so that the back of his left hand took the brunt of the collision. That was a good thing, too, because pain shot up his arm and he figured he might have busted a couple of his knuckles. It hurt so bad he went to one knee, but he didn't stay down long, pushing back onto his feet and turning to face the cabin and the stunned, angry, disbelieving faces of the Burkett clan.

"There he is," Raider said, waving his right hand at Cleavon's crumpled, senseless form. "I fought him just like you said, Burkett. Now I'm ready to carry out the rest of the deal, the deal you gave your word of honor on. How about you? You gonna live up to it?"

Burkett sputtered and cursed and finally burst out, "You cheated! Damn it, you cheated!"

"Looked like a fair fight to me," Jess said. "Hand to hand, man to man."

"He kicked poor Cleavon in the balls!"

"You never said he couldn't. You know the rules of a rough an' tumble fight like this, Burkett. Anything goes as long as nobody uses a weapon. I didn't see no guns or knives or clubs bein' used."

Burkett's face was brick red with rage above the white beard, but he couldn't dispute anything that Jess said. Raider had won the fight fair and square, at least according to the standards of these hillfolk.

"All right, damn it," Burkett said at last, spitting out the words as if they tasted bad. "We had a deal, and me an' mine'll honor it." He pointed a blunt finger at Raider. "But you got to get out o' the Ozarks, and if you ever set foot in 'em again, the feud's back on! You hear me, boy?"

"I hear you," Raider said. He dragged the back of his right hand across his mouth and then looked down at his left hand. He flexed the fingers, slow and careful-like. The knuckles were swollen and hurt like blazes, but there was a chance none of them were broken.

"You all right, Ray?" Johnny asked in a low voice.

"Yeah, I'll be fine." He took his gunbelt from the saddle and buckled it on, wincing, as he had to use his left hand to do so. Then he settled his hat on his head and said, "Let's get the hell out of here."

"Today!" Burkett yelled after Raider had mounted up and turned his horse away from the ramshackle cabin. "I want you gone today, you hear me, you bastard?"

Raider didn't look back or give any sign that he had heard. He would keep his part of the bargain. Other than that, he was through with the Burketts.


"It ain't fair," Johnny said when they were about halfway back to Uncle Jess's farm. "You worked hard to make a life for youself here, Raider. You shouldn't have to give it all up just because a bunch o' hillbillies are crazy as loons."

Raider chuckled despite the pain in his hand and as-sorted other aches and bruises. "If life was fair, then folks wouldn't be born handsome as me and ugly as you, now would they?"

"You know what I mean, damn it!"

"Yeah, I know," Raider said as he grew more serious. "Sometimes we just have to do things whether we want to or not. Part o' the price o' bein' born, I guess."

Uncle Jess rubbed his jaw and said, "Yeah, but this don't sit right with me. You're the one givin' up everything, Ray. The rest of us get to go on with our lives, and you got to start all over somewheres else. You were plannin' to spend the rest o' your life here."

"Folks plan a lot of things that never come about. Any-way, it's true that I figured on settlin' down and raisin' a family, but that already wasn't workin' out too well. Don't see me gettin' hitched up with any gal, now do you?"

"You just ain't found the right one yet."

Raider shook his head. "Maybe there *ain't* a right one for

96

everybody, Uncle Jess. Maybe some gents are just fated to live on their own." *And die on their own,* he added to himself.

"I don't believe that," Jess said stubbornly. "There's somebody for everybody."

"Well, say that's true." Raider looked over at his uncle. "What if the gal for me ain't even in the Ozarks?"

Jess frowned but didn't have any answer for that question.

Now that the decision had been reached and the deal struck with the Burketts—and now that he had survived the fight with Cleavon—Raider was starting to feel a mite better about things. Even though he had enjoyed the time he had spent in the Ozarks, there had been some nights when sleep had been slow to come, when he had felt the sort of yearnings and longings that called out to him to be on the move again, answering the call of distant trails. When a man had been fiddlefooted for so many years, it was hard to give it up.

In a way, Raider thought, he was looking forward to moving on. And even though he had promised not to return to the Ozarks, when enough years had gone by, it might be possible for him to come back, once some of the Burketts who hated him the most were dead.

Assuming, of course, that he lived that long . . .

The three riders came in sight of the farmhouse a short time later, and Jess reined in sharply as he said, "What the hell! Who's that buggy belong to?"

Raider and Johnny pulled their horses to a stop, also. Raider had seen the buggy parked in front of the farmhouse at the same time Jess had. A mule was hitched to the front of the vehicle, and as Raider saw that, a powerful flash of memory went through his brain. He seemed to see an enclosed apothecary wagon being pulled by a single mule, with a derby-hatted, gray-suited driver perched on the seat.

But that was a buggy parked at the house, not an apothecary wagon, and old Judith, Doc Weatherbee's mule, was long since dead.

"It's hardly ever good when city folks come visitin'," Jess

said with a worried frown. "Most o' the time they're from the gov'ment, come to tell you all about how they're goin' to help you . . . only that help turns out to be no help at all, and expensive to boot."

"If that dude's come to make trouble, we'll send him packin'," Johnny said. "Give him a buttful o' buckshot and make him drive that sissified buggy standin' up."

"Take it easy, you two," Raider advised. "I've dealt with plenty o' city folks, and they ain't all bad. Just most of 'em. Let's get down there and see what this one wants."

They rode on down the hill, hurrying more now. The people inside the cabin must have heard the hoofbeats of the approaching horses, because Hannah and Joanie stepped out onto the porch, Joanie with Enos perched on her hip. The women had known that the menfolk were going to parley with the Burketts, so relief was obvious on their faces when they saw that Raider, Jess, and Johnny had all returned, evidently unharmed.

"Thank God you're back," Joanie exclaimed as the men drew rein in front of the porch. "I was afraid those crazy Burketts would shoot all three of you!"

"We're fine," Johnny said. He nodded toward the buggy. "Who's that belong to?"

"We got comp'ny, Hannah?" Jess asked.

"We've got a visitor, all right," Hannah said. She stepped aside so that a medium-sized, well-built man in a gray suit could step out of the cabin onto the porch. He had sandy hair and held a gray derby in one hand. Hannah went on, "Says he's a friend of Raider's."

Raider stared at the man, remembering all the times they had argued and cussed each other and a few times even come to blows over a woman or a particularly tricky case. But despite those rough patches, they were friends, all right. They had saved each other's lives too many times to count.

"Hello, Raider," Doc said. "Are you ready to get back to work?"

# Chapter 14

"I ain't signin' on with the Pinkertons again," Raider said a short time later as he and Doc sat at the table in the farmhouse's kitchen, cups of coffee laced with whiskey in front of them. "By God, I just won't do it! I had my fill of that."

"I'm not asking you to sign on with them," Doc said. "I'm not working for them, either, although—and you'll appreciate this, Raider—they've been working *for me* recently."

Raider frowned. "You hired the Pinks?"

"That's right. I'm trying to track down a man who embezzled nearly eighty thousand dollars from my brother's bank in Boston. When it comes to finding one man in this big land of ours, no one is better at it than the Pinkertons, as you and I have ample cause to know."

Raider drank some of the spiked coffee and then said, "So you sicced the Pinks on this thief. How come you don't just leave the job to Wagner and his operatives? Why'd you come west yourself?"

"Because part of the mission is personal." Doc's face grew solemn. "When Ned Montayne—that's the name of

99

the embezzler—fled from Boston, he took my niece Katie with him."

Raider's eyes widened in outrage. "Kidnapped her, did he?"

Doc shook his head and said, "No, that's the worst of it. She went with him willingly. Evidently there's, ah, some sort of romance going on between the two of them. When I confronted Montayne with the evidence against him, Katie was there, too, unknown to me until she put a gun to my head and helped Montayne escape."

Raider let out a low whistle and asked, "How old's this little girl?"

"She's not so little. She's eighteen and, I suppose, mature for her age. I'm afraid I never really paid that much attention."

"So you want to catch this fella Montayne, get as much o' the bank's money back as you can, and take your niece home to her folks."

Doc nodded. "Yes. That sums it up nicely. If it were just a matter of bringing Montayne to justice and recovering the money, I probably would have left the entire thing in the hands of the Pinkertons. But Katie's involvement . . . well, that complicates things. I felt that I ought to handle this myself."

"I reckon I can understand that," Raider said. "Family always makes things a mite trickier. I reckon the Pinks must've got a line on Montayne, or else you wouldn't be here."

"That's right. I had a pretty good idea that Montayne and Katie headed west when they left Boston. Montayne is one of those Easterners who is fascinated by the West. Evidently he spent most of his time—when he wasn't embezzling money from my brother or seducing my niece—reading dime novels."

Raider made a face. "One o' those fellas, huh? Probably believed all that made-up shit, too."

"Evidently. According to the landlady in the rooming house where he lived, he had a revolver of some sort and a holster, and he spent a lot of time—"

"Let me guess," Raider cut in, "practicing his fast draw." A tone of contempt edged his words.

"Exactly," Doc said.

"Doc, you know a fella like that's bound to get himself in trouble out here. Ain't nothin' more dangerous than a greenhorn who thinks he knows what he's doin'."

"Yes, I know. That's why I want to locate him and Katie as soon as I possibly can. Pinkerton agents in Boston were able to discover which train they left the city on, and they sent word on down the line to other operatives, who picked up the trail. They traced Montayne and Katie to Chicago, then Kansas City, and finally on to Texas. The last time they were seen, they were on a Santa Fe Railroad train bound for Fort Worth."

"The Pinks got agents in Texas," Raider pointed out.

"Yes, but I think I know where Montayne is headed." Doc reached inside his coat and took out a newspaper clipping. He set it on the kitchen table in front of Raider.

Raider's frown deepened as he read the story. "What sort o' damn fool would put on a gunfightin' contest?" he asked.

"A man with more money than sense," Doc said. "This fellow Corrigan seems to fit the bill. A competition such as the one he's staging at his ranch would certainly appeal to a man like Montayne."

"He'll get himself killed!"

Doc shook his head. "The contestants won't be shooting at each other. It's not like a series of actual gunfights, with the winner being the only one who survives. It's just a shooting competition. We've run across them before."

"Yeah, but never one with such a fancy grand prize," Raider muttered. "A Golden Eagle. What do you reckon it's worth?"

"I have no idea. A small fortune, certainly. *That* would appeal to Montayne, too."

"You don't think there's any chance o' him winnin' it, do you?"

"I honestly don't know," Doc replied. "Perhaps he really is fast on the draw and a good shot. There's no law that

101

says someone from east of the Mississippi can't handle a gun well, you know."

Raider's snort made it clear just how likely he thought *that* was.

Doc frowned. "I'm quite proficient with firearms, as you'll recall, and I'm from Massachusetts."

"You were passable," Raider said, "and that was a few years back. Hell, you're probably out of practice by now. Lost your shootin' eye, more'n likely."

"I have not! If you want to step outside, we'll set up some targets—"

Raider lifted a hand to stop him. "You're just as prickly as ever, that's for sure. Ain't lost your touch there." He changed the subject by asking, "What is it you want from me, Doc?"

"I'm on my way to Fort Worth to pick up Montayne's trail. I thought perhaps you'd like to come with me."

"You an' me trackin' down some owlhoot, eh?" Raider grunted. "Just like the old days."

"Yes, except we won't be doing it for the Pinkertons this time. However, I'd be glad to hire you as a freelance operative—"

Doc stopped short as he saw the glare Raider directed toward him. "You're right, I shouldn't have said that. I'm asking you to accompany me as a favor, old friend, and to be honest, I thought you might enjoy getting back into the harness for a little while."

"I swore off killin'."

"I know. My hope is that there won't be any violence involved. I'd like to take Montayne into custody in such a manner that he won't have a chance to fight back."

"Yeah, but what we want ain't always what we get."

Doc's face fell. "Then you won't come with me?"

"I didn't say that." Raider gulped down the rest of the whiskey-laced coffee. "As a matter o' fact, you got here just in time. I'm leavin' the Ozarks. Plan on bein' gone before the day's over."

Doc shook his head in confusion. "Why would you do that?" he asked. "I thought you liked it here."

"I do. Leastways, I did 'fore a clan o' crazy hillbillies decided to have a blood feud with me and my kinfolks over somethin' they blame me for."

Raider sketched in the events of the past few days for Doc, who grew angry as Raider told him about the Burketts and the violence that had already resulted from Roscoe Burkett's obsession with Chastity Doolittle.

"They sound like they truly are insane," Doc said when Raider was finished. "You should report them to the authorities."

Raider laughed. "This is the Ozarks, Doc, not Boston. The nearest law is forty miles o' bad road away over the mountains. Folks around here settle things their own selves. I made a deal with Asa Burkett. He'll keep his word . . . I think."

"And if he doesn't?"

Raider's eyes narrowed. "If I ever hear tell o' him or his kin hurtin' any o' my kin, I'll come back to the mountains, all right. I'll come back and kill him, first thing, and he knows it. That's why I said I reckon he'll live up to his part of the bargain."

Doc thought that over for a moment and then nodded. "I'm sorry for your troubles, Raider," he said. "I really am. But under the circumstances, it's obvious you should go to Texas with me. If I believed in such things, I'd almost say that fate must have brought me here today."

"I believe in fate. Can't be raised up in the mountains and not believe in it."

"Then you'll come with me and help me find Montayne and Katie?"

Raider nodded and stuck his hand across the table. "Yeah. I reckon we're partners again."

"Partners," Doc said with a smile as he gripped Raider's hand.


Doc had made the trip up to Uncle Jess's place from Fort Smith, where the closest rail line came through Arkansas.

Raider returned with him, riding alongside the buggy as it negotiated the steep, narrow mountain trails.

"The Ozarks are beautiful," Doc muttered as he carefully took the buggy around a hairpin turn, "but they're not meant for civilized transportation."

"You'd've been a lot better off puttin' a saddle on that mule instead o' hitchin' it to a buggy," Raider told him. "If God had meant for the mountains to be easy travelin', He wouldn't't'a made 'em so up and down."

When they reached Fort Smith, Doc returned the buggy to the wagon yard where he had rented it. As Raider looked at the big, red brick courthouse on the bluff overlooking the Arkansas River, he said, "You reckon we ought to stop and say howdy to Judge Parker?"

He and Doc had crossed trails with the famous hanging judge on several occasions in the past, and it hadn't always been on friendly terms.

"No, that's all right," Doc said. "I think we'd best get down to the depot we can catch the next train bound for Texas."

That train wouldn't roll through until that night, so they had time to get some supper in a café not far from the station. As Raider washed his food down with gulps of strong black coffee, he said, "I got to admit, it feels sorta good to be back on the trail of an owlhoot again, Doc. Never thought I'd miss manhuntin' until I wasn't doin' it no more."

"The thrill of the chase," Doc mused. "It's a powerful intoxicant, to be sure."

They returned to the depot, bought tickets, and were on the train when it pulled out, bound for Fort Worth. They hadn't been able to secure sleeping compartments, so they dozed sitting up in one of the club cars. That certainly wasn't the first time either of them had slept that way on a train, but Raider was stiff and sore and groggy by the next morning. Living a normal life for a couple of years had softened him up, he thought. Lord knew what would happen when he had to actually spend a night out on the trail.

The train was not an express, which meant it stopped in

every little two-bit town in the southwest corner of Arkansas and across East Texas. Because of that, it was after noon when it pulled into the depot at Fort Worth. Raider and Doc climbed down to the platform carrying their gear, which amounted to one bag and one rifle apiece.

Doc pointed to a cigar stand that also sold newspapers and said, "Let's see if there's anything in the local paper about that shooting competition."

Raider picked up some cigars while Doc scanned the first page of the newspaper he bought. He turned to Raider and said with some excitement in his voice, "There's an exhibition going on this very afternoon, featuring the contestants in Corrigan's competition."

The elderly black man who ran the cigar stand said, "You gents interested in enterin' that contest?"

Without hesitation, Doc pointed at Raider and said, "He is."

Raider frowned. This was the first time he'd heard anything about him being in the shooting contest.

"Best get a move on, then," the proprietor advised. "From what I hear, those folks are all leavin' for Mr. Corrigan's ranch later today."

"Yes, that's what it says in the paper," Doc agreed. "Come on, Raider."

"Come on where?" Raider asked as he followed Doc away from the cigar stand.

"To the stockyards, north of the river. That's where the exhibition is being held."

"Hell, Doc, that's more'n a mile from here." They had been to the Fort Worth stockyards before, during a case that had brought them to Fort Worth several years earlier.

"We'll rent some horses," Doc said with a decisive nod.

Raider had left his horse at the wagon yard in Fort Smith, so that Jess could pick it up the next time he came to town. Before leaving the farm, Raider had made a present of the animal to Johnny, who had always admired it.

"All right," Raider said. "But what's this about me enterin' that dang fool contest? We ain't talked about that."

"It's the perfect way to find out if Montayne is one of the contestants. I'll have to stay out of sight, because he and Katie would recognize me, but neither of them ever saw you before." Doc rubbed at his chin in thought. "You'll need a nom de plume, though."

Raider frowned. "Whatever that is, it don't sound like somethin' I need. Sounds too Frenchy."

"It's a pen name, a pseudonym," Doc explained. "Or in this case, perhaps 'alias' would be a more appropriate term."

"Because your niece has heard you talkin' about your ol' pard Raider, right? About how he was the smartest, handsomest, best Pinkerton agent there ever was?"

"Yes," Doc said. "Something like that. How about Wagner for a false name?"

Raider made a face. "Aw, Doc, you ain't gonna saddle me with that, are you?"

"It's easy to remember. From here on out, you're Bill Wagner."

Raider sighed. He supposed Doc was right. Having worked for William Wagner for years, it was a name neither of them would forget. And while Wagner was certainly an important cog in the Pinkerton machine, he wasn't well-known like Allan Pinkerton himself, so no one would think twice about Raider using the name.

"Wagner it is," Raider said, shaking his head at the injustice of it all.

They found a livery stable, rented a couple of saddle horses, and rode north along Main Street, over both of the Trinity River bridges, and followed their noses to the stockyards. There was a big crowd in front of a large, Spanish-style building. Doc pointed at it and said, "That must be where the exhibition is. I'll wait here. You go find Edmund Corrigan and tell him you want to enter the contest."

"You sure about this, Doc?"

Doc nodded. "I'm sure."

Raider took a deep breath and started shouldering his way through the crowd toward the front. During the trip from Arkansas, Doc had showed him several photographs of his niece, Katherine Weatherbee, better known as Katie, and he had described Ned Montayne as well. Since they were fugitives, it was likely Montayne had changed his appearance, at least somewhat, and Katie might have, too. But Raider thought he stood a good chance of recognizing either of them.

He ignored the resentful glances he got from those he shoved past, and once they saw how big and mean-looking he was, most of them turned their attention elsewhere in a hurry. As he reached the front of the crowd, some fancy-dressed galoot standing on the porch of the building was hollering into a megaphone. A couple of dozen men were standing on the porch with him, and Raider figured out that they were the contestants. A few of them didn't look like gunfighters at all, but for the most part they appeared to be a pretty salty bunch. Raider's gaze lingered on a tall, Indian-looking fella in a brown tweed suit and a flat-crowned brown Stetson. The hombre had a sweeping long-horn mustache that curled on the ends, and his face was tanned to the color of old saddle leather. Something about him struck Raider as familiar, but he couldn't put his finger on whatever was tickling at the back of his mind.

The gent in charge, whom Raider figured was Edmund Corrigan, said something about getting the exhibition started, so Raider knew he couldn't wait any longer. He stepped forward, raised his voice, and called, "Hold on there! How does a fella get signed up for this here contest?"

# Chapter 15

Longarm looked at the big, dark-haired man who stepped out of the crowd, and for a second it was almost like gazing into a mirror. There was definitely a resemblance between him and the stranger.

But there were differences, too. The man with the Arkansas twang in his voice had darker hair, and his mustache was smaller than Longarm's. He wasn't quite as tall, either, although his shoulders were equally as broad. He wore his Colt in a regular holster on his right hip, rather than in a cross-draw rig on the left. His black Stetson had a slightly curled brim. His nose had been broken more times and healed back with just a little crook in it.

So on closer inspection, they didn't look like brothers after all, but they might have passed for cousins.

Edmund Corrigan lowered the megaphone and frowned, clearly irritated by the interruption. He motioned for the stranger to come forward. As the big man approached, Corrigan said, "Do I understand you correctly, sir? You want to enter the competition I'm staging?"

"That's right," the man said. "You must be Corrigan. Big skookum he-wolf around here, ain't you?"

"I'm the man who's putting on this contest, if that's what you mean," Corrigan snapped.

"Didn't mean no offense. Yeah, I want to sign up. I'm a pretty fair hand with a smokepole."

"What's your name?"

Longarm thought there was the least bit of hesitation before the stranger answered, "Bill Wagner." Longarm pegged it as an alias.

"Well, Mr. Wagner," Corrigan said, "in order to take part in my contest, you have to demonstrate a suitable level of skill. That's the real purpose of this exhibition."

"Point me out a target and I'll hit it," Wagner said with complete confidence.

"*And* you have to pay a two-thousand-dollar entry fee."

Wagner's dark brows drew down in a frown. "Two thousand! Where the hell am I supposed to get—" He broke off, glanced over his shoulder at the crowd as if looking for someone there, and then said, "All right, what the hell. I'll get the money."

"You'll have to have the fee before you can officially enter the contest."

"I said I'll get the money! Now, you want to see me shoot or not?"

Corrigan considered for a second and then nodded. "I'm going to give you the benefit of the doubt, Mr. Wagner. You can participate in the exhibition. But all the contestants are leaving for my ranch this evening, and if you don't have the entry fee by the time the train leaves, that's it. No second chances."

Wagner glared, but he had no choice except to agree if he wanted to take part in the contest. Corrigan was, as Wagner had put it, the big skookum he-wolf.

Corrigan lifted the megaphone again and called through it, "All right, gentlemen, if you'll please take your places on the lawn . . ."

Targets had been set up in the open, grassy area in front of the Livestock Exchange Building. The bull's-eyes were attached to thick bales of hay. At Corrigan's order, another bale was wrestled into place and had a target fastened to it so that Wagner would have something to shoot at.

The contestants lined up. Longarm was careful to take a place at the far end of the line from Felix Gaunt, even though he was confident the outlaw wouldn't recognize him. Kid Montana was next to him, with the dark-faced man called Sale on the other side of the Kid. Wagner was about in the middle of the bunch.

"We'll start by having all of you put six shots in your target, as fast as you can," Corrigan called. "Ready, gentlemen? *Draw!*"

Hands flashed to gun butts. Guns leaped from holsters. And with a roar that made small children in the crowd clap their hands over their ears, shots blasted out from more than two dozen weapons. There was no way to distinguish individual reports. It was one continuous rumble of Colt thunder as the contestants emptied their weapons into the targets.

But it didn't last very long—no more than ten seconds. Quite a few of the men finished even faster than that. It was only a handful of stragglers who took that entire time to trigger off six shots. As the gunfire died away, cheers and applause from the crowd welled up to take its place.

Corrigan let the enthusiastic response go on for more than a minute before he signaled for quiet. It took another minute before the noise actually died down. Then Corrigan called to the contestants, "Holster your weapons, gentlemen, and we'll see how you did!"

Men who worked for him went to each of the bales in turn and unfastened the bullet-torn targets. They held up the targets so that the crowd could see just how accurate each shooter had been. Some of the contestants had hit their piece of paper with all six shots, while some had missed with one or two bullets.

Kid Montana had done pretty well, Longarm saw, grouping all six shots fairly close to the center, although none of them had struck the bull's-eye itself. The bullet holes on Sale's target were clustered even closer together.

Longarm hadn't wanted to draw attention to himself, so he had scattered his shots a little, hitting the target with all six of them but making sure none of them were in the bull's-eye. If he had wanted to, he could have put all six rounds in a space about the size of a man's palm. That wasn't bragging or overconfidence on his part, just practical knowledge of what he was capable of.

On down the line the results went, some better than others but none of them terrible. The big man who called himself Wagner had done slightly better than Longarm, which prompted an odd thought: What if Wagner had been holding back, too?

For that matter, most of these men could have deliberately shot worse than their best. It was the same as nudging along a raise in a poker game in which you've drawn really good cards; you don't want to show your hand too soon. The more Longarm thought about it, the more he reckoned that was the case with some of the contestants.

Some, though, like the Kid, were too excited to do anything like that. The youngster, who dressed like a character out of a dime novel, had clearly been doing his best.

Felix Gaunt shot well, Longarm noted, putting all his bullets fairly close to the center of the target. That came as no surprise. Longarm already knew that Gaunt was pretty good with a gun.

But even the best shot sometimes hurried and missed, as the soiled dove called Betsy had had the bad luck to find out in Wichita a few nights earlier.

Corrigan called for volunteers to shoot at colored glass balls that were tossed into the air by one of his helpers. Longarm passed on that challenge, as did Sale, Wagner, and Gaunt. The Kid took Corrigan up on it, though, stepping forward to draw and fire as the glass balls sailed upward. He hit two out of the five that were thrown during his turn, and Longarm thought that was fine shooting. The Kid seemed upset that he hadn't blasted all five of the balls to smithereens, though. He cussed under his breath as he jammed his right-hand Colt back in its holster.

More volunteers paired off and shot at moving targets that were waved in the air on the ends of long sticks. A few men shot from the backs of running horses. It was the sort of flashy trickery that you saw in Wild West shows back East, like the one that Buffalo Bill Cody had started putting on. It looked impressive but didn't have a damned thing to do with the sort of shooting that men who lived by the gun had to do in real life. Longarm stayed back and didn't take part. He figured he had already done enough to prove that he belonged in the contest.

Feeling eyes on him, he glanced over his shoulder and saw Anita Corrigan standing on the covered porch of the Livestock Exchange Building. She turned away rather than meet his gaze, and he knew she was still angry with him for turning her down in her hotel room. He had a feeling she was used to getting what she wanted, especially when she was nude.

He was sure she could find one of the other contestants to play up to, though.

Maybe that big fella Wagner, assuming she was the sort who liked her hombres a mite rough around the edges . . .

Doc was gonna kill him, Raider thought as the exhibition wrapped up a short time later. He hadn't known what else to do, though, except to promise Corrigan that he would get the two-thousand-dollar entry fee before the train left for West Texas that evening.

Raider sought Doc out in the dispersing crowd. He spotted the pearl-gray derby and made his way toward it through the press of people. When he reached Doc's side, the man from Boston asked, "Did you see Katie or Montayne?"

Raider shook his head. "Afraid not, but there were a heap o' people here this afternoon, Doc. I mighta missed 'em."

A worried frown creased Doc's forehead as he said, "You might not have seen Katie in the crowd, but you should have been able to pick Montayne out among the other contestants."

"Did *you* see him?"

"No, but I didn't dare get too close, for fear Montayne would see *me*."

"Well, I saw all of 'em, and none of 'em matched the description of Montayne you gave me, at least not exactly. There was one young fella who was dressed real fancy, like you might expect from somebody who thinks them damn dime novels are real, and he had blond hair, too, but it was long and curly, down on his shoulders like he was Bill Hickok or General Custer. Montayne ain't had time to grow hair like that since lightin' a shuck outta Boston, has he?"

Doc sighed and shook his head. "Unfortunately, no. But just out of curiosity, did you get that young fellow's name?"

"Nope, never heard it, just saw him with the other contestants." Raider rasped a hand along his jaw and took the plunge. "Speakin' o' contestants, Doc, did you happen to hear what Corrigan said to me about the entry fee everybody has to pay when they sign up?"

Doc stared at him. "Entry fee? No, I didn't hear anything about that. How much is it?"

"Two thousand bucks."

"*Two—*" Doc's startled exclamation broke off into a strangled gasp. After a moment he was able to go on. "Two thousand dollars? Are you serious?"

"Serious as a tombstone. Corrigan let me go ahead and take part in the exhibition, but he said I got to come up with the cash before the train pulls out for his ranch this evenin' or I can't be in the contest."

Doc thought it over, frowning and taking off his hat to turn it around in his hands. "I was so sure that Montayne planned to enter that shooting contest," he said. "All my instincts still say that he's here somewhere."

"For what it's worth," Raider said, "my gut tells me the same thing. You know how it is when you've been a manhunter for a while. You get to where you can almost

113

smell the fella you're after, like an ol' bloodhound on the trail o' some poor devil."

Doc nodded. "Exactly." He put his derby back on, squared his shoulders, and nodded. "Very well. We've come too far to give up the chase over a matter of two thousand dollars. I'll send a wire to Aaron right now and have him get in with one of the local banks. I'm sure he can arrange to have the money delivered to us."

"Best make it quick," Raider advised. "In the mornin' ain't gonna be soon enough. Corrigan and all them contestants will be gone by then. I suppose we could buy those horses we rented and ride out to his ranch, but that might take a few days. Montayne and Katie could be gone by then."

"Indeed. Do you know where Corrigan is staying?"

"Yep. The Palace Hotel."

"Go there now and keep an eye on the place. You might still spot Montayne or Katie. I'll meet you there later, hopefully with the cash for the entry fee."

Raider nodded. He found that he still didn't much cotton to taking orders from Doc, but he was willing to go along with his old partner. For one thing, Doc was right. It made sense for Raider to keep an eye on the hotel where the contestants were staying.

As he rode back along Main Street toward the hotel, he asked himself what they would do if it turned out Doc was mistaken and Montayne didn't have anything to do with Corrigan's big contest. He supposed they would have to try to pick up the fugitive's trail some other way, but by then it would be mighty cold.

They had followed plenty of cold trails before, Raider reminded himself, back in their Pinkerton days. They could do it again.

He reached the livery stable, turned the horse over to the hostler, and walked the rest of the short distance to the Palace Hotel. Dusk was settling down over Fort Worth, and Raider's stomach growled, reminding him that it had been quite a while since the meager lunch he and Doc had had on the train. He wondered if he ought to get something to eat.

The lure of the arched entrance into the hotel dining room on the other side of the big lobby proved to be too much. Mouthwatering smells drifted from the dining room and made Raider's stomach grumble again. He thumbed his hat back and headed in that direction.

He was only about halfway across the lobby when someone moved alongside him and linked an arm with his. Surprised, Raider looked over to see that a woman was walking beside him. She smiled up at him and said, "There you are! I've been looking all over for you, you know."

Raider didn't know. As far as he could recollect, he had never seen this female before in his life.

But she was pretty, about twenty-five years old, tall and redheaded with a nicely shaped body in a stylish but not too fancy gown, and the smile she gave him was warm enough to make his stomach do flip-flops in something other than hunger.

"I was fixin' to have some dinner," he said. "Reckon you'd like to join me?"

Her smile grew even warmer. "I thought you'd never ask, Mr. Wagner."

Even though the name still bothered him a mite, Raider figured that under the circumstances, he was more than happy to be Bill Wagner for a while.

# Chapter 16

She wasn't a whore, Raider decided. That had been his first thought, that she was just a soiled dove who had approached him and pretended to know him so she could try to get him to hire her services for the night.

But she had too much class for that, as anybody could tell once they had been around her for more than a few moments. She carried herself with poise and grace and spoke like she was well-educated.

He wondered if somebody was trying to give her trouble. She might have latched on to him and pretended they were acquainted to keep some lowlife varmint from bothering her.

When they were seated at one of the tables in the dining room, Raider said, "I reckon you know who I am, ma'am, but you've got the advantage on me."

She smiled, and that made her green eyes light up so that she was even prettier. "I know who you're *not*," she said. "You're not William Wagner, the second-in-command to Mr. Allan Pinkerton, no matter what name you gave Mr. Corrigan this afternoon."

Raider tensed. "I, uh, don't know this other Wagner fella you're talkin' about, but that's the name my mama saddled me with—"

"Nonsense. You're the legendary Raider. And I know you're not William Wagner because *I* work for him now."

Raider couldn't keep the surprised expression off his face. "You're a Pinkerton agent?"

He knew that females occasionally worked as operatives for the agency. Back in the old days, he and Doc had run across one or two of them.

"Colleen Gallagher," the redhead introduced herself. "I thought that by pretending I knew you, out there in the lobby, I could make you curious enough to have dinner with me."

"You got that right," Raider admitted.

He would have said more, but a waitress arrived just then to take their orders. When the waitress was gone, Colleen went on, "I suppose you wonder what I'm doing here."

"Well, Doc Weatherbee told me he hired the Pinks to give him a hand on a problem he's got, so I suspicion that you're tied up with that." Raider didn't mention Ned Montayne or Doc's niece by name, just in case he was wrong about Colleen Gallagher being involved in that case.

He wasn't wrong, though, because Colleen nodded and said, "I'm one of the agents who was assigned to track down Mr. Weatherbee's niece and the man who stole all that money from the bank in Boston. We know they were heading for Fort Worth the last time we were able to pin down their whereabouts."

Raider nodded, more comfortable now about discussing the case with her. It felt good to be talking to a fellow detective again, although in most of the ways that counted, Colleen Gallagher was about as far from being a fellow as possible.

"Doc's taken over the investigation his own self now, and asked me to pitch in," he said.

"I know," Colleen said. "I'm not happy about it, either. The other operatives and I did some good work in trailing Montayne this far, and now Mr. Weatherbee has cut us out of the case."

"I don't reckon that's really how he intended it to seem," Raider said. "He just wanted to handle the rest of this business personally, since one of his relatives is involved and all."

"He came to *you* for help," Colleen pointed out.

Raider shrugged. "Doc and me go back a heck of a long ways. We were partners for a long time. He knows he can trust me."

"He ought to know that about the agency's operatives, too." Colleen leaned forward and looked squarely at Raider. "That's why I want back in."

His bushy black brows drew down in a frown. "Back in the case, you mean?"

"That's right."

Raider made a face and shook his head. "I reckon that'd be up to Doc, and it seems like he's already made up his mind—"

"You could change it for him."

Raider grunted and tried not to laugh. "You act like you've heard stories about Doc and me—"

"As I said, you're legendary."

"Then you ought to know that the two of us butted heads as much as we worked together. Doc may look like a dude, but he's got a stubborn streak a mile wide in him. Changin' his mind about somethin' ain't all that easy, and I know that better'n anybody."

"But you could at least ask him to consider my request," Colleen argued. "I'm a good detective, Raider. I can help find Montayne and Miss Katherine Weatherbee." She sat back in her chair and gave him a faint smile. "For instance, I already know that Doc suspects Montayne has entered that shooting competition being staged by Edmund Corrigan."

The conversation had been carried out in low voices, so with all the talk and laughter and clinking of crystal and silverware in the dining room, their words were pretty much inaudible except at the table Raider shared with the attractive redhead. He glanced around anyway, worrying that someone would overhear what Colleen was saying. No

118

one seemed to be paying any attention to them, however—except for the admiring glances that other men in the room stole toward the young woman, that is.

"Look, I can talk to Doc," Raider said, "but I don't know that it'll do any good. I ain't promisin' nothin'."

"Just some consideration, that's all I ask."

"I'll see what I can do," Raider promised. It might be good to have a Pink backing them up as they headed west to Corrigan's ranch. That would put all the considerable resources of the agency at their disposal, should they be needed.

Besides, Colleen Gallagher was a smart, attractive woman, and it never hurt to have one of those around, either.

The waitress brought their food, and Raider and Colleen spent the next half hour eating and talking. She had heard many stories about the cases on which Raider and Doc had worked, and she wanted to know his version of the tales. Raider wasn't a naturally modest hombre, but he didn't embellish his role in the adventures *too* much. No more than any man would have while talking to a pretty girl . . .

Doc came into the dining room, looked around, and spotted Raider sitting at the table with Colleen. His eyebrows rose in surprise, then settled back down into an irritated frown. He started across the room toward them.

"Uh-oh," Raider muttered under his breath. "Here comes Doc, and he don't look happy."

As Doc came up to the table, Raider half rose to his feet and began, "Doc, this is—"

"I know who Miss Gallagher is," Doc cut in. "More importantly, I know *what* she is."

Colleen smiled. "Some ladies would find your tone insulting, Mr. Weatherbee."

Doc took off his derby and held it as he said, "I mean no offense, Miss Gallagher. I know you and your associates did some fine work on my case, and I appreciate that."

"Why don't you sit down and join us, Doc?" Raider suggested. "Me an' the lady got somethin' to talk to you about."

Doc took one of the empty chairs and set his derby on

the table in front of him. "I suspect I know what you want to say, Raider. And while I appreciate the work that the agency did, as I said, I prefer to handle the rest of this case with just your help."

"Might be a good thing to have the Pinks with us," Raider argued. "They got informants all over the country."

"Montayne is *here*," Doc insisted. "I'm sure of it."

Colleen spoke up, saying, "I agree. The trail led straight to Fort Worth, and based on what we know about Montayne, it's inconceivable that he wouldn't enter Corrigan's contest. A man as obsessed with the West and gunfighters and such things as he is would have no choice in the matter."

"Then where was he this afternoon at that exhibition?" Raider asked. "I got a good look at all the contestants."

"Have you ever seen Montayne in person?" Colleen wanted to know.

"No, but Doc gave me a good description of him."

"Hold on a moment," Doc said. "Why are the two of you discussing the case as if Miss Gallagher is still working on it? I sent Wagner a telegram saying that I would take over the investigation. He should have reassigned you to some other case by now, Miss Gallagher."

Colleen flushed. "I don't work for the agency on a full-time basis," she admitted. "They call me in when they need a female operative. Mr. Wagner thought that might be necessary on this case, since one of the people we were looking for was a woman. Your niece, in fact, Mr. Weatherbee."

"I know," Doc snapped. "So in reality you want to get involved in the case again in hopes of impressing the men in Chicago so they'll hire you full time. Is that it?"

"Now, Doc," Raider said. "No need to get snippy."

Colleen looked hard at Doc and said, "You're right, Mr. Weatherbee. But I also thought I might genuinely be of help to you and Raider. I'm a good operative, whether you want to believe that or not."

"I have no reason to doubt it," Doc replied. "But I also have no reason to think that Raider and I can't handle this by ourselves."

Colleen took a deep breath and reached for her bag. "I should go, then. There's no point in continuing this discussion."

"I'm afraid not," Doc told her.

Raider gritted his teeth. Doc could be a mighty stiff-necked bastard when he wanted to. And it wouldn't do any good to argue that it would be good to have Colleen around because she was so pretty. Doc was a happily married man now—if there was such a thing—and he was more worried about his niece's safety and his brother's money than he was about anything else.

Colleen looked at Raider. He shrugged and said, "Sorry. I reckon Doc is the boss on this case."

"Very well." Colleen opened her bag. "I should pay for my meal—"

"Not hardly," Raider said. "We got that, don't we, Doc?"

"Of course," Doc said. "And I honestly do appreciate your concern for my niece, Miss Gallagher. Perhaps if things were different . . ."

Colleen nodded, snapped her bag closed again, and turned to leave. Raider watched her go across the dining room and sighed in regret.

"There goes one *fine*-lookin' woman, Doc," he said.

"I suppose so," Doc admitted, "but we have more important things to think about right now."

That was where Raider and Doc would never see completely eye to eye. To Raider's mind, there was nothing more important than a good-looking woman, although things like life and death came mighty close. On the other hand, what good was life without good-lookin' women in it?

"Are you listening to me?" Doc asked.

"Uh, yeah, go ahead. What were you sayin'?"

"I have the entry fee," Doc said. "It took several telegrams and Aaron calling in some favors that he was owed, but the cash is right here." Doc tapped his coat, indicating an inside pocket. "We need to find Corrigan and give it to him. Or rather, you do. I still need to lie low, in case Montayne or Katie are around."

121

"All right. Maybe you shouldn't even be in here talkin' to me."

"Probably not." Doc reached into his pocket, took out an envelope, and handed it to Raider. "Take care of this. Don't lose it before you give it to Corrigan."

Raider frowned. "I ain't ten years old, you know."

"No, the way you were gazing in lovestruck rapture at Miss Gallagher, I would have taken you more for fifteen or sixteen."

Raider's eyes narrowed. He didn't want to make a scene and call attention to them, so he would cut Doc some slack on snide comments like that one, he decided. Doc had to be worried sick about Katie.

"I'll go find Corrigan right now," Raider said. "You make yourself scarce."

"I'll be on the train with you, but you may not see me."

Raider nodded. "I'll find you if I need you."

They parted company, Doc leaving the dining room through a rear door, Raider striding openly into the lobby again. It was good timing, too, because Corrigan was descending the broad staircase with what appeared to be his whole entourage, including a fussy, four-eyed secretary type of gent and a beautiful woman with hair black as midnight. Raider figured she was Corrigan's wife, the way she was hanging on to his arm, as if she was afraid that some other gal would snatch her rich fella away from her.

Raider met the group as they reached the bottom of the stairs. "Told you I'd get it," he said as he held up the envelope.

"The entry fee, Mr. Wagner?" Corrigan reached out and took the envelope from Raider. He opened it for a second, riffled through the bills inside, then turned and handed it to the secretary. "Everything appears to be in order. Take care of this for me, Millard."

"Yes, sir, Mr. Corrigan," the man said.

Corrigan turned back to Raider and held out his hand. "Welcome to the competition, Mr. Wagner. From what I

122

saw at the exhibition this afternoon, you're a good shot. I wish you the best of luck."

Raider gripped the cattleman's hand and nodded. "Much obliged. I reckon I'll need it."

"You might as well come with us to the train station, since we're ready to depart." Corrigan glanced over at the raven-haired woman. "If that's all right with you, my dear?"

"Of course," she said. "I'm sure we'll be seeing a lot more of Mr. Wagner in the next few days, so we might as well start getting to know him."

Raider made an effort not to frown as he felt the woman's eyes on him. He kept his face carefully expressionless. But he had seen the interest in the woman's gaze and recognized it for what it was. Corrigan's wife was on the prowl, and he was going to have to be careful not to let her start stalking him.

*That* would be a complication this case just flat-out didn't need.

# Chapter 17

The train leaving Fort Worth that evening was a special, which showed how much pull Edmund Corrigan had with the railroad. No freight cars were included, only a baggage car, a club car, and a couple of sleepers.

Traveling west overnight, the train would arrive in Big Spring early the next morning. Corrigan's Box C Ranch was located north of that settlement, beyond the Cap Rock, the escarpment that divided the Staked Plains from the rest of Texas. For the most part, the countryside was flat and semiarid, although it was broken here and there by rugged hills and mesas and badlands formed by knife-edged gullies. The grazing was good enough to support vast herds of longhorns, but quite a bit of acreage was required for each head of stock. Ranches in this part of Texas were sometimes the size of small states back East. The Box C, from everything Longarm had been able to learn about it, was one such ranch.

He turned his warbag, McClellan saddle, and Winchester over to a porter for stowing away in the baggage car, then went to the club car for a drink.

When he came into the car, he heard someone call, "Hey, Parker, over here!"

Longarm turned to look and saw Kid Montana sitting in one of the booths, along with the blond girl the Kid had pointed out during the exhibition and the gunman called Sale. A glance around the interior of the car told Longarm that Felix Gaunt wasn't there, so he walked over to join the Kid and the other two.

"This is my girl, Kitty," the Kid said as Longarm slid into the booth beside them.

Longarm gave the young woman a polite nod, touched a finger to the brim of his Stetson, and said, "Pleased to meet you, ma'am."

She smiled. She was very pretty in a fresh, wholesome way, although Longarm wasn't sure just how wholesome she could really be if she was traveling with Kid Montana this way, without benefit of clergy, as the old saying went.

"Thank you, Mr. Parker," she said. "Montana has told me a lot about you."

"Don't reckon he knows all that much about me," Longarm drawled, "since we just met this afternoon."

The Kid laughed. "I know enough to be able to tell that you're going to be one of the top competitors in the contest, Parker." He pointed a finger at Longarm. "You were holding back during the exhibition, admit it."

Longarm shrugged and said, "I thought I was doing the best I could."

"Don't believe him, Kid," Sale put in. "He's good. Take my word for it."

The gunman sounded so certain in his statement that for a moment Longarm wondered if Sale had recognized him. That didn't appear to be the case, though, so he said, "I reckon we'll just have to wait for the contest. Like the old hymn says, further along we'll know more about it."

In truth, though, Longarm hoped that things wouldn't have to go that far. He would prefer to take Gaunt into custody before the contest got under way. It was all a matter of finding an opportunity to arrest the killer when there was a smaller chance of innocent people getting hurt.

Longarm didn't really want to participate in the contest. As a federal lawman, even if he were to win, he couldn't accept the prize. That fancy Golden Eagle would have to go to somebody else.

"Both of you may be good," the Kid said to Longarm and Sale, "but I plan on winning." He put a hand under Kitty's chin and tipped her head up a little. "And I always get what I want, don't I, darlin'?"

"Sure you do, Kid," she said.

Despite her apparent agreement, Longarm thought he saw a flash of something in her blue eyes. Anger? Resentment? Maybe not everything was as good between Kid Montana and his girl as he thought it was.

But that was none of Longarm's business, so he put the thought out of his head.

More of the contestants began drifting into the club car, intent on getting drinks and sampling the free food that was laid out. Longarm sipped from a glass of Maryland rye and kept an eye on the entrances at each end of the car, watching for Felix Gaunt. Gaunt didn't seem to be in any hurry to put in an appearance, though, so Longarm was left to make small talk with Kid Montana, Kitty, and Sale.

The Kid was getting drunk, and the more booze he put away, the less Longarm liked him. The fancy-dressed young man had an arrogant, boastful streak in him. As the liquor took effect, his accent began to slip, too, so that he sounded more and more like an Easterner. Longarm wondered if he and Kitty had come all the way out here to Texas just so the Kid could take part in Corrigan's contest, which had evidently been publicized all over the country.

It was only a matter of time before the Kid had gotten drunk enough that he began to become loud and boisterous. When some of the other contestants started casting angry glances toward the young man, Longarm leaned toward him and said, "Maybe you'd better call it a night, Kid. You're already gonna have one hell of a hangover in the morning."

"Don't need you to tell me . . . how much to drink, Parker," the Kid replied in an unsteady voice. "You're not my father or anything."

"Nope, but even though I ain't your pa, I don't want to see you getting yourself in trouble."

"What the hell does it matter to you? Scared I'm gonna . . . beat you in the contest?"

"I hadn't given it a whole lot of thought," Longarm answered honestly. "Anyway, if that's what I was worried about, wouldn't I want you as sick and hungover as possible?"

The Kid lifted his hat and scratched at his head as he frowned, trying to wrap his mind around what Longarm had just said. "Yeah, I . . . I guess."

"Anyway, I think Miss Kitty here wants to leave—don't you, ma'am?"

The blonde nodded in relief. "Yes, come on, Kid, you've had enough to drink tonight."

The Kid reached for the whiskey bottle on the table. "No, I haven't. There's still whiskey in the bottle . . . ain't there?"

Longarm moved the bottle out of reach before the Kid could grasp it. The Kid glared at him.

"Hey! Put that back!"

Kitty looked at Longarm, pleading for help, and even though he knew Kid Montana wouldn't take it well, he reached over and grasped the young man's arm. "Come on. I'll help you back to your berth."

Longarm glanced at Sale, who was pointedly looking the other way. The gunman wanted no part of this affair, which had the potential to turn into an ugly scene.

The Kid tried to pull away from Longarm's grip. "Damn it, Parker—"

"Why don't you leave him alone?" one of the contestants at the bar asked Longarm. "Let him drink himself into a stupor, the young fool. That's that much less competition we'll have to worry about."

The Kid finally twisted free of Longarm's hand and lurched to his feet. He ignored Kitty plucking at the sleeve

127

of his fringed buckskin jacket. "Hell, I can shoot better drunk than you can sober, mister!" he yelled at the man who had just spoken.

Longarm wasn't surprised that the hombre at the bar didn't like that. He stood up and swung toward Kid Montana, his movements slow and deliberate. He was around thirty, well-dressed in a dark suit and cream-colored Stetson and string tie. A holstered Colt hung on his right hip. He moved the coat back on that side so that he could reach the gun easier and said, "I know you're young and stupid, so I won't hold that remark against you. But you'd better not say anything else."

Sale said in a quiet voice that still carried over the clicking of the rails, "You should listen to him, Kid. That's Cleve Endicott. He's pretty fast with a gun."

"Not as fast as me," the Kid boasted. "And I'll prove it anytime he's ready, if he's got any guts."

Longarm's eyes narrowed. This was turning into the sort of showdown that took place all too often in Western saloons, where pride and liquor mixed into a dangerous combination. A railroad club car wasn't much more than a saloon on wheels, and given the nature of the passengers on this train, there was more than enough pride to go around.

He knew he could put a stop to this by revealing that he was a lawman, but that would expose him and severely hurt his chances of capturing Felix Gaunt. The Kid was a grown man, and so was Cleve Endicott. They would just have to take their chances—although given the fact that Kid Montana was almost too drunk to stand up, Longarm didn't give him much of a chance of surviving a shoot-out.

The Kid's challenge had prompted most of the other men in the club car to move out of the way. They didn't want to be caught in the line of fire if shots began to ring out. Sale stood up, taking his drink with him, and clasped Kitty's arm with his other hand.

"Come on, miss," he said. "We'd better move."

"No," she said as she pulled away from him. She stood

up and went to the Kid. "Don't do this," she pleaded in a low voice.

With a sneer on his face, Kid Montana shoved her away. "Lea' me alone," he snarled. "I can take care o' myself."

Based on what he had seen so far, Longarm seriously doubted that. He muttered, "Hell," and reached over to tap the Kid on the shoulder.

The Kid's head jerked around. "What in blazes do you want?" he demanded, his face darkening with rage.

"Sorry, old son," Longarm said.

Then he slugged the Kid in the jaw, pulling his punch a little so that he wouldn't break any bones in his hand. The blow landed with enough power to slew the Kid's head around anyway. His knees unhinged, and he would have pitched forward onto his face, out cold, if Longarm hadn't caught him before he could fall.

With the Kid's unconscious form draped over his shoulder, Longarm straightened and asked Kitty, "Where do you want me to put him?"

She sighed. "In our berth, I guess." She touched Longarm's hand. "Thank you, Mr. Parker. But you know he's going to hate you when he wakes up."

"At least he'll be alive to hate me."

Kitty led the way. As Longarm followed her past Endicott, the man nodded and said, "I'm obliged to you for doing that, Parker. I didn't want to kill him."

"I know you didn't. That's why I did it. No point in anybody dying."

They left the club car. Sale remained behind, going to the bar to get a refill on his drink. Longarm, Kitty, and the Kid went into the sleeper that was directly behind the club car, and the blonde led Longarm to one of the curtained-off berths. She opened it, and Longarm dumped the Kid's senseless form on the lower bunk.

"I'll steer clear of him in the morning, so's I won't irritate him," Longarm said. "Could be that his head will hurt bad enough he won't be thinking about anything else."

"You don't know him the way I do," Kitty said. "He'll nurse a grudge against you from now on."

Longarm smiled. "He won't be the first."

As he started to turn away, she stopped him with a hand on his arm. "Mr. Parker," she said, "you saved his life back there."

"I expect so," Longarm said with a nod. "I never met that Endicott fella before, but now that I think about it, I've heard of him. He's pretty fast, fast enough so that he's killed half a dozen men in gunfights. Fact is, I'm a mite surprised he came back to Texas. I think he's still wanted here."

He stopped, not wanting Kitty to start wondering how come he knew so much about wanted men. In truth, Longarm thought several of the contestants, in addition to Felix Gaunt, probably had charges outstanding against them. They had been unable to resist the challenge of competing against the other fast guns, and they wanted that Golden Eagle, too.

"Even though things haven't worked out like I thought they would, I'm glad you kept him from getting killed," Kitty said. "I'd like to thank you for that."

"You already did," Longarm pointed out.

"No." She moved closer, close enough that Longarm could smell the subtle scent of her perfume. "I'd like to really thank you. You have a berth here, too, don't you?"

The train swayed a little as it click-clacked along the rails, speeding westward. The corridor of this sleeping car was dimly lit, and Longarm and Kitty were alone in it. Longarm leaned his head toward the bunk where Kid Montana had started snoring and asked, "What about him?"

"He won't wake up for hours. I know that from experience. And even if he did, he wouldn't be any good to me tonight, if you know what I mean."

Longarm's eyes narrowed. "Beggin' your pardon if this is an indelicate question, but just how old are you, ma'am?"

"I'm twenty-four."

Longarm grunted. He had taken her for at least four years younger than that. But he knew that some women were older than they looked, and in his experience, it was rare for a female to claim more years than she actually possessed.

And she *was* mighty pretty, there was no denying that.

The train swayed again, harder this time, and Kitty sort of fell against him. Even as his arms came up and went around her, he suspected her of acting, suspected that she really hadn't been thrown off balance all that much. But either way, she was in his embrace now, and as she slid her arms around his waist and tipped her head back a little with an inviting look in her heavily lidded eyes, Longarm said a silent *what the hell* and brought his mouth down on hers.

Men and women put on an act with each other all the time, he told himself. If they didn't, hardly any of them would ever get together, so Longarm wasn't going to worry about Kitty's motives right now. As he kissed her, he reached behind him with one hand and drew the curtain closed across the berth where Kid Montana continued to snore.

# Chapter 18

"We'll have to be quiet," Longarm said as he closed the curtain of his own berth a few minutes later.

Kitty laughed. "I can manage that . . . I think. I suppose it depends on how you make me feel, Mr. Parker."

He began unfastening the buttons on her dress. "Maybe under the circumstances, you ought to be calling me Custis. And seeing as how I don't know your last name, I reckon I'll just keep on calling you Kitty."

She didn't volunteer her last name in response to his comment. She was already busy unbuttoning his shirt.

The only light in the sleeping compartment came from the corridor and filtered in around the curtain. But that was enough illumination for Longarm to see the sleek, beautiful lines of Kitty's body as he undressed her. When her breasts were revealed he thought for a second that they had no nipples, but when he cupped them in his hands he could feel the little buds of flesh hardening against his palms. The nipples were such a pale pink that at first glance they blended in with the creamy flesh around them.

She pushed his underwear down and freed his stiffening

shaft. "Oh," she breathed as she tried to wrap her hands around the hard, thick length of him. "I've never seen one that big before. Or done anything with one like it, either." She looked up at Longarm and asked somewhat nervously, "Will it fit?"

"Only one way to find out," he told her.

When they were both nude, he lay back on the bunk and pulled her on top of him. She had shaken her long blond hair loose. It fell around both their faces as she sprawled atop him and kissed him. Her full breasts flattened against his broad, muscular chest. He slid a hand down the smooth sweep of her back until it reached the swelling curves of her rump. As her lips parted and his tongue delved into the heated recesses of her mouth, he squeezed and kneaded each cheek in turn and even slipped a finger into the cleft between them. Kitty groaned in passion against his mouth and began to squirm harder.

Her legs parted as she straddled his hips. The rising tide of desire she felt caused her to grind her pelvis against the thick pole of male flesh trapped between their bellies. The feel of her furred thatch against it made Longarm's shaft throb with need. He grasped her hips and moved her up a little so that his erection popped up between her spread thighs. When she settled back, that brought him in contact with the already damp opening between her legs. The moist folds of her sex caressed his manhood like lips bestowing a tender kiss.

She lifted her mouth from his and whispered, "I'm still not sure I can do it, but I'm ready to try."

Longarm thought she was wet enough so that she wouldn't have any trouble, and he was sure ready to be inside her, so he lifted her hips and guided her into position. With an unused bunk above them, she couldn't sit up straight, but she managed to raise herself enough so that the tip of his shaft teased her opening. She braced her hands on his chest and began to lower herself onto him.

The sensation of penetrating her was one of the best Longarm had ever felt. She wasn't a virgin, which came as

133

no surprise, but she hadn't had a lot of experience. She was very tight and hot, and she gasped and squirmed as she tried to fit more and more of Longarm's massive member inside her. He was careful not to thrust too hard as he worked his way in. Kitty paused several times as if she thought that surely he had reached the end, but he was always able to insinuate himself just a little bit deeper.

Finally he was all the way in, stretching her to the limit. They stayed that way for a while, just reveling in the ultimate closeness of their connection. But then Kitty began to rock her hips back and forth a little, and Longarm flexed his hips, meeting that rocking motion with short thrusts of his own.

Even though they weren't moving much, they were generating enough friction to increase his arousal and swell his shaft even more. Kitty moaned as she felt it growing inside her. Her hips moved faster. Sensing that she might not be able to remain quiet after all, Longarm cupped a hand behind her head and brought her mouth down to his. He gave her a hard, passionate kiss, and when she thrust her tongue into his mouth to duel and dance with his tongue, he accepted it with an eagerness that matched her own.

Shudders of culmination began to roll through Kitty's body. Longarm's climax had been building up, and feeling her reach her peak tipped him over the edge into releasing his own. He slammed up into her with his hardest thrust yet. Reaching an even greater depth than before, he held himself there as his juices boiled up his shaft and burst out into her in thick, white-hot spurts. Both of them shook from the intensity of their shared climax as he emptied himself into her. They were drenched by the time their spasms subsided.

With a long sigh, Kitty pillowed her head on Longarm's chest. He stroked her flanks, which were still quivering a little from the aftereffects of her climax. Her hands moved on his body as well, caressing and exploring.

"I should go back to the Kid," she said after a few minutes of companionable silence, although her tone made it clear that she didn't really want to.

"How well do you know him?" Longarm asked.

She stiffened. "Well enough," she said. "Why do you ask?"

"Any chance he's gonna hold a grudge against you when he wakes up, for trying to settle him down earlier?"

"Are you asking if I'm going to be in danger from him?"

"That's about the size of it," Longarm admitted.

Kitty raised her head and shook it. "No, I don't think so. He has a bad temper sometimes, especially when he's drinking, but he's never taken it out on me. I trust him."

"Well, I reckon you'd know better than anybody else," Longarm said, but he wasn't completely convinced.

Kitty kissed him again. "I just hate to leave you, Custis. I never knew it could be like that. I . . . I'm really glad I met you. Maybe we can spend some more time together on Mr. Corrigan's ranch, while the contest is going on."

"Maybe," Longarm said. He wasn't sure that would be a good idea, though. He didn't want to have to face the Kid in a showdown, either. He had killed enough young varmints who thought they were fast on the draw to last him a lifetime.

They lingered a few moments more, then slipped out of the bunk. Kitty started getting dressed. Longarm just pulled on the bottom half of his long underwear and moved the curtain aside enough to check the corridor outside the sleeping compartments.

"Nobody around right now," he reported to Kitty.

She finished buttoning up her dress and settled her hat on her blond hair, which she had pinned up again. When she was ready to go, she stepped close to Longarm and kissed him again. "Good night, Custis," she whispered.

He told her good night, too, then she left the berth and headed toward the one she shared with the Kid. Longarm watched her until she reached it. Then she cast a last look over her shoulder at him before disappearing behind the curtain again.

He hoped she was right about her being safe from Kid Montana's wrath. If the Kid woke up in the morning and hurt her . . .

With a shake of his head, Longarm forced that thought away. He found a cheroot in his pocket, lit it, and stretched out on the bunk to smoke for a few minutes before he went to sleep. He tried to think about Felix Gaunt and how he would handle things when they reached the Box C.

But he found himself pondering something odd he had noticed about Kid Montana. When the Kid had scratched his head back there in the club car, for a second Longarm would have sworn that there was something wrong about those long, Hickok-like curls. Then, when Longarm had dumped the Kid onto the bunk, his hair had again looked unnatural somehow. Longarm thought he understood *what* he was seeing.

But he was danged if he could understand why a grown man would be vain enough to wear a long, curly wig like that.

Longarm was drinking coffee in the club car the next morning when an angry voice came from behind him.

"Parker!"

Taking his time about it, Longarm placed his cup on the bar and then turned around. Kid Montana stood there, his hair and clothes disheveled, with no hat on. His face was twisted in angry lines, and a purple bruise stood out plainly on his jaw. His hands were curled over the ivory-handled butts of his Colts. He stood in a slight crouch, ready to slap leather.

"Howdy, Kid," Longarm drawled. "Want some coffee?"

"You . . ." The Kid sputtered for a few seconds before he could go on. "You son of a bitch! You sucker-punched me!"

Longarm didn't bother denying it. Instead, he said, "Couldn't have done it if you hadn't been drunk and foolish, old son. And if I hadn't done it, you'd be dead now."

"I could've beaten that bastard!"

Endicott wasn't in the club car, and Longarm was grateful for that fact. If Endicott had been there to hear the

Kid's insult, they would have been right back where they'd left off the night before, getting ready to shoot each other. Longarm didn't much care what the Kid called him. He'd been cussed so many times in his career that it rolled off his back like water off a duck.

Before the Kid could say anything else, Kitty hurried into the club car behind him. "Kid!" she said. "Don't do this! Come on back to the compartment with me."

Few men in their right minds would refuse an invitation to adjourn to a sleeping compartment on a train with a gal who looked like Kitty. Unfortunately, the Kid wasn't really in his right mind at the moment. He was too angry to be thinking straight.

And his rage was directed at Longarm, who knew he was probably making it worse by standing there calmly like that. By refusing to get rattled, he was just infuriating Kid Montana that much more.

Longarm didn't feel like killing anybody so early in the morning, though. In an attempt to be reasonable, he said, "I'll bet your head hurts like blazes, Kid. What you really need is to sit down and have some coffee, maybe a little something to eat if you think your stomach can stand it. You need something to soak up what's left of that who-hit-John you guzzled down last night."

"Damn you, Parker, are you gonna draw, or are you nothin' but a yellow-bellied coward?"

Kitty turned a tense, pale face toward Longarm and said, "Please don't kill him, Mr. Parker."

Longarm was glad she'd had the presence of mind not to call him Custis. If the Kid suspected what had gone on between the two of them the night before, he would be more determined than ever to force Longarm into a gunfight.

Longarm took a step toward the furious, hungover youngster, looked into the Kid's bleary eyes, and said, "So I'm a yellow-bellied coward, am I? That's a good line, Kid. Where'd you get it? From Ned Buntline or Colonel Prentiss Ingraham? You know Buntline ain't even that scribbler's real name? He's from back East somewhere, a fella name of Judson. He don't know much about the West, and what he don't know he just makes up. You ever read any of those yellowbacks by Frank Reade? *The Steam Man of the Prairie*? All about an hombre made out of tin who's got a steam engine inside him? Can't get much more far-fetched than that. How about Deadwood Dick? You ever read any of those books? I've met the real Deadwood Dick a time or two, you know that? He was a stagecoach driver up in the Black Hills named Dick Cole. He claimed to be the real Deadwood Dick, but of course there's no way of knowing if that's true or not. When I knew him, most folks called him Little Dick, and I ain't sure it was because of how short he was, either. That's how those dime novel fellas are, though. They don't care whether they get it right or not—"

Kid Montana lifted both hands, clenched them into fists, and shook them at Longarm. "Damn it!" he howled. "Will you *shut the hell up*!"

Longarm moved closer and said, "I'll shut up, all right, and I'll shut your mouth for you, too, Kid, if you don't wise up. The men on this train are the genuine article, not some dime novel fantasy, and they ain't impressed with you. Most of 'em could probably kill you without halfway trying, and they'll do it if you push 'em. Now, either sit down and have some coffee with me, or get the hell out of here. What's it gonna be?"

The Kid managed to glare at Longarm for another tense minute or so, then his face turned a sickening shade of green.

"Get out of his way!" Longarm warned Kitty.

She stepped aside in a hurry as the Kid turned and rushed past her, headed for the platform at the end of the car. He slammed out through the vestibule. Longarm hoped he made it in time and didn't puke all over his buckskins. He didn't care about the Kid, but it would be a shame to ruin clothes that fancy.

"Thank you," Kitty said to him.

Longarm nodded toward the door where Kid Montana

had rushed out of the club car. "You know, if you stay with him, sooner or later you'll wind up crying over his coffin."

"I know, but . . . I've come this far. I can't just leave him."

"Nothing stopping you," Longarm told her. "Turn around and go back where you came from."

A look of inutterable sadness came into Kitty's eyes. "I wish I could," she said. "You don't know how much I wish I could."

# Chapter 19

Raider worried that he might have to fend off advances from Mrs. Corrigan during the trip to the ranch, but thankfully she disappeared with her husband into their private car and didn't show up again until the next morning when the train rolled into the station at Big Spring.

Raider had been here before and knew the town's history. Sitting on the edge of the Cap Rock as it did, the geologic conditions of the area were perfect for bringing water to the surface in a huge natural spring on Sulphur Draw. At least, that was the way Doc had explained it to him.

In the mostly dry West Texas landscape, that spring had attracted visitors for hundreds of years. It had been a principal stop on the Comanche War Trail, and as the buffalo herds had migrated south from the Great Plains, it had drawn millions of those huge, shaggy beasts as well. As a young man, Raider had worked for a while as a buffalo hunter, and he had been part of a group that had come out from Fort Griffin. They had killed and skinned their share of buffalo, and they had fought the Comanch', too. Some of the fellas had lost their hair.

Those days, though not really so far in the past, were already receding from memory. The Comanches were all on reservations now, and the buffalo herds had been thinned out so that they were merely a small fraction of their once impressive numbers. The railroad had come to Big Spring, and what had once been nothing more than a tent settlement of buffalo hunters had grown to be a real town.

As Raider stepped down onto the platform from the car where he had spent the night, he looked around for Doc without thinking. A second later, he remembered that he wouldn't be seeing Doc again for a couple of days. During a hurried conference in an isolated corner of the hotel in Fort Worth the night before, it had been decided that Doc would take a later train. Riding Corrigan's private special would be running too great a risk that Doc would be spotted by Katie or Montayne, and he was insistent that they not be tipped off that pursuit was closing in on them.

Raider thought that maybe Doc was being a mite too careful, but Doc was running this operation. It was his niece and his brother's money they were after, so Raider was willing to go along with his ideas, even if they were a little harebrained. If everything went according to plan, Doc would reach Big Spring a day or two behind Raider and then rent a wagon or a horse to go the rest of the way to Corrigan's ranch. Raider expected that when Doc finally showed up, he would be in disguise. Doc dearly loved his disguises. He might not want to admit it, but he had a downright sneaky nature.

Corrigan had a couple of buckboards waiting at the train station for the contestants' bags and other gear. A fancy buggy for Corrigan and his wife was parked there, too, along with several wagons brought from the ranch. Those vehicles wouldn't be enough to carry all the contestants, but wranglers from the Box C had brought in a dozen saddle horses, too. Most of the men were used to riding, so Corrigan told them that anyone who wanted to travel by horseback to the ranch could claim one of the mounts and use it as long as they were there.

141

Raider was anxious to get back in the saddle again, so he headed for the remuda right away. He picked out the horse he wanted, a rangy dun with a mean eye and a darker stripe down the center of its back, but as he reached for the animal's reins, so did one of the other men in the group.

Raider saw that the other hombre was the tall gent with the longhorn mustache. They traded looks, then the man said, "Match you for it."

That sounded good to Raider. He'd always trusted his luck. He dug out a coin as the other fella was doing likewise. "Evens," he said.

They flipped the coins. Both came up heads. Raider took the reins.

"No hard feelin's?" he asked.

"I reckon not. That lineback dun's the best of the bunch, though. He may not look like much, but I'll bet he can run all day and still be ornery enough to take a bite out of your hide if you don't watch him."

Raider chuckled, thought about who he was supposed to be, and stuck out his hand. "Bill Wagner," he said, giving the phony name.

The other man shook with him and introduced himself as Custis Parker.

Raider frowned and said, "That name's a mite familiar for some reason. We ever cross trails before?"

"Not that I recollect," Parker replied. "But I've been a lot of places, so you never can tell."

Raider nodded. "Yeah, I reckon. Well, it's good to meet you, Parker. Maybe we can have a drink together, once we get out to Corrigan's ranch."

"I'd like that," Parker said with a nod of his own. He moved off to select another horse and get ready for the ride to the Box C.

It took a while for such a large group to get organized, of course, but eventually all the baggage was loaded, the men who were going to ride had swung up into their saddles, and the others had boarded the wagons. Corrigan climbed into the fancy buggy next to his wife and off they went, heading north from Big Spring toward the Box C. As the group strung out across the prairie, Raider thought they looked a mite like a tribe of nomads, on their way to a new home.

The headquarters of Corrigan's ranch was about thirty miles north of Big Spring. It would take most of the day for the caravan to reach it. When the sun was directly overhead at the middle of the day, the travelers stopped for lunch on the banks of a creek lined with mesquite trees. Corrigan's cook had packed baskets of food in one of the wagons that had come into town to pick up the guests. Plenty of fried chicken, biscuits, beans, and apple fritters to go around.

Raider noticed that Mrs. Corrigan didn't join the others but remained in the buggy instead, eating lunch from a smaller basket she had with her. He didn't know what was in it, but he saw her pouring wine from a bottle into a crystal glass, so he suspected her vittles were a mite fancier than everybody else's. Corrigan, though, got down on the ground and ate with everybody else. Raider didn't particularly like the man, but he felt some respect for him.

Denied the lineback dun by the luck of the coin flip, Custis Parker had selected a big roan instead. He was letting the horse drink at the creek when Raider strolled over and nodded a howdy.

"Ever been through these parts before?" Raider asked, making idle conversation.

Parker nodded. "A few times." He didn't offer any details, and Raider didn't ask for them. West of the Mississippi, being too curious about another fella was what Doc would call a social four paw, whatever the hell that meant.

"Yeah, me, too," Raider said. "That was before Corrigan came out here from the East and built up his spread, though."

"I'd never heard of him until I read about this contest he's putting on," Parker admitted. "Seems like a good enough hombre, for a rich fella."

"Yeah. I'm not so sure his wife likes it much out here, though. She seems a mite standoffish."

Parker chuckled as if he knew something that Raider

didn't, which irritated Raider. "I say something funny?" he snapped.

"No, not really," Parker said with a shake of his head. "I agree with you that Mrs. Corrigan ain't your usual ranch wife, but I wouldn't call her standoffish—"

Whether or not Parker would have gone on to explain that comment, Raider never knew, because at that moment, loud, angry curses filled the air. Both of the big men standing beside the stream turned around to see what was going on.

The long-haired, fancy-dressed gunfighter Raider had seen at the exhibition the day before was yelling at one of the other contestants, a shorter, bland-faced man.

"Damn it," Parker said. "Not again."

"What's going on?" Raider asked.

"Kid Montana's an asshole, that's what's going on. He's already tried to force a showdown once with Endicott. I hoped he had more sense than to try it again."

Raider frowned. "Cleve Endicott? The gunslinger?"

"One and the same," Parker confirmed.

"He's killed half a dozen men. He's wanted by the law, too. What's he doin' down here?"

"I reckon he must want to win that Golden Eagle." With a grim expression on his face, Parker started toward the confrontation, leading his horse. Raider followed. He was interested in Kid Montana. Other than the long hair, he matched the description of Ned Montayne.

Montana . . . Montayne . . . Raider stiffened, and under his breath said, "Son of a bitch." It was possible, all right. That long hair could be a wig. A disguise, just like he had been thinking about earlier, only instead of Doc carrying out a masquerade, it was the man Doc was pursuing.

From the looks of what was happening, though, Doc might not have a chance to catch his quarry. Kid Montana was saying, ". . . damn sick and tired of you making comments behind my back, mister."

Endicott shook his head. "I wasn't talking about you specifically, Kid. I just commented that some of the men entered in this contest didn't really deserve to be here."

"I know good and well you were talking about me!"

Endicott shrugged and said, "If you want to go ahead and prove my point for me by acting loco like this, have at it."

The other men had drawn back so that an open circle had formed around the Kid and Endicott. Nobody wanted to be in the line of fire. Corrigan stepped forward, though, and said in a loud voice, "Stop it right now, you two. I won't tolerate such behavior."

"Talk to this fool youngster," Endicott said with a nod toward the Kid. "He's the one trying to make trouble."

"That's a damned lie," the Kid said. "He's been ragging me ever since we left Fort Worth. It's time we settled things."

In a deceptively mild voice edged with steel, Endicott said, "I don't cotton to being called a liar."

Kid Montana sneered. "That's what you are, mister. A no-good liar."

Endicott's face went pale, and Corrigan tried, perhaps foolishly, to get between the men. Raider was the closest to the rancher, so he grabbed Corrigan's arm to hold him back and keep him from blundering into some flying lead.

"You son of a bitch," Endicott grated as he stared at Kid Montana. His hand stabbed toward his gun.

Raider fully expected Kid Montana to be dead a blink of an eye later. But instead, the Kid moved with blinding swiftness, and he had filled his hand by the time Endicott was clearing leather. The ivory-handled Colt boomed first—only by a fraction of a heartbeat, but that was ample. Endicott was thrown backward by the Kid's bullet boring into his chest, and his own shot whined off harmlessly into the air, well above the heads of everyone there.

Endicott landed hard on his back, with his arms and legs sprawled. The gun slipped out of his hand, so he couldn't try for a second shot. His body shook with spasms as blood welled from the hole in his chest and stained his shirt crimson.

Kid Montana walked over to his fallen opponent and gazed down at him. Endicott's mouth opened and closed a couple of times, but nothing came out except a trickle of blood from the corner of it.

Coolly, the Kid shot him three more times, hammering the first two slugs through Endicott's body and then planting the third one in the middle of the gunslinger's forehead. Endicott jerked and died.

A hush hung over the group gathered on the creek bank. Kid Montana looked around at them and said in a loud, clear voice, "You all saw what happened. Endicott drew first. It was a fair fight."

"It was a fair fight," Corrigan admitted grudgingly with anger in his voice. "But you had no right to do that, Kid. I asked you not to. I ought to—"

The Kid turned his cold gaze on the rancher. "Ought to what? Not let me compete in the contest? That wouldn't be fair, Mr. Corrigan. A man's got a right to defend himself, doesn't he? It all comes back to the fact that Endicott reached for his gun first."

Corrigan had no argument for that. He shrugged and turned away. But then he said, "The next man who causes trouble will be barred from the competition. No exceptions."

That rule was a mite late to help Cleve Endicott, Raider thought.

His opinion of Kid Montana had changed. Most men who dressed like that weren't the genuine article. Raider had figured that while the Kid might be fast on the draw and a good shot where targets were concerned, he wasn't a real gunman.

Raider had been wrong about that, though, and now he knew the truth.

Kid Montana was a stone-cold killer.

And if he really was Ned Montayne, that meant Doc's niece Katie was traveling with a very dangerous man.

# Chapter 20

The gunfight and Cleve Endicott's death cast a pall of sorts over the procession, and after lunch most of the men were quiet as they rode toward the Box C . . . for a while.

But for the most part these were hard-boiled hombres, men who had seen death many times and dealt it out themselves on more than one occasion. Although they remained subdued, talk and laughter among them soon returned.

Longarm wasn't surprised very often, but the fact that Endicott was dead and Kid Montana was still alive surprised him. Downright shocked him, in fact. He had never expected the Kid to be that fast on the draw and icy-nerved under fire. The cruel streak that the Kid had displayed by firing three more bullets into Endicott after downing him came as no shock, though. Longarm had seen the hatred and recklessness in the Kid's eyes the night before. Kid Montana was a cold-blooded killer.

Longarm was going to have to remember that from here on out, because the Kid had a grudge against him, too. Sooner or later, the youngster would probably try to settle that score.

If the Kid had known about Longarm bedding Kitty, chances were he would have come after the big lawman before he prodded Endicott into a fight. So it was unlikely the Kid had discovered that yet. Longarm hoped Kitty had enough sense to keep to herself what they had done.

Kitty was subdued today, staying close to the Kid in one of the wagons. Being an Easterner, as Longarm had him pegged, the Kid hadn't jumped at the chance to ride horseback all the way to the Box C. He might be caught up in the whole dime-novel view of the West, but even so he didn't want his ass pounding a saddle all day. Give him credit for that much sense, anyway.

Felix Gaunt was one of the riders, but even though he didn't seem to be all that friendly to anybody, he always had men around him. Longarm was getting tired of waiting. Patience and discretion went only so far. He wanted to arrest Gaunt and be done with it, so that he could put an end to this charade of entering Corrigan's shooting contest.

By the time late afternoon rolled around, the caravan was nearing the headquarters of the Box C. The travelers had been on Corrigan's range most of the day, and Longarm had spotted quite a few head of cattle. Not only longhorns, but also some of the shorter-horned, more stockily built breeds. This was all open, unfenced range. Barbed wire had made considerable incursions into Texas, but it hadn't gotten this far west yet. It was only a matter of time, though. Right here were some of the last vestiges of open range days.

Give it another ten years, Longarm thought as he rode along on the roan he had picked out that morning after Bill Wagner claimed the dun. Ten more years and the frontier as he had known it would be gone, except maybe in isolated places.

Would there still be a job for him as a deputy U.S. marshal if he survived that long? Longarm figured there would be. The coming of civilization had never meant that crime would disappear completely. If anything, the more folks crowded in, the more lawbreaking there was. It was just the natural order of things. Look not too far under the surface, even in some genteel, civilized hombre, and you would find a bloody-handed reaver.

The road went through a big, arched, wooden gate, even though there were no fences to either side of the gate. The Box C brand was marked on the heavy posts that supported the arch, where the name CORRIGAN had been burned into the wood. The gent was a mite fond of himself, Longarm thought.

The ranch house stood by itself with only a couple of small trees around it. It was a huge, whitewashed, three-story building with a covered porch that appeared to run around all four sides. About fifty yards away, numerous outbuildings were scattered, including a long bunkhouse, a blacksmith shop, a smokehouse, a cook shack, some storage buildings, a few cabins for the hands who had wives and families, and a couple of massive barns with pole corrals sprawled around them. As far as Longarm could tell, everything was in good repair and kept up quite nicely. The Box C was no greasy-sack outfit. If Corrigan kept taking in more range, it might grow to be the equal of the XIT or the Four Sixes, up in the Panhandle.

When the group had come to a halt in front of the house, Corrigan stood up in the buggy and turned to face them. "There's enough room for everyone in the house," he announced, "but if any of you would be more comfortable staying in the bunkhouse, that can be arranged. I want you to know that we'll be having a big barbecue and fandango tonight to welcome all of you and celebrate the beginning of the contest tomorrow." He grinned. "I'll just warn you that it might be wise not to overindulge in food or drink tonight. You want to be at your best when the shooting starts tomorrow." He started to sit down, then straightened and added, "One more thing. No guns tonight. There'll be time for that tomorrow, so leave them wherever you're staying."

Longarm frowned a little, and so did some of the other men. Most of them would feel a mite naked without their guns. As the old saying went, they had packed iron for so long that without it they walked slanchwise. But it was

Corrigan's spread and his contest, after all, and Longarm supposed that the cattleman made the rules.

Still, he planned to have the derringer in its usual place in his vest pocket, no matter what Corrigan said.

Gaunt chose to take one of the rooms in the house, so Longarm did likewise. He wanted to stay close to his quarry, just not so close that Gaunt got suspicious.

Longarm noticed that Kid Montana and Kitty were staying in the house as well. He knew Kitty wanted a chance to get together with him again, and Longarm wouldn't have minded that, either. He had his doubts about it happening, though. From here on out, things were likely to be all business.

After Doc had left the Pinkertons and gone back to Boston to get married and work for his brother, Raider had operated on his own as an agent for several years. On occasion another detective would be teamed with him for a particular case, but most of the time he was on his own. He had gotten to like it after a while.

But right now he wished that Doc was here. Now that he had started to suspect Kid Montana and Ned Montayne were the same hombre, he wasn't sure how to proceed. His worry increased when he saw the Kid entering Corrigan's house with a young, pretty blonde. That pretty much clinched it in Raider's mind. The girl had to be Katie Weatherbee. Raider hadn't noticed her before now because there were always quite a few people around, and she seemed to be trying to blend into the crowd.

That certainly wasn't true of the Kid. He liked to be the center of attention. He reveled in it, in fact. Katie wouldn't be able to do anything about that, but at least she could keep herself inconspicuous.

The thing to do was to be patient, Raider told himself as he unsaddled the dun and turned the horse over to one of Corrigan's men, a tall, broad-shouldered hombre with dark hair and a hawklike nose who introduced himself as Walt.

"Don't worry about this old fella," Walt assured Raider in a deep, musical voice. "I'll take good care of him."

Raider shrugged. "He's Corrigan's horse, not mine. Seems to be a good mount, though."

Walt patted the dun on the shoulder, then jerked his hand back as the horse twisted his head around and snapped at the wrangler's hand. "I'll give him a surroundin' of grain," Walt said with a grin, "since he seems to be a mite hungry."

Carrying his gear, Raider left the horse in Walt's capable hands and walked toward the house. Kid Montana and the girl Raider had taken to be Katie Weatherbee had gone in there to claim a room, so Raider supposed he ought to stay in the house, too—although his natural inclination would have been to grab an empty bunk in the bunkhouse.

Corrigan's little four-eyed secretary was waiting inside the house. He directed Raider up to the second floor and told him to stow his gear in any of the empty rooms. Raider did so, tossing his bag on the bed and crossing the room to raise a window. As he lifted the glass, he heard the strains of fiddle music and looked out to see several cowboys gathering in the large open area between the house and the outbuildings. A couple of them carried fiddles, while the others had guitars. Musicians for the big barbecue and party that night, Raider figured. He watched as the men began to tune their instruments and other members of Corrigan's crew brought tables and chairs from one of the storage buildings and started setting them up. Mexican women appeared carrying colorful tablecloths and spread them over the tables. From the looks of things, it was going to be quite a fandango.

Raider sniffed as the breeze brought the scent of cooking beef to his nose. Laden with spices, it was a delicious aroma. Lunch had been good but a mite sparse for a man of his appetites. His mouth started to water at the thought of that barbecue.

Since he wasn't absolutely certain about Kid Montana really being Ned Montayne, there wasn't anything he could do except keep an eye on the Kid and the girl until Doc got there. It would be up to Doc to make a positive identification. Once that was done, then they could take action.

Until then, Raider decided, he would enjoy himself, starting with a heap of good food and maybe some dancing tonight, assuming that some of those gals who worked for Corrigan were unmarried and unspoken-for.

Recalling Corrigan's rule about not bringing any guns to the party, Raider unbuckled his shell belt and coiled it around the holstered Colt, then stashed the revolver in his warbag. He took a sheathed knife *out* of the bag, slipped it behind his belt at the small of his back, and tucked his shirt in over it so that it couldn't be seen.

Most of the time, cold steel wasn't the equal of hot lead, but Raider was damned if he was going anywhere without some kind of weapon on him!

Once he was in his room, Longarm decided to change into range clothes rather than wear the brown tweed suit to the barbecue. He had been sporting town duds for too long. He took the turnip watch and put it in the pocket of the denim trousers he pulled on, along with the chain and the .41-caliber derringer welded to the other end. It wouldn't be as handy that way as it was when he wore it as a watch fob in his vest pocket, but it was better than nothing.

He had just finished buttoning his shirt when a knock sounded on the door of his room. Longarm wasn't expecting anybody, but he supposed his visitor might be one of Corrigan's servants who'd come to tell him something.

Habitual caution made him ask, "Who's there?" and then step to one side in case whoever was in the second-floor corridor blasted a shot through the door at him.

"It's me," a woman's voice called softly. "Kitty."

A frown creased Longarm's forehead as he opened the door. Kitty stood there looking as pretty as ever, even though she was frowning, too. The worried expression told Longarm that something was wrong.

"What is it?" he asked. It didn't take much effort to make a guess. "The Kid?"

Kitty nodded. "He's got a flask of whiskey he's been nipping at all afternoon, ever since he killed that man on the way out here. I think he's going to come after you next, Custis."

Following the fatal shoot-out, Cleve Endicott's body had been wrapped up in a blanket and placed in one of the wagons with the baggage for the rest of the journey to the Box C. The ranch had its own cemetery, and Corrigan had announced that there would be a small burial service first thing in the morning. It seemed a mite grotesque that everybody else would be enjoying a barbecue and party tonight while Endicott's body was lying in one of the barns, waiting to be put in the ground the next morning, but such things weren't all that uncommon. Life was still hard and sometimes harsh on the frontier, and folks took their pleasure where they could, meaning no disrespect to the dead by doing it.

"Corrigan said no guns at the party," Longarm pointed out.

Kitty shook her head. "I'm afraid the Kid won't pay any attention to that. Even if Mr. Corrigan has men posted to enforce the rule, the Kid will try to sneak a gun in."

Since Longarm was planning to do the exact same thing, he couldn't say too much about that.

He told Kitty, "I'll be careful, but I don't reckon Corrigan will let anything else happen tonight. He was mad as hell about that shoot-out between the Kid and Endicott. It'll be all right."

Kitty sighed. "I hope you're right." She moved closer to Longarm, came up on her toes, and put her arms around his neck. "I'd surely hate to see anything bad happen to you, Custis. I've been thinking all day about what happened between us on the train . . ."

Longarm lowered his mouth to hers, forgetting for the moment that Kitty had left the door open a crack when she came into the room. He was reminded of it when he heard a floorboard creak in the hall and glanced in that direction over her shoulder. Somebody was passing by out there, but he couldn't tell who.

It probably wasn't Kid Montana, though, because the Kid likely would have gone loco if he'd seen his girl kissing another man. Longarm didn't really care who else might have caught a glimpse of Kitty in his arms.

She broke the kiss and whispered, "Custis, is there time for us to . . . ?"

"Later," Longarm told her. "If the Kid's been drinking all afternoon, chances are he'll pass out before the night's over. You know, you might give some thought to leaving him when this is over."

"I plan to. Things . . . well, things haven't worked out the way I hoped they would when the two of us got together."

"If you need any help, you let me know."

"You should watch your own back," she said. "He's crazy. I didn't want to admit it, but after seeing how he goaded poor Mr. Endicott into drawing on him today . . ." She shuddered as her voice trailed off.

"Don't spend a lot of time feeling sorry for Endicott," Longarm said. "He was a pretty bad hombre himself, even though he looked a little like a clerk in a dry goods store. Chances are he would've wound up at the end of a hangman's rope sooner or later."

"The West really is still a barbaric place, isn't it?" Kitty said.

"Only the parts where people live," Longarm said.

# Chapter 21

*Well, son of a bitch,* Raider said to himself as he went down the stairs.

He wasn't the sort of hombre to go peeking into other folks' rooms, but he had glanced in the direction of one of the doors he was passing in the hallway, which was open an inch or two, and had spotted the shine of long, fair hair. Even though he had barely broken stride, he had gotten a good enough look to recognize the girl he suspected of being Katie Weatherbee. She had been in there hugging and kissing a fella, and it was a mighty passionate embrace, too.

But it wasn't Kid Montana—or Ned Montayne, if that was who he really was—kissing Katie.

No, it was the tall drink of water with the longhorn mustache, Custis Parker.

*Son of a bitch,* Raider thought again.

He didn't know what to do now. The two times he had spoken to Parker, he'd felt an instinctive liking for the man. But if that girl really was Doc's niece, then Raider felt duty-bound to look after her and defend her honor—not that there was a whole lot left of it to defend, he reminded himself, since she had put a gun to her own uncle's head and then run off with a lowlife snake like Montayne.

Still and all, she was Doc's kin—and until Doc got here to confirm or deny that, Raider had to assume that she really was Katie—and he couldn't let her come to harm if he could do anything about it. Parker didn't look like the sort of gent who had the best of intentions when it came to willing, good-looking young women.

Of course, Raider reminded himself, considering his own history with the ladies, he didn't have much room to talk. He had a habit of obliging the ladies whenever he got the chance.

He would have a talk with Parker, he decided, and warn the man that it might be a good idea to steer clear of Katie. That was all he could do, other than hope that Doc got here pretty quick-like.

By the time darkness settled down over the Cap Rock country, the tables set up outside were groaning under the weight of platters piled high with food. The fiddlers were sawing away with their bows and the guitar players were strumming along with them. A clean-cut young cowboy got up and sang a song or two, backed up by some of the other ranch hands. The contestants milled around, heaped food on their plates, and accepted cups of wine and beer from the pretty serving girls. A few of them danced with the gals, who seemed quite willing to go along with that. Raider figured they would go along with other things, too, if anybody was interested.

He contented himself for the time being with plenty of the spicy beef, eating the barbecue along with beans and cornbread and washing it all down with beer. After filling his plate for the second time, he spotted Parker sitting at one of the tables and sauntered in that direction.

Before he could get there, a woman came up beside him and linked her arm with his. Raider looked over in surprise and saw Mrs. Corrigan smiling up at him.

"Come sit with me, Mr. Wagner," she said, and Raider didn't see any tactful way he could refuse. He tried not to look down the low-cut neck of her gown at the inviting swell of her breasts as he nodded and said, "Yes, ma'am."

Longarm was sitting one table down from Felix Gaunt, keeping an eye on the man. A part of him wanted to pull out the derringer and arrest Gaunt right then and there, but he didn't do it because he figured Gaunt probably had a hideout gun, too. Anita Corrigan had been wandering around the party talking to people, and Kitty and several other women were there, too. Longarm wasn't going to take a chance on endangering them if he didn't have to.

He was looking around when he spotted Corrigan talking to one of the ranch hands. Something was familiar about the fella, who was a tall, dark-haired, hawk-nosed gent. Longarm suddenly stiffened as recognition punched him in the belly. He knew that cowboy.

Only the man wasn't a cowboy at all.

Before Longarm could ask himself what in blazes Walt Scott was doing here, a voice called from behind him, "Mr. Parker! Howdy!"

He looked around and saw the young man named Riley Hutchins striding toward him. Riley was dressed like he had been the last time Longarm saw him in Fort Worth, only he wasn't wearing a gun now. Two people were with him, a medium-sized man with a salt-and-pepper beard and a nice-looking woman with red hair.

Longarm got to his feet as Riley came up to him. He shook hands with the young man and said, "I didn't expect to see you out here so soon, old son. Thought it would take you longer to ride out."

"I got the next train," Riley said with a grin. "Brought my horse with me and everything. Once you told me that Mr. Corrigan might be willin' to hire me, I wasn't gonna let anything stand in my way."

Longarm had passed along to Riley what Corrigan had said, making it clear that there was no guarantee Riley would wind up with a riding job on the Box C. Obviously, the young man had quit his job at the hotel anyway and gotten out there as fast as he could.

"Good thing I came along, too," Riley continued. "Otherwise these folks would've been in trouble. The buggy they rented in Big Spring to come out here had a wheel come off."

"And with this fine young man helping us, we were able to repair it," the bearded man said. He extended his right hand to Longarm. "The name's Abelard Finch. I'm a journalist, come to write up Mr. Corrigan's contest for *Harper's Weekly.* And this lovely lady is my assistant, Miss Galloway."

The redhead smiled at Longarm and said, "Mr. Finch underestimates me, sir. I'm a journalist as well, and we'll just see whose account of these festivities winds up in the pages of *Harper's.*"

Longarm shook hands with Finch and tried not to grimace at the thought of a pair of reporters sticking their noses into this affair. He had never gotten along too well with representatives of the press. They had a habit of fouling things up, all in the name of journalism.

Finch and Miss Galloway might prove to be even more annoying than the usual run of scribblers, because there was an air of prickly hostility between them. Longarm had a feeling their rivalry was far from friendly.

Luckily, that was none of his business, and if the breaks went his way, he would be out of there before the actual contest got under way.

But there was still the worrisome fact that Walt Scott was on the Box C to contend with. Something unusual was going on, and Longarm had no idea what it was. But since he had recognized Scott, it was entirely possible that Scott would recognize him. He thought he could trust Scott not to blurt out the fact that gunslinger Custis Parker was really Deputy U.S. Marshal Custis Long, but accidents sometimes happened.

Longarm felt a little like a man watching a bad storm blow up. He knew it was going to raise holy hell, but there wasn't a thing in the world he could do to stop it.

Scott had disappeared somewhere after talking to

Corrigan. The rancher went back to the table where he had been sitting with his wife and several of the contestants, including Bill Wagner. Corrigan's secretary came up to the table carrying a box, and from the way the little fella was straining, it had to be heavy. He set it down in front of Corrigan, who waved him away.

"Ladies and gentlemen, if I could have your attention, please," Corrigan called. The conversations died down as everyone turned to look at the cattleman. Corrigan had raised his hands as he called for attention. He lowered them now to the top of the box in front of him and lifted it. Reaching inside, he pawed aside some packing material and grasped the item that the box contained. "I thought you'd like to see what you're competing for. I give you the Golden Eagle!"

He raised the statue out of the box and held it up high in front of him. A little more than a foot tall, it was just about lifesized, Longarm thought, and he could tell from the way Corrigan handled it that it was heavy. The Eagle had its wings spread as if it were attacking. Its beak was open, and Longarm could almost hear a screech coming from it. The surface of the thing gleamed in the light from the oil lamps that were set up all around the tables, but it was a dull shine. Longarm didn't know how thick the gold coating was. The Eagle was supposed to be worth a small fortune, though.

"Worth competing for, gentlemen?" Corrigan asked with a smile as he turned from side to side, holding the Golden Eagle in front of him so that everyone could get a good look at it.

One of the contestants called, "Hell, yeah!" and the others laughed. Someone started to clap his hands. That prompted more applause to swell up. Corrigan basked in it for a moment, clearly enjoying himself.

Then a shot rang out, changing everything.

Raider had had women play up to him before, so that was nothing new or uncommon. Rarely, though, had any married gal gone after him so blatantly right in front of her husband.

He had stiffened in more ways than one when Anita Corrigan reached under the table and started caressing his manhood through his trousers.

She smiled sweetly at him, like butter wouldn't melt in her mouth, and continued eating with her other hand as she rubbed his groin. Raider fought off the impulse to bolt up from the table. It wasn't that he didn't enjoy what she was doing; it felt mighty good, in fact. But there was a time and a place for such carrying on, and this damn sure wasn't it.

Raider took a deep breath, leaned closer to Anita, and asked in a half whisper, "Ma'am, just what the hell is it you want, anyway?"

Her smile didn't waver as she said, "You should be able to guess, Mr. Wagner."

Corrigan had gotten up to go talk to one of his ranch hands, the man called Walt who had taken care of Raider's horse earlier. Raider leaned his head toward the rancher and said, "Your husband is right over yonder, Mrs. Corrigan. I don't reckon you should be doin' what you're doin'."

"You don't think the risk of being discovered makes it even more exciting?"

"As a matter of fact, ma'am, I don't."

She pouted for a second. "Then I'm disappointed in you, Mr. Wagner. I was about to invite you to come up to my room later."

Raider's brain waged war with certain other parts of his anatomy. Anita Corrigan was beautiful, no doubt about that, and Raider had to admit that he liked a certain amount of boldness in a woman. And while he generally didn't fool around with married women, that wasn't a hard-and-fast rule. Under some circumstances he would at least consider it.

But not here and now, he decided. Corrigan was an older gent, and maybe he wasn't able to satisfy his wife the way Anita wanted to be satisfied, but that didn't mean the responsibility for that chore fell to Raider. He reached under the table and put his hand on hers, about to move it gently but firmly off his lap, when Corrigan's secretary staggered up and plopped a heavy box down on the table.

Corrigan called for everybody's attention, and that distracted Anita, for which Raider was grateful. He squeezed her hand, friendly-like, as he turned in his chair. No point in making his host's wife any angrier with him than he had to, he thought. This was a good excuse to slow things down a mite.

Corrigan opened the box and took out the Golden Eagle. Raider had to admit that it was an impressive little statue. Corrigan's eyes gleamed with pride of possession as his hands clasped around the Eagle's body. Seeing the way the rancher held the thing, like he never wanted to let it go, Raider was a little surprised that Corrigan planned to give it away. Corrigan looked like he would rather just keep the Eagle for himself.

The people at the tables began to clap as Corrigan turned from side to side, showing off the gold-plated statue. Raider joined in the applause, and so did Anita, although she seemed a little reluctant about it. Clapping meant she had to take her hand off Raider's crotch.

There was no telling how long the applause would have gone on if the sudden, unexpected blast of a gunshot hadn't put an abrupt end to it. Instinct sent Raider's hand toward his hip, but there was no gun there, he recalled. His only weapon was the knife hidden at the small of his back.

Confused yells filled the air for a second as men leaped up from their chairs and looked around for the source of the shot. A loud, powerful voice cut through the hubbub.

"Everybody elevate!" the commanding voice bellowed. "In the name of the State of Texas, you're all under arrest!"

Men carrying rifles strode out of the darkness at the edge of the big circle of light. They came from the bunkhouse, the barns, and the ranch house itself. Striding in front and taking the lead was the cowboy Raider had spoken to earlier, the man called Walt. But now he didn't look like some harmless wrangler. His face had the same sort of hunting look to it that was on the face of the Golden Eagle, and that beak of a nose made the resemblance even stronger. His fists were filled with twin

Colts that had come from the black holsters belted around his lean hips.

And pinned to the breast of his bib-front shirt was a badge the likes of which Raider had seen on several occasions in the past. A silver star set in a silver circle, hammered out of a Mexican ten-peso piece.

The emblem of the Texas Rangers.

# Chapter 22

Longarm figured there were at least a dozen Rangers springing the trap, led by Walt Scott. A few years earlier, during a dustup down in the border country, Longarm had met Scott and worked with the big Ranger. At the time, Scott had been posing as an owlhoot himself, the hombre known to the peons as *El Aguila*, the Eagle. Pretty damned appropriate, Longarm thought, that Scott was mixed up in this Golden Eagle business—which was clearly a sham. There was no contest. There never had been.

That realization burst in Longarm's brain like a bomb, and as it did, he saw the simple elegance of it. Why go to the trouble of chasing down a bunch of gunmen and killers when you could have them come to you instead?

The presence of Felix Gaunt and Cleve Endicott should have tipped him off to the possibility this was a trap, he thought. Probably at least half of the men who had entered the contest had charges leveled against them somewhere, with warrants out for their arrests. One thing about fast guns, they were vain as all get out. They hadn't been able to resist the temptation of showing off in front of their peers, and the prospect of winning the fabulously valuable Golden Eagle had been a strong lure, too.

Sure, some of the contestants wouldn't have any reward dodgers out on them. They would be angry about being fooled, too, not to mention being put under arrest. But the Rangers could sort all that out later, once they had everybody under lock and key. They would probably apologize to the few innocent men who had gotten caught up in their net. In the end, it wouldn't matter, because a dozen or more of the most dangerous men in the West would wind up behind bars where they belonged.

It was enough to make Longarm chuckle. He understood now why Corrigan had insisted that the contestants be unarmed when they came to this party.

But he had the derringer in his pocket, he reminded himself, and it was likely he wasn't the only one in the crowd with a hideout gun. This situation could still blow up in the faces of the Rangers who had come out of the shadows to cover the men at the tables.

That was exactly what happened. A couple of the men lunged to their feet, clawing at guns hidden in pockets or under their shirts. Women screamed and men yelled curses as Scott pivoted toward the gunmen and flame spouted from the muzzles of the Colts in his hands.

One of the gunmen spilled over backward as Scott's slugs hammered into his chest, but the other forced the Ranger to duck as he sent a bullet whistling past Scott's ear. Crouching, the gunslinger ran along the table, and the other Rangers had to hold their fire for fear of hitting innocents.

Surprisingly, as the man passed the two journalists Longarm had encountered earlier, Abelard Finch launched himself in a tackle that sent him crashing into the fleeing gunman. Both of them went down. Finch's fist rose and fell, cracking against the gunman's jaw. Stunned by the blow, the man went limp.

Finch pushed himself to his feet. His beard was hanging

askew from his jaw, and Longarm realized that the man was wearing a disguise. Finch reached up, pulled the fake beard free, and dropped it.

"Doc!" Bill Wagner exclaimed.

Walt Scott came up, covering both Finch—or Doc— and the gunman who had been knocked out. "Who are you, mister?" the Ranger demanded.

"My name is Weatherbee," Doc replied. "I'm a Pinkerton agent."

The pretty, redheaded Miss Galloway spoke up. "No, he's not," she said, "but I am. My name is Colleen Gallagher. Mr. Weatherbee used to be a Pinkerton agent, but he retired."

"Retired or not, what in blazes are you folks doing here?" Scott asked.

Doc turned and pointed dramatically at Kid Montana. "Looking for him!"

The Kid came halfway out of his chair, snarling at Doc. "You bastard. I should have killed you back in Boston."

Beside him, Kitty put her hands over her face and began to sob. "I . . . I'm sorry," she said to Doc Weatherbee. "I never meant to hurt you. I wouldn't have pulled the trigger."

Longarm's brain was whirling now. Obviously, a lot had been going on that he didn't know anything about.

But he still had a job to do, and the man who had brought him here was still sitting at one of the tables, unwilling to make a break and risk getting gunned down by the Rangers. Longarm stood up, causing Walt Scott to wheel quickly toward him. The heavy revolvers in the Ranger's hands covered Longarm.

"Take it easy, Scott," Longarm said. "Remember me? I'm Custis Long."

A smile creased Scott's face and relieved its grimness somewhat. "Marshal Long," he said. "Sure I remember you. What are you doing here?"

"Same as you, trying to round up owlhoots. I'm just after one fella, though." Longarm pointed at Gaunt. "That one."

Gaunt's features twisted in a grimace of hate. "You were that son of a bitch in Wichita," he guessed, spitting the words out angrily.

Longarm nodded. "Damn right."

"You can have him, Marshal," Scott said, "providing that the State of Texas doesn't have a prior claim on him. We'll have to work that out."

"All right," Longarm said, even though he was making a promise to himself that he wouldn't let the Rangers take Gaunt away from him. The federal charges against the killer ought to outweigh any state charges.

With a grin, Walt Scott looked around the group and raised his voice to ask, "Any other lawmen working undercover here?"

The man called Bill Wagner pushed himself to his feet next to a stunned Anita Corrigan, who looked like she hadn't known a thing about the plot hatched between her husband and the Rangers. "That'd be me," Wagner said. "I used to be a Pinkerton agent, too, and I'm workin' with this fella here"—he gestured toward Doc Weatherbee and went on—"who could've told me he was here instead o' skulkin' around in a fake beard."

"I just hadn't had a chance to inform you of my presence yet, Raider," Doc said.

Longarm's eyes narrowed. He remembered hearing about a couple of Pinkerton agents named Raider and Doc, but he had never crossed trails with them before. Since he hadn't heard anything about them in several years, he had assumed they were either dead or no longer working as detectives. Obviously, neither of those things was true.

Scott poked a gun barrel in the general direction of Kid Montana. "And it's this fella you were after, Weatherbee?"

"Precisely," Doc replied. "I don't know what he's calling himself down here, but his real name is Ned Montayne. He worked for my brother's bank in Boston, where he embezzled approximately eighty thousand dollars. *And* he kidnapped my niece, Miss Katherine Weatherbee." Doc

166

nodded toward the young woman Longarm had known as Kitty.

"That's a damned lie," Montayne said. "I never kidnapped anyone. Katie came with me of her own free will." He sneered. "She thought she was in love with me."

"Yes, well, that was a mistake," Katie said. "I never knew you were so rough and brutal, Ned."

"I never heard you complaining about me being too rough while I was making love to you," Montayne shot back, still with a sneer on his face.

Longarm, Doc, and Raider all clenched their fists as a humiliated flush colored Katie's face. Longarm had to rein in the impulse to step forward and smash a punch into Montayne's face, and he reckoned Doc and Raider felt about the same way.

Walt Scott said, "Keep talkin' like that, Montayne, and you'll wind up a mite bruised when you go back to Boston to face charges there. We plan on extraditin' the hombres we corraled tonight who aren't wanted in Texas to wherever they've got charges against 'em. But that doesn't mean we have to make your stay here any too pleasant."

Montayne didn't lose the look of disdain, but he kept his mouth shut after that as the rifle-toting Rangers moved in and disarmed their prisoners. Each man was questioned, and it was soon determined that only a few of them besides Longarm and Raider weren't wanted. Most of the wanted ones tried to lie their way out of it, but the Rangers had thoroughly investigated the entrants in Corrigan's so-called contest and knew who they were dealing with. They also had what was sometimes called the Rangers' Doomsday Book, which contained detailed descriptions and in some cases even photographs of the most wanted men in Texas.

One of the Rangers came over to where Scott stood with Longarm, Raider, and Doc, and asked, "You'll vouch for these hombres, Walt?"

Scott nodded. "I reckon so. I know Marshal Long personal-like. He and I once raised hell and shoved a chunk under the corner. And I've heard plenty about these other two gents. If the lady here"—he gestured toward Colleen Gallagher—"can prove that she's a Pinkerton agent, and she vouches for them, I will, too."

Colleen opened her bag. "I have all my identification papers, and I assure you they're in order, Captain."

Scott took the documents she handed him and said, "I'm not a captain, ma'am. That'd be my boss, Cap'n McNelly. I'm just a Ranger."

Longarm knew that wasn't quite true. Scott was the Ranger that Captain McNelly trusted to handle the most important missions, like rounding up a whole passel of wanted men with a fake contest and a fake prize . . .

"What about the Golden Eagle, Scott?" Longarm asked as that thought crossed his mind. "I reckon it must be phony, too, like the contest?"

Scott handed Colleen's identification papers back to her and nodded his acceptance of her bona fides. In reply to Longarm's question about the Golden Eagle, he said, "Nope, not at all. It's as real as can be. Mr. Corrigan was having it made anyway, so when we approached him with the idea of staging a contest to lure some fugitives out of the woods, he suggested using it as the prize." Scott grinned. "It made good bait, too."

The prisoners—nineteen of them in all—were herded off at riflepoint toward the sturdy storage building that would serve as a makeshift jail. There were no windows and only one door, and it would be padlocked and guarded at all times by at least two Rangers, as Scott explained.

"I reckon that wraps this up," Scott concluded.

"What about my niece?" Doc asked. "She *did* help Montayne escape from Boston. Technically, there should be charges against her, too."

It looked like it pained him to say that, but he felt duty-bound to do so, Longarm figured.

Scott thought about it for a moment and then shrugged. "That's up to you, Mr. Weatherbee. We sure can't lock her up in the storage building with those owlhoots, though."

Katie paled at the thought of that.

"No, of course not," Doc said quickly. He turned to her and went on, "Do you give me your word that you won't try to escape?"

"Of course I won't," she promised. "I *want* to go back to Boston. Falling in love with Ned and agreeing to help him get away was the worst mistake I ever made in my life."

"Well, at least you're smart enough to realize that." Doc turned back to Scott. "I'll take the responsibility for her," he told the Ranger. "You can consider her to be in my custody."

"Good enough for me," Scott agreed.

Edmund Corrigan came over to them. "Is everything all right?" he wanted to know.

"It sure is," Scott said. "Thank you for your help in rounding up those coyotes, sir. You have the gratitude of the State of Texas."

"I was glad to do it. Texas is my home now, and I intend to make it so for the rest of my life." The rancher looked at Longarm and Raider. "Did I understand correctly? You two are lawmen?"

"I am," Longarm replied. "A deputy U.S. marshal."

Raider said, "I reckon I'm a civilian, but I used to be a Pinkerton. I ain't no outlaw, anyway, that's for sure."

Corrigan shook his head. "You had me fooled. I thought you were real gunslingers, like the rest of them." He turned and went to rejoin his wife, taking her arm and leading her toward the massive ranch house. Anita Corrigan cast a glance over her shoulder, but Longarm couldn't tell if she was looking at him or at Raider.

Any plans she had made for cheating on her husband during the contest were pretty much ruined, Longarm thought. She was probably disappointed that things hadn't worked out right for her.

Remembering how Anita had opened her dressing gown and tried to tempt him into bedding her, Longarm didn't feel any envy for Edmund Corrigan. The man might have a pile of money and one of the biggest spreads in Texas—he even had a gold-plated statue of an eagle worth even more money—but he had a wife who despised him and he didn't even know it. Longarm wouldn't have traded places with the man for all the money and all the range in Texas.

# Chapter 23

With all the fugitive gunmen locked up, most of the rooms on the second floor of the ranch house were empty again. The Rangers had gone through them and gathered up the possessions left in them by the prisoners.

Doc and Colleen Gallagher were each given a room on the second floor, and Katie would keep the room where she was supposed to have stayed with Ned Montayne, also known as Kid Montana. Doc, Raider, and Colleen were gathered in Katie's room a short time after the trap set by the Rangers had been sprung, talking over everything that had happened—and everything that would happen in the future.

"I never meant to hurt anybody," Katie was saying with a look of contrition on her beautiful face. "It's just that . . . well, you know how strict my parents are." She looked at Doc for support.

His heart went out to his niece, but he kept a stern expression on his face. "Parents are supposed to be strict," he said. "That's the only way children will learn how they're supposed to act."

"I hope that works with your little boy," Katie said, "but it didn't with me."

"Maybe what Doc's brother shoulda done was put you over his knee and blistered your bottom more often," Raider put in. "No offense, Doc."

Doc just shook his head, too tired to be worried about being offended by Raider's blunt advice right now.

"Anyway," Katie went on in a more defensive tone, "I didn't really mean to do anything wrong when I fell for Ned. And I didn't know he was stealing from Father's bank until after . . . until he and I had . . ." She looked down at the floor, her face burning with shame.

"Don't you worry about it, honey," Colleen told her. "Don't you let these men browbeat you, either. And you sure don't need to feel like you're the first woman who was ever taken in by the slick lies of some fast-talking scoundrel."

She glared at Raider and Doc, as if daring them to say anything else disapproving to Katie.

"All right, all right," Doc muttered. "All that can be hashed out when we get back to Boston. I'm just glad that Montayne is in custody and that you're safe, Katie. I think the man is somewhat mentally unhinged."

Raider said, "A fella'd have to be loco to dress up in flashy duds like that, put a wig on his head, and call himself Kid Montana. I'll say one thing for him, though: He really is fast on the draw. He slick-ironed Cleve Endicott, and Endicott was no slouch with a six-gun."

A little shudder ran through Katie at the memory of the way Montayne had gunned down Endicott on the way out to the ranch.

Raider turned to Colleen and went on, "Not to change the subject or nothin', but how'd you come to be travelin' with Doc and pretendin' to be a journalist? I thought Doc told you the Pinkertons' part in this deal was over."

"I did tell her that," Doc said, "but she didn't listen to me."

Colleen's chin had a defiant tilt to it as she said, "Didn't the two of you ever have a case you just didn't want to let go of, even though technically the assignment was over?"

172

Raider shrugged. "Doc never did like to let go once he'd sunk his teeth into somethin'."

"Me?" Doc said. "What about you? You defied orders and kept poking around in more cases you weren't supposed to than I ever did!"

Colleen smiled and said, "You see? I didn't do anything that the two of you wouldn't have done."

"She caught the next train out of Fort Worth after Corrigan's special left, just like I did," Doc explained. "When I spotted her at the train station in Big Spring and confronted her, she said she was coming out here to the Box C whether I liked it or not, so I decided I might as well work with her rather than have her working against us." He frowned at Colleen. "I intend to send a telegram to Wagner in Chicago, though, reporting your actions and making it clear that I'm not going to pay for anything you did after the agency's part in this case was officially concluded."

"I didn't do anything when I came out here, anyway," Colleen pointed out with a smile. "But I got to see the case through to the end, and that was what I wanted."

Raider rubbed his jaw. "I reckon that wraps everything up, then."

"What are you going to do now, Raider?" Doc asked.

"I ain't quite sure yet. Can't go back to the Ozarks, leastways not as long as all them Burketts are still alive. I gave my word to 'em."

"To a bunch of murderous, inbred hillbillies," Doc pointed out.

Raider shrugged. "Don't matter. It's still my word. Anyway, I thought I might drift on out toward California. Ain't been there in a good long while."

Colleen said, "I'm sure Mr. Wagner would hire you back at the agency."

"Don't be too sure o' that. Wagner an' me butted heads plenty o' times. Anyway, that part o' my life is over. I got no hankerin' to be a Pink again."

"Well, I'm certain that whatever you do, you'll be a success at it," Doc said. "Thank you for all your help, old friend."

"I didn't do much of anything. The Rangers are the ones who grabbed Montayne."

"That's just the way it happened to work out. We found Montayne, just like we set out to do."

That was true enough, Raider thought. He had already tumbled to the fact that "Kid Montana" was wearing a wig and was probably Ned Montayne, just as he had figured out that "Kitty" was likely Katie Weatherbee. If the contest had been real instead of a ruse by the Texas Rangers, Raider was confident that he and Doc would have succeeded in exposing and capturing Montayne.

Now there was only one thing left to do, and Doc didn't need to know about that.


Longarm was standing on the porch of the ranch house smoking a cheroot when he heard a footstep behind him. After everything that had happened, he didn't feel like turning in yet, so he had lingered out there to have a smoke. It rankled a mite that he had followed Felix Gaunt all the way down to Texas, biding his time, only to have the Rangers arrest the varmint first. Even though he had no doubt the State of Texas would turn Gaunt over to him so that the outlaw could be prosecuted on federal charges, it still seemed wrong somehow.

But not every assignment worked out all nice and neat, Longarm had learned over the years. Sometimes you just had to accept the hand that fate dealt you and make of it what you could.

When he heard the footstep behind him, he turned to see Bill Wagner standing there. No, not Wagner, Longarm reminded himself. The hombre went by Raider, although Longarm had no idea what his real name was.

Longarm nodded and said around the cheroot, "Evening, Raider."

The former Pinkerton agent rested his hands on the railing around the edge of the porch and said, "It's gotten mighty quiet out here, considerin' the fandango that was goin' on earlier."

Raider was right about that. The food and drink had been carried back into the house, the tables and benches stored away, and the lamps blown out. A dim light still burned inside the bunkhouse, and faint orange glows marked the tips of the quirlies being smoked by the two Rangers who were standing guard over the prisoners. Other than that, the Box C seemed to be sleeping.

"I guess there ain't no reason to be celebrating anymore," Longarm said. "The Rangers got what they wanted."

"Yeah. That was a pretty slick deal they set up. Why chase killers when you can trick them into comin' to you?"

"I reckon you're right. But I got to admit, it goes against the grain for me somehow."

"I'll tell you what else goes against the grain," Raider said. "A grown man takin' advantage of a gal who ain't old enough to know better."

Longarm frowned and took the cheroot out of his mouth. "What are you talking about?" he asked.

"Katie Weatherbee," Raider said in a flat, angry voice.

"The girl who was calling herself Kitty? The one with Kid Montana?"

"That bastard's name is Montayne. But yeah, she's the one I'm talkin' about."

Longarm shook his head. "You're following the wrong trail, Raider. She's twenty-four years old. Told me so herself."

"And you never had a gal lie to you before?"

Longarm's frown deepened. He didn't like the way this conversation was going. "Are you saying she's *not* twenty-four?"

"She's eighteen. That's accordin' to her uncle, so I reckon he'd know."

Longarm rasped a thumbnail along his jawline, not liking the way he felt right now. He had known that Kitty—or Katie—was young, but he hadn't figured that he was more than twice her age. She sure as hell didn't *look* eighteen. And it was true that out on the frontier, a lot of gals were married and even had young'uns of their own by the time they were eighteen. It wasn't like he had deflowered her and besmirched her maidenhood, or anything like that. Longarm figured Montayne had taken care of that chore long before the two of them even came west.

Still and all, he preferred his women older. It was just more respectable that way, and while Longarm wasn't the sort of gent who had ever lost much sleep over being respectable, some things were more important than others.

He put the cheroot back in his mouth and clenched his teeth on it. "The gal ain't related to you, is she?" he asked Raider.

"No, but her uncle's my friend, so don't go sayin' it ain't any o' my business."

"It *ain't* any of your business," Longarm said, "but for what it's worth, I thought she was older, and I'm sorry I carried on with her. How in hell did you know about that, anyway? She didn't tell you about it, did she?"

Raider shook his head. "No, I just happened to catch a glimpse of the two of you earlier this evenin', and the way you were kissin' her it was pretty easy to see that you'd done more before that. Don't worry, I ain't gonna tell Doc. He'd probably feel like he had to kill you, and I don't figure he's quite as gun-handy as you are, Long."

"I ain't worried . . . and anyway, it's Montayne that Doc ought to be gunning for, if anybody. When I met the gal, she was no virgin, that's for sure."

As soon as the words were out of his mouth, Longarm knew he'd said the wrong thing. Raider tensed and turned toward him, saying, "You son of a bitch."

The former Pinkerton agent threw a punch at Longarm's head.

Longarm saw the blow coming and tried to get out of the way, but Raider was too fast. Longarm couldn't avoid his fist completely. It clipped him on the jaw and staggered him. The cheroot went shooting out of his mouth.

Anger welled up inside him as he caught his balance. Sure, he had been too blunt with his comment about Katie not being a virgin. But even so, Raider hadn't had any call to punch him. Besides, Longarm wasn't in the habit of letting himself be walloped without striking back.

So he blocked the next wild swing Raider made and stepped in to crash a short, hard right into the man's face.

Raider was driven backward by the blow. He hit the railing at the edge of the porch and flipped over it, falling to the ground below. Longarm hoped that had knocked some sense into him. He went down the steps and started toward Raider, saying, "All right, now, just hold your horses, old son—"

Raider surged up off the ground and tackled Longarm around the waist. It was Longarm's turn to fall backward, knocked off his feet by the impact of the collision. He hit the ground hard enough so that the wind was knocked out of him. As he gasped for air, Raider landed on top of him, driving his knees into Longarm's stomach and making the situation even worse. Loco with anger, Raider swung his fists at Longarm's head.

The big lawman knew he couldn't just lie there and let Raider pound him into the dirt. He heaved upward with his body, and at the same time he hammered a fist against the side of Raider's head. Raider sprawled to one side. Longarm rolled the other direction.

Longarm came up on a knee and stayed there, his chest heaving as he tried to catch his breath. He said, "Damn it, Raider . . . there ain't . . . no need for this."

Raider pushed himself up. A dark trickle of blood came from one corner of his mouth. He wiped the back of a hand across it and said, "I feel like beatin' the hell outta somebody. That's reason enough."

With that, he charged again, rushing forward just as Longarm made it back to his feet.

Longarm barely had time to get himself set before he found himself standing toe to toe with Raider, slugging away and trading punches with the big man from Arkansas. They were both strong, powerful men, long accustomed to brawling, able to endure a great deal of punishment as well as dish it out.

But they were also evenly matched, so as their fists thudded against flesh and bone, neither man gained an advantage. The sounds of their struggle drew the attention of the Rangers who were posted at the storage building where the prisoners were locked up. One of the lawmen came running up to them and demanded, "What in blue blazes is goin' on here?"

Longarm and Raider both ignored the Ranger. The muscles in Longarm's arms and shoulders were starting to feel like lead, and he could tell that Raider was tiring, too. He threw a punch but missed and stumbled forward a step. The same thing happened to Raider. They found themselves leaning on each other like punch-drunk prizefighters, and Longarm supposed that was sort of what they were. There was no prize for them to win, but they were punch-drunk, sure enough.

A strong hand gripped Longarm's shoulder, steadying him and pushing him away from Raider. At the same time, the man who had taken hold of Longarm did the same to Raider, putting an end to the fight as he separated the two combatants. Walt Scott's deep, powerful voice asked, "Aren't there enough outlaws on the frontier for you two to tussle with, without having to whale away on each other?"

Raider spat blood from his mouth and rasped, "This here's a personal ruckus, Scott. Got nothin' to do with the law."

"Yeah, I figured as much." Scott had come from the house, where he had heard the sound of blows smashing home. He looked back and forth between Longarm and Raider and went on, "I reckon you'd better call it a draw before both of you break every bone in your hands. Did you settle anything?"

"Ain't nothing to settle," Longarm said. "Raider just wanted to punch somebody, and I got elected."

"That ain't all of it, and you know it, Long." Raider shrugged. "But I reckon sometimes I'm a mite too hotheaded for my own good. I don't hold what happened against you." His face darkened into an ominous glower. "Just don't let it happen again."

"Don't worry," Longarm told him. "It won't."

Raider jerked his head in a nod. "Good enough." He stuck out a hand. "Shake on it?"

Longarm didn't hesitate. "Sure," he said as he gripped Raider's big paw and squeezed, meeting the firm pressure with strength of his own.

Scott said, "Well, now that you fellas have settled that—whatever it was—maybe we can all get some rest around here."

Longarm nodded. That sounded good to him.

Fighting with Raider was enough to wear an hombre plumb out.

# Chapter 24

Long had a punch like a Missouri mule. Raider had to give him that much. And as much as he wanted to hate the big lawman for bedding down with Katie Weatherbee, it wasn't all Long's fault. Raider had to admit that Katie looked older than she really was, and if he hadn't known her and she had told him she was twenty-four—plenty old enough to make up her own mind whether or not she wanted to have a tumble with a fella—he probably would have believed her.

As long as Doc didn't find out, everything would be all right, Raider decided. Doc already hated Ned Montayne, and after all, Montayne was likely the skunk who had taken Katie's innocence.

When Raider got back to his room, he was more than ready to turn in and get some rest. He was going to be bruised and stiff and sore in the morning because of the pounding he had taken from Long's fists.

It looked like sleep was going to be postponed at least for a little while, though, because as soon as he stepped into his room on the second floor of the ranch house,

Raider's instincts warned him that someone else was there.

He darted to the side so that he wouldn't be silhouetted in the doorway by the light from the hall. At the same time, he reached for the handle of the knife tucked under his shirt at the small of his back. The blade was still the only weapon he was carrying.

"Raider, no!" a woman's voice cried as he whipped the knife out and dropped into a crouch. "It's me, Colleen Gallagher."

Raider frowned as he straightened from his fighting stance. "Colleen?" he rasped. "What the hell are you doin' here?"

She moved forward so that she was in the light that spilled through the doorway. He saw that her thick red hair was loose around her shoulders and she had a sheet from the bed wrapped around her. Evidently that was the only thing she was wearing, because the sheet parted a little as she walked and he saw the flash of bare legs underneath it.

"What do you think?" she asked. "You're a legend, Raider, not just as a Pinkerton agent but with the ladies, too."

Raider growled as he heeled the door closed behind him, plunging the room into darkness. "Lurkin' in a fella's room is a good way to get yourself hurt, or even killed," he said. "You ever think about that?"

"I thought about it," she admitted. "But I was thinking even more about how I wanted to get into your bed."

He heard a rustle of fabric and knew that she had dropped the sheet. Sensing that she was standing there nude before him, he slid the knife back in its sheath and then tossed it aside. He stepped forward and put his arms out. Her warm, naked form came eagerly into his embrace.

Raider wasn't sure that bedding Colleen was really a good idea, but after everything that had happened, including the ruckus with Marshal Long, his nerves were drawn painfully tight. It had been a good while since he'd been with a woman. Might be just what he needed, he thought as he leaned forward and found her mouth with his.

Her lips were hot and sweet and wanting, and they made him forget that his mouth was sore from being punched. All his other aches and pains disappeared, too, banished for the moment by his desire for Colleen. Her body surged against him as he swept his big hands over her bare flesh, stroking her back and her hips. He slipped his tongue into her mouth. She accepted it without hesitation, using her own tongue to meet the invader in a sensuous dance.

Raider felt his manhood growing hard, and Colleen must have felt it swelling against the softness of her belly. She moaned and insinuated a hand between them to squeeze his shaft through his trousers. She pulled her mouth away from his and whispered, "You need to get out of those clothes and into me."

Raider sure as hell couldn't argue with that.

Colleen gave him a hand as he began stripping out of his duds. The feel of her deft fingers on his body just made him harder. When she tugged his underwear down and allowed his member to spring free, she wrapped her hands around it and said, "Ahhh! That's what I've been waiting for. It's as big as I hoped it would be."

"Anybody ever tell you that you're a mite shameless, ma'am?"

Colleen laughed. "As a matter of fact, yes. And before this night is over, you're going to be very glad that I am, Raider."

As if to get started proving that, she dropped to her knees in front of him and pressed her lips to the head of his shaft in a heated kiss. Then she began licking the thick pole of male flesh, starting at its base and working her way up one side and down the other. When she was finished with that, she opened her mouth wide and took the head inside it.

Raider closed his eyes in sheer pleasure as Colleen began sucking gently on his manhood. He ran his fingers through her thick red hair and then rested his hands on her head as it bobbed up and down a little while she sucked. Bit by bit she swallowed more of him until the warm, wet cavern of her mouth was stuffed with his flesh. What she was doing felt so good that Raider had to grit his teeth and struggle to keep from giving in to temptation and flooding her throat with his climax. He wanted to postpone that as long as he could.

Colleen sucked him until her jaw had to be getting a mite tired. Raider kept himself distracted by thinking about some of the old cases he and Doc had worked on, as well as all the times he had been shot and beat up and come close to death. It was a long list, and it did the trick—but just barely. He was still throbbing with passion when Colleen finally lifted her head and let his shaft slide out from between her lips.

"My turn," she said in a husky voice.

She found Raider's hand in the dark, grasped it, and led him over to the bed. He finished kicking off the last of his clothing along the way. His eyes had adjusted to the darkness, so he could see the dim glow of her naked body as she sprawled out on the bed and spread her legs wide open. He knelt between her thighs and reached down to find the damp grotto of her femininity.

She was very wet already. He parted the moist folds and slipped a couple of fingers inside her. Her inner muscles were like heated butter, slick and accepting. Her hips bucked a little as his thumb found the hard nubbin of flesh at the top of her opening and strummed it. He plunged his fingers in and out of her for a moment as he continued working her button, then he leaned over, slid his fingers out, and replaced them with his tongue.

Colleen groaned softly as Raider licked and thrust and nibbled. Her juices smeared his face. She brought her knees up and pressed her thighs hard against his head as shudders ran through her. Raider's tongue flicked her most sensitive part again and again as he moved his hand down to the puckered opening between the cheeks of her rump. Some of her juices had trickled down there and lubricated it so that he had no trouble pushing his middle finger into the tight, scalding hot passage.

That pushed her all the way over the edge into a screaming, bucking climax. At least, she would have screamed if

183

she hadn't grabbed one of the pillows and stuffed it into her mouth to muffle the sound. Raider was grateful for that, since he didn't especially want anybody knocking on his door and asking what was going on in there.

Colleen's hips surged up and down and her thighs clamped on his ears again, holding him in place as her culmination rolled through her. At last the spasms began to ease. Her legs parted again, falling to the sides as if every muscle in her body had gone limp. She pushed the pillow aside and gave a long, satisfied sigh.

But Raider wasn't satisfied yet. In fact, his erection was still like a bar of iron. It pulsed with the need for release. He made an effort to wait a couple of minutes, giving Colleen a chance to catch her breath, and then he moved so that he was poised above her.

She realized what he was doing and said, "Lord, Raider, you're going to kill me! But I'll die a happy woman."

He brought the head of his shaft to her drenched opening and sheathed it with a hard, swift thrust of his hips. Colleen's legs came up and locked themselves around him as if they had minds of their own. She wrapped her arms around his neck and pulled his head down for a passionate kiss as he began to stroke in and out of her.

His hips pumped in a steady rhythm. With each thrust he seemed to reach even deeper inside her. He braced his hands against the bed on either side of her head and steadily increased his pace until his hips were flying. Colleen thrashed underneath him, meeting his thrusts with her own, matching his eagerness, intensity, and need. He could tell from her breathing that even though she had already climaxed once, she was building up to another explosion.

His own culmination came on him so suddenly that he couldn't hold it back. He slammed into her a final time and stayed there, buried as deeply within her as he could possibly get. His juices burst forth inside her in spurt after throbbing spurt. Raider emptied himself and filled her to overflowing. He kissed her, as much to keep himself from groaning as to stifle her cries of satisfaction.

Having crested the peak together, they started the long, slow, sensuous slide down the far slope. Raider tightened his arms around her and rolled over, taking her with him so that she wound up sprawled on top of him with his shaft still lodged inside her. He felt the pounding of her heart against his chest and knew that she probably felt his slugging away, too.

She rested her head on his chest. Delicious shivers went through her as he stroked her body. After a few minutes she lifted her head a little and began to kiss his chest, lingering on his nipples.

"That was magnificent, Raider," she whispered. "I understand now why you're such a legend."

"You can stop that legend talk," he told her. "I'm just a fella who does the best he can."

"Your best is a whole lot better than most men's. I'm glad I got this chance."

"Too bad the case wrapped up without any of us havin' to do much of anything." Raider chuckled. "Who could've figured that the Texas Rangers would take a hand?"

"I'm not talking about the case," Colleen said. "I don't really care about that anymore."

Raider had known what she meant. He cupped her chin and kissed her again. His erection had softened, and now he slipped out of her. But he was still semi-hard, and he knew it wouldn't take long for him to be ready to go again.

"You plannin' to stay the night?" he asked.

"Are you inviting me?" she replied.

"It'd be fine with me. If you let me rest up a mite, I'll bet we could think of a few more things to do . . ."

"That sounds like a good idea." She reached down to cup his still-swollen manhood and give it a gentle squeeze. "I told you I was shameless, but I haven't gotten to give you enough evidence of that yet."

Raider thought that if she gave him much more evidence, they might both be dead by morning.

But as Colleen had said, they would die happy.

# Chapter 25

Following the battle with Raider, Longarm returned to his room, stripped down to the bottom half of his long underwear, and then took a bottle of Tom Moore from his warbag for a long, soothing swallow before he turned in. The smooth fire of the Maryland rye eased the aches that he felt. By morning he would be stiff and sore, but a good night's sleep would help.

The soft knock on his door told him that he wasn't going to get it right away.

Longarm put the cork back in the bottle and set it on the table next to the bed. He took his Colt from the holster hanging on the chair and went to the door.

"Who's there?" he asked, the revolver held ready to return fire if anybody tried to ventilate him through the door.

"It's Katie," a soft voice replied. "Katie Weatherbee."

Longarm frowned. He opened the door and said, "Damn it, girl, what are you doin' here?"

She stood there with a thick dressing gown wrapped around her. "I know I shouldn't be here—" she began.

"You got that right," Longarm said.

"But I just wanted to apologize, Custis. I never should have lied to you, and I shouldn't have . . . Well, you know what I shouldn't have done."

Longarm nodded.

"It's just that I had already started thinking that I ought to leave Ned," Katie went on. "I . . . I thought if I did that with you, you'd be more likely to help me."

In a gruff voice, Longarm said, "You didn't need to do that. If you wanted help, all you had to do was ask for it."

"I understand that now." A shy smile appeared on her face. "But I have to admit, I enjoyed it, too. I enjoyed it a great deal."

"We'd better not talk about that," Longarm advised. "And what you'd better do now is get on back to your room before your uncle finds out what you're doing. He ain't gonna be too happy if he finds you standing in front of my door, with both of us dressed like we are. He might figure you were just leaving, instead of getting here."

"All right." But instead of leaving, she stepped forward and came up on her toes to brush her lips against his cheek. "I want to thank you first, though. Thank you for everything, Custis."

"Maybe you better call me Marshal Long."

She looked offended at his curt tone for a second, but then she nodded and said, "Yes. You're right about that, too."

With that, she turned and walked away. Longarm watched her move a few yards along the corridor, then eased the door shut. He stuck the Colt back in its holster, then picked up the bottle of Maryland rye again.

He had planned to stop with one swig before he went to bed, but he figured that after that little encounter, he was justified in taking another.

Longarm wasn't sure how much time had passed since he'd dozed off, but he suddenly found himself wide awake and knew that something must have happened to rouse him from slumber. Without making a sound, he reached over and closed his hand around the butt of his gun. He listened hard for any sounds of movement, trying to determine if his instincts were warning him that someone was in his room. He didn't hear a thing, and after a few moments he decided that he was alone after all.

But *something* had disturbed him, and he knew he wouldn't rest again until he found out what it was.

He swung his legs out of bed and stood up. Holding the Colt, he went to the door first and put his ear against it. The house was quiet, as if everyone were asleep. Longarm padded barefoot across the room to the window and used the barrel of the gun to push the curtain aside enough to let him look out. He didn't see anything unusual, so he raised the window, being careful not to make any noise in doing so. Then he listened again.

Spring had reached West Texas, meaning that the days were warm but the nights could still be chilly. Tonight certainly was. A cool breeze brushed against Longarm's chest as his keen ears listened for sounds that didn't belong in the night. He didn't hear anything and wondered if he had just imagined or dreamed whatever it was that had roused him from sleep.

He wasn't prone to imagining things, so he didn't want to accept that explanation. Still, he might have to, he told himself, because from the looks and sounds of things, nothing unusual was taking place on the Box C tonight.

That thought was going through his head when he heard the muffled groan that was cut off with abrupt, shocking finality.

Longarm knew something bad had just happened. Somebody was hurt, and either a hand had been clapped over their mouth to muffle that sound—or the injured man had been silenced by a more permanent method.

Either way, Longarm knew he had to find out what was going on.

He leaned forward as he saw a shadow flit through the darkness. It was near the building where the prisoners had been locked up, but whoever was hurrying in the night was moving away from there. A second later, Longarm caught a glimpse of more movement like that.

"Son of a bitch," he muttered as he wheeled away from the window. He had to move fast. The Texas Rangers needed to be alerted to this suspicious activity.

Longarm paused just long enough to yank on a pair of denim trousers, then hurried out of the room. The second-floor hallway was deserted. He ran to the landing and bounded down the stairs. He was aware that he could have roused the house by firing a couple of shots into the ceiling, but he didn't want to take a chance on the bullets going through and hitting someone on the third floor. Nor did he want to alert whoever was skulking around outside to the fact that they had been discovered.

Longarm wanted to keep the element of surprise on his side as long as he could.

Only a few lamps were lit in the big house, and the wicks on them were turned so low that they gave off little light. The glow was enough for Longarm to see where he was going, though, and he made his way to the front door without wasting any time. He eased it open and stepped out onto the porch, then paused to listen again.

The sound of running footsteps came to his ears from somewhere near the corrals. Horses stirred and nickered. Those sounds *might* be innocent, but every instinct in Longarm's body told him they weren't. He sprinted toward the building where the prisoners had been locked up.

Before he got there, he almost tripped over a figure sprawled on the ground. Spotting the dark shape just in time, Longarm skidded to a stop and then dropped to one knee beside the motionless figure. He put out his free hand, found the man's shoulder, and shook it. There was no response.

Longarm moved his hand over the man's chest and found a large wet spot on his shirt. The big lawman didn't need light to know he had found a bloodstain. It took Longarm only a moment longer to press his fingers to the man's throat and determine that there was no pulse. Whoever the hombre was, he was dead.

Since Longarm hadn't heard a shot, he figured the wound in the man's chest had come from a knife. He got to his feet and hurried on toward the makeshift lockup. He wasn't surprised to see when he got close enough that the door stood open. Another motionless shape lay on the ground beside it, with its head in the middle of a dark circle. Longarm took a lucifer from his pants pocket, knelt, and snapped the match into life.

The lucifer's glare revealed the pain-twisted face of one of the Texas Ranger guards. The man lay on his back, and the gaping slash in his throat looked like a bloody second mouth below his chin. The dark circle on the ground around his head was a pool of blood. He was just as dead as the other man Longarm had found, who had to be the second guard. Longarm figured this gent was the one he'd heard groaning, and the sound had been cut off by the knife that had ripped open the poor fella's throat.

Now there was no time to waste and no longer any need for stealth. Longarm surged to his feet, pointed the Colt at the sky, and squeezed the trigger twice, sending a pair of gun blasts rolling through the darkness.

"Rangers!" he bellowed. "Texas Rangers! Prisoners escaping! Rangers!"

Then he dashed toward the corral where he had heard horses moving around and the jingle of bit chains.

Before he could get there, Colt flame bloomed in the darkness. He heard the wind-rip of a bullet's passage close beside his ear as lead fanged through the night. With a whirlwind rataplan of hoofbeats, riders burst from the corral gate, a dozen or more of them, all shooting.

More bullets clawed through the air around Longarm as he left his feet in a long dive that carried him behind a water trough beside the corral. He grunted as he hit the ground hard, the wind knocked out of him for a second. Slugs thudded against the trough.

As the gunblasts died down for a second, Longarm raised up and triggered several shots at the fleeing riders.

Then another storm of lead drove him down. Blended in with the thunderous volley of gunshots, he heard a woman's scream that chilled his blood. Had the escaped prisoners managed to get their hands on one of the gals who were there at the Box C?

Hot lead kept Longarm pinned down behind the water trough for long moments. The firing died away, though, as the gunmen put more distance between themselves and the ranch headquarters. Longarm had thumbed fresh cartridges from his pocket into the Colt, filling the wheel. Now he risked leaping to his feet and pointing the revolver in the direction of the dwindling hoofbeats, but he bit back a curse and held off the trigger at the last instant, recalling that scream he had heard. Since it was possible the fugitives had taken one or more of the women as hostages, he couldn't risk firing blindly after them. One of his slugs might find an innocent target.

Doors slammed in the house and men ran toward him, yelling in alarm. Longarm swung toward them and shouted, "Hold your fire! It's Marshal Long!" He didn't want anybody getting trigger-happy and blasting him by accident.

"Long!" That was Walt Scott's voice. "What happened?"

"Your prisoners got loose somehow," Longarm told the Ranger. "They've taken off for the tall and uncut. They're gone, Scott—and I think they've taken at least one woman with them as a hostage."

When the commotion erupted outside, Raider rolled over in bed and reached for his gun. He had the revolver gripped in his hand before he realized that Colleen wasn't beside him in the bed, as she had been when he had dozed off.

"Colleen?" he said as he swung his legs out of bed and stood up. There was no answer. He grabbed his trousers, stuffed his legs in them, and headed for the door. When he threw it open, he glanced back and saw that the room was empty. Colleen was no longer there.

But just because she wasn't there and he didn't know where she was, that was no reason to assume she was in some sort of trouble, he reminded himself. He'd been told that he snored sometimes. Maybe he'd been sawing wood and she had gone back to her own room to get some sleep. Lord knew she had plenty of reason to be tired. She and Raider had plumb worn each other out.

Something was sure wrong. Somebody was yelling outside, and shots blasted in the night. By the time Raider reached the front door of the ranch house, the shooting had stopped, but men were still shouting in confusion. He bulled his way outside and looked around.

Spotting several men standing near the corral, Raider thought he recognized one of them as Marshal Long and another as Walt Scott, the Texas Ranger. He started down the steps, intending to go ask them what was going on, but before he reached the ground Doc called from behind him, "Raider, wait!"

Raider stopped and looked around. Doc had come out of the house wearing long underwear and carrying a pistol. For some unfathomable reason, Doc had grabbed his derby, too, and clapped it on his head, which meant he looked downright ridiculous. Raider sensed there was nothing ridiculous about the situation, though. Something had gone mighty wrong.

"I heard shots," Doc said. "Do you have any idea what's happening?"

"Not a damn clue," Raider replied. "But there's Long and Scott, over yonder by the corral. Figured I'd go ask them."

"Good idea," Doc agreed. "Come on," he added as if it had been his idea to talk to the marshal and the Ranger in the first place.

On the way over there, Raider noticed the open door on the storage building where the prisoners had been locked up, and he grunted in surprise. When he pointed it out to Doc, the man from Boston cursed with uncharacteristic vehemence.

"They got loose somehow. That means we're going to have to track down Montayne all over again." Doc shook his head in frustration and dismay. "Thank goodness Katie's safe now, and we don't have to worry about her."

Raider felt the same way. But he also experienced a slight tingle of excitement at the prospect of another manhunt. They had found Montayne once, and they could do it again.

"Did they all escape?" Doc asked as he and Raider came up to Long and Scott.

"I reckon we'd better make sure, one way or the other," the Ranger replied. Unlike the other three, he appeared to be fully dressed except for his broad-brimmed Stetson. He led the way over to the storage building, drawing both of his black-butted six-guns as he did so.

Long lit a match. As the flame flared up, all four men pointed their guns through the door. The building was empty, though. All of the former prisoners had fled.

With a sigh, Scott holstered his guns and knelt beside the Ranger whose throat had been cut. "This is Weary Ames," he said. "We rode together on many a long, hard trail." He turned his head to look at the other sprawled form several yards away. "That's Steve Bennett, another good Ranger. I don't know how those polecats managed to get the better of them. But I give you my word, fellas, I'll find those varmints and even the score for you."

Raider knew Scott was talking to the dead Rangers now. He said, "They must've had help. Somebody got the drop on your men and killed them before they knew what was going on, Scott. Then they let the prisoners out. Has to be the way it was."

"I agree," Doc said. "That building is sturdy, and there's only one way in or out. And look at the lock. It's been opened with a key, not shot open or forced in any other way."

Marshal Long held the match so that its glare shone on the lock and confirmed Doc's words.

"So somebody in there had a partner who didn't get rounded up with the others," Scott speculated. "The partner snuck in tonight, killed the guards, and turned the prisoners loose. They'll scatter, but the Rangers will hunt them down. You can count on that."

"That may not be the worst of it," Longarm said. "Like I told you, Scott, I heard a woman scream. If they've got a hostage, we'd better find out who she is."

"A woman?" Raider repeated, feeling a chill go through his bones as he remembered that Colleen hadn't been where he expected her to be when he woke up. "You sure about that, Marshal?"

"Sure enough," Long replied. "Let's get to the house and see if there's anybody missing."

Despite the fracas he'd had with Long earlier, Raider respected him and knew he was a good lawman. He dimly recalled hearing yarns about a deputy marshal called Long-arm who was supposed to be hell on wheels. He figured Long was the one the stories were about. As with most such tales, they were probably exaggerated—but there was almost certainly some truth to them, too.

So he knew Long was right about checking on the women in the house. The four men hurried to do just that.

"Anybody seen Corrigan since all the commotion started?" Long asked as they went up the stairs after grabbing a couple of lamps to give them more light.

"I haven't," Scott replied, and Raider and Doc shook their heads, too.

That was curious, because it seemed like all the shooting should have roused everyone on the ranch, but looking in on Corrigan could wait. Right now they wanted to make sure Katie and Colleen were safe. Lines of worry were etched on Doc's face as he muttered, "Montayne could have gotten to her somehow and forced her to go with him."

Raider was worried about Colleen, too. She could have gotten up, started back to her room for some reason, and run smack-dab into whoever was helping the prisoners to escape. He stopped at the door of the room she had been given, while Doc hurried on to Katie's room.

Colleen didn't answer when Raider pounded on the door and called her name. He didn't give a damn about propriety. He reached down, grabbed the doorknob, and twisted it. The door opened.

The room inside was empty. Colleen's bed hadn't even been slept in.

"She's gone," Doc was announcing in a strained voice as Raider stepped out into the hall from Colleen's room. "Katie's gone."

"So's Miss Gallagher," Raider said.

"We'll search the whole place," Walt Scott said, "just to make sure they're not here somewhere."

"You know they're not," Doc said. "Those bastards grabbed them somehow."

A faltering step from the landing and a groan of pain made the four men spin around, their guns coming up. They held off the triggers and stared in surprise at the big, powerful form of Edmund Corrigan, who didn't look nearly as impressive in rumpled pajamas as he leaned on the banister after staggering down from the third floor. His face was pale, which made the smear of blood from the gash on his head stand out that much more.

"Gone!" he croaked. "Gone!"

Raider and the other men rushed to Corrigan's side. Long gripped his arm to steady him. "Are you talking about your wife?" the marshal asked. "Is Mrs. Corrigan missing?"

"Anita?" Corrigan seemed to be struggling to form coherent thoughts. "Yes . . . yes, they . . . they took her, too. But . . . it's gone!" He looked utterly stricken as he gazed around at them and went on, "They've stolen the Golden Eagle!"

# Chapter 26

Longarm didn't know whether to be angry, disgusted, or both. Judging from the expressions on the faces of Raider, Doc Weatherbee, and Walt Scott, they felt the same way as they looked at the man who slumped in a heavy, ornately carved chair in a room dominated by a massive four-poster bed. This was Edmund Corrigan's bedroom. He had told them how several men had burst into the room, clouted him over the head with a gun barrel before he could get a good look at any of them, and dragged his wife out, taking the gold-plated statue with them, as well.

"It was right over there," Corrigan said, waving a trembling hand in a weak gesture toward a table. "It was right there, and now it's gone."

"You might want to forget about that Golden Eagle," Longarm advised him, "and start worrying about your wife. If she's been carried off by that bunch, she's in danger."

"I know, I know." Corrigan held a wet cloth to his head where he'd been pistol-whipped. "I just can't stop thinking about how they stole the Eagle, too."

Longarm exchanged a glance with the other men and saw that they, too, were pretty much disgusted with Corrigan.

Assisted by some of the Box C cowboys, the Rangers had searched the house and the grounds around the ranch headquarters without turning up any sign of Anita Corrigan, Colleen Gallagher, or Katie Weatherbee. The only conclusion that could be drawn was that the escaping prisoners had taken the women with them. Longarm still couldn't figure out who had helped them to escape, though. No one else seemed to be missing . . .

Corrigan lifted his head and looked around. "Where's Millard? Has anybody seen Millard?"

"Who?" Longarm asked.

"Benjamin Millard, my secretary," Corrigan snapped. Longarm realized he had never heard the little hombre's name before. "He has to go to Big Spring and get some wires sent off immediately. I want every lawman in the State of Texas alerted to be on the lookout for that statue!"

"Corrigan, I'm gettin' mighty fed up with you—" Raider began, but Doc held up a hand to stop him. It was true that the rancher was being a royal pain in the ass about that damned statue, Longarm thought, but for now they might need Corrigan's cooperation in order to rescue the hostages and bring those escaped killers back to justice.

"Even if Millard started out to Big Spring right now, he wouldn't get there until morning," Scott pointed out. "Anyway, I can't spare a man to escort him. We'll all be pulling out as soon as it's light enough in the morning to follow the trail those varmints left."

"You're not going after them now?" Corrigan demanded.

"The moon's nothing but a sliver tonight. There's not enough light to read sign, and if we chase after them blindly, we run the risk of losing their trail entirely. That means it'd be that much longer before we caught up to them." Scott's stern voice softened a little. "I know you're worried, Mr. Corrigan, but the smart thing to do is wait until morning to set out after them."

"All right, all right, whatever you say. But I still want to talk to Millard. I'm going to put up a reward for the safe return of the Golden Eagle!"

"Where's his room?" Scott asked. "I'll tell him to come up here and talk to you."

"First floor, next to my library and office."

"You'll need to go to Big Spring yourself and have a doctor look at that cut on your head. It may need stitching up."

"I don't care about that. I just want those bastards caught and my property returned!"

Longarm didn't have much respect for a man who thought of his wife as property, but then he realized Corrigan was still talking about the Golden Eagle. There was a bad taste in his mouth as he left the room with Raider, Doc, and Walt Scott.

"I know you fellas are worried," Scott said to Raider and Doc, "but you might as well try to get a little more sleep. We'll be hitting the saddle mighty early in the morning. I reckon the two of you are coming along?"

"Damn right," Raider said. "Just try an' stop us."

Scott smiled. "I wouldn't want to do that. I know your reputation as manhunters. Figure we can consider you honorary, temporary Rangers."

Doc sighed and said, "I don't think I can sleep for worrying about Katie, and Miss Gallagher, too, I suppose. And someone needs to worry about Mrs. Corrigan. Lord knows her husband isn't doing a very good job of it!"

"Some fellas just don't deserve the luck they've had," Raider growled.

Longarm couldn't argue with that. He said, "I'll go fetch Millard."

"I'll let my men know we'll be picking up the trail first thing in the morning," Scott added.

Longarm went down the stairs with the Ranger, then turned toward Corrigan's library and office when he reached the first floor. Scott went on outside. Longarm found the door of Benjamin Millard's room and knocked on it. He found it hard to believe that the secretary could have slept through all the uproar. Millard was a mousy little fella, though—when he heard guns going off, he might have just pulled the covers over his head and stayed there.

No answer came from inside Millard's room. Longarm knocked again, then rattled the doorknob. It seemed to be unlocked, so he turned it and went in.

Millard wasn't there. Longarm stood in the doorway for a moment, frowning. He reached up and tugged a couple of times on the lobe of his right ear, an unconscious habit he had when he was deep in thought, then scraped a thumbnail along the line of his jaw. It was too early to assume that Millard was gone—he could still be somewhere else in the house—but if he was, Longarm wondered, was it possible that his disappearance was tied in with the prisoners' escape, the kidnapping of the three women, and the theft of the Golden Eagle?

Longarm went outside and found Walt Scott talking to some of the other Rangers. "Millard's gone," Longarm said.

Scott frowned and said, "Who?" then nodded and went on, "Oh, yes, Corrigan's secretary. The little fellow's a mite forgettable."

"You think those gunmen grabbed him, too, when they took the women out of the house?"

"What reason would they have for taking him along?" Scott asked. "You'd think the women would be enough hostages for them."

Longarm rubbed at his jaw. "Yeah, you'd think so. But the only other explanation is that he went after them himself. I don't hardly see him doing that, do you?"

"Nope," Scott said with a shake of his head. "But I don't know the hombre all that well. I'm not sure what he's capable of."

They went to the bunkhouse, where the Box C hands were still awake after having been jarred from sleep by the gun battle that had gone on. A few minutes of questioning established that none of the cowboys had seen Benjamin Millard during all the commotion. When Longarm brought up the possibility that Millard had gone in pursuit of the escaping gunmen, Corrigan's foreman, Jeff Holman, shook his head.

"That don't seem likely," Holman said. "I don't recollect ever seein' the little fella on a horse before, and I ain't sure he even knows which end of a gun the bullets come out of."

"Well, he's gotten off somewhere," Longarm said. "I don't reckon we can worry about him overmuch right now, though, what with those women missing."

Holman's face was grim as he said, "When the Rangers start after 'em in the mornin', me and the rest of the crew are comin' along."

"No, you're not," Scott declared. "This is a job for the Rangers, and we'll do it. You men need to stay here and tend to the business of running Mr. Corrigan's ranch."

"We ride for the brand, damn it! Those varmints stole from the boss and carried off his wife."

Scott nodded. "I understand how you feel, Holman. But my decision stands. The posse will be composed of Rangers, Marshal Long, and those two former Pinkerton agents."

Holman and some of the other cowboys grumbled about that, but they had no choice except to go along with Scott's decision. As the commander of the Ranger detail, he had the final say.

Longarm didn't think anybody was going to be getting much sleep the rest of the night, but he went back up to his room and stretched out for a while anyway, smoking a cheroot as he stared at the ceiling and thought about everything that had happened. As far as his job was concerned, his primary goal was still to take Felix Gaunt into custody.

But his biggest worry was now the safety of the captives, and he couldn't change that. It was just the way he was.

Would the fugitives split up or stay together? Longarm was betting that they would split up. They weren't all members of the same gang or anything like that. In that case, what would happen to the women? Would the smaller groups each take one of the prisoners with them?

Longarm didn't know and told himself to be patient, to take his own long-standing advice about eating an apple one bite at a time. When the sun came up, the trail would tell the story.

It always did.


Longarm surprised himself by dozing off for a while, but he didn't sleep for long. He was up and around when the eastern sky was beginning to turn gray with the approach of dawn. The smell of coffee filled the air when he got dressed and went downstairs.

The Rangers were already in the dining room of the big house eating breakfast, washing down the stacks of flapjacks with cups of strong black coffee. Longarm joined them, and a few minutes later, so did Raider and Doc. The two former Pinkertons looked as haggard as Longarm felt. His eyes were gritty and his sore muscles had grown stiff as he rested.

For the most part, a grim silence hung over the table as the men ate, broken only by the clatter of silverware. Jeff Holman came in to report that the posse's horses were all saddled and ready to go, and to ask again if Scott had changed his mind about letting the ranch hands come along.

Scott hadn't.

When the meal was over, the manhunters checked their guns, some of them taking the opportunity to grab a quick smoke as they did so. Then they trooped out to their horses and mounted up.

Edmund Corrigan stepped out onto the porch as the men were getting ready to ride. A bandage was wrapped around his head now, but it wasn't much whiter than his face, which was drained of blood and drawn with fatigue and strain.

"Listen to me, all of you," the cattleman said. "I'm offering a five-thousand-dollar reward to anyone who returns the Golden Eagle safely to me."

"The only ones who could claim a reward are Raider and Mr. Weatherbee," Scott said in a cool voice, not bothering to hide his disdain for Corrigan. "The rest of us are sworn peace officers."

"The reward stands," Corrigan insisted. "Five thousand for the Golden Eagle." He didn't mention his wife.

Scott just shook his head and turned his horse so he could look at the other men. "Let's ride," he said, and the posse galloped out of the yard in front of the Box C.

# Chapter 27

Although the sun was not quite up yet, the eastern sky was ablaze with enough reddish-gold light for the men to follow the tracks left by the fugitives' horses as they escaped from the ranch. The group of men, roughly the same size as the posse that now pursued them, had headed due north but soon veered slightly to the west. Longarm knew there wasn't much in that direction except the flat wasteland of the *Llano Estacado*—the Staked Plains.

The region had gotten its name from the fact that the first explorers to cross it many years earlier, Spanish priests and *conquistadors,* had driven stakes into the ground to mark their route, for fear that otherwise they would get lost in the featureless landscape and travel around and around in circles until they died of thirst. Even now, it was a dangerous area to cross, and there wasn't much reason to do so. On the far side lay the border between Texas and New Mexico Territory, and there wasn't much over in New Mexico except more wasteland that stretched for miles before a range of mountains rose from the plains.

The fugitives had stayed bunched together for several miles, but then the inevitable defections had begun. The tracks indicated that one man headed north; another two cut off to the northeast. A short distance farther on, a single rider turned and set off to the south.

Scott called a halt. Addressing his men, he said, "Richmond, go after this fella who headed south. Tompkins, Chadwick, backtrack and follow the ones who went northeast. Gardner, pick up the trail of the one who rode due north."

"You sure it's a good idea to split your force this way?" Longarm asked.

"Those men were in Ranger custody," Scott said. "The Rangers are going to get them back. You other fellas can do whatever you want."

Raider spoke up, saying, "Looked to me like none o' the horses that left the main bunch were carryin' double. I'd bet the gals are still with the ones who are stickin' together."

"That's what I think, too," Doc said, "so we'll continue to ride with you, Scott."

The Ranger nodded. "That's fine. I've got a hunch the women are still with the men we're following, too. How about you, Marshal?"

"Let's keep going," Longarm said. "They've still got a big lead on us."

The Rangers Scott had assigned to follow the other trails galloped off, and the rest of the posse continued northwest across the Staked Plains. This was still part of Corrigan's range, Longarm supposed, but they didn't see many cows. The grass was too sparse up there, and waterholes too few and far between, to make good cattle range. Most of the ground was sandy and bare, dotted with clumps of bunch grass, some scrubby catclaw bushes and cactus, and the occasional mesquite tree that was so stunted it barely deserved to be called a tree. Here and there the earth was slashed by dry washes that carried water only during the very rare cloudbursts.

At least the trail was easy to follow. The horses' hooves left fairly clear marks in the sandy soil. The dozen or so fugitives remained together, surprising Longarm a little. He had thought that once they started to split up, they might all scatter to the four winds. Maybe one of the fugitives knew of a hideout in this direction and had offered to share it with the others. Or maybe none of them wanted to give up possession of the Golden Eagle or the hostages.

Longarm worried about what would happen to Anita Corrigan, Katie Weatherbee, and Colleen Gallagher when their captors finally called a halt to rest their horses. That would give the men the opportunity to molest the women if they were of a mind to. Most Western men, even outlaws, wouldn't stoop that low, and Longarm knew that gunslingers, even wanted ones who had killed wantonly and ruthlessly, had their own peculiar code of honor.

But he didn't want to count too heavily on the hope that they would leave the women alone. Some of the fugitives probably wouldn't participate in any attacks on the women, but they might not stop the other men, either.

The members of the posse were all well mounted, but even so, Scott had to call several halts during the day to allow the horses to rest. Corrigan's cook back at the Box C had packed several bags of supplies for them before they left, so during those stops the men were able to make meals from strips of beef, tortillas, and biscuits. It was mighty plain fare, but it would keep them going. They washed the food down with swigs from their canteens, which the men would be sure to refill every time they came across any water that was fit to drink.

Scott had kept the posse moving at a fast pace. They would reach the edge of Corrigan's range soon, if they hadn't left the Box C already. It was another thirty or forty miles to the New Mexico line. They wouldn't get there today, if indeed the trail continued in that direction.

It did, although it curved more and more to the west as the afternoon went on. The sun began to sink toward the horizon, casting a glare over the landscape. The men had been in the saddle for long, long hours, and everyone was tired, men and horses alike. But they would push on, Scott announced, until it was too dark to follow the trail. None of the others objected to that decision.

Longarm leaned forward in the saddle as he suddenly heard a faint popping sound in the distance. Scott heard it, too, as did Raider and Doc. "Sounds like shootin'," Raider blurted.

"Yep," Scott agreed. "Two men, one with a rifle and the other with a handgun. Let's go see what it's about, gents." He heeled his big black horse into a run.

The others followed close behind him. Longarm spotted something lying on the ground ahead of them, and as they came closer he realized it was the body of a horse. A man lay behind the animal, using its carcass as cover while he fired a revolver at a clump of mesquites. Powder smoke spurted from that concealment, accompanied by the crack of a rifle. It looked to Longarm like someone had been waiting in the scrubby trees to ambush the man whose horse had been shot out from under him.

The bushwhacker must have seen the dust being raised by the posse, because the rifle fell silent and a moment later a man on horseback burst out of the trees and raced toward the west. Scott shouted over his shoulder, "Look after that fella!" and sent his horse thundering after the rifleman. Longarm and Raider went with him, while Doc and the rest of the Ranger troop stopped to check on the other man.

The bushwhacker's horse seemed to be fresher—no telling how long he had lurked there in the mesquites, waiting to see if any pursuit was going to show up—but Scott's horse still had plenty of speed and stamina. He drew ahead of Longarm and Raider and closed in on the fleeing man.

The hombre had shoved his Winchester in a saddle boot, but he twisted and fired back at Scott with a Colt. Not surprisingly, none of the shots came close to their target. Drawing accurate aim from the back of a galloping horse was next to impossible.

206

As Scott narrowed the gap even more, the fleeing man's horse must have stepped in a prairie dog hole or some such, because the animal suddenly fell in a welter of dust and wildly flailing legs. The bushwhacker was thrown clear, sailing through the air with a startled yell as his arms and legs pinwheeled. He crashed to the ground, rolled through a patch of cactus, and screamed as hundreds of the razor-sharp needles penetrated his hide. When he finally came to a stop, he lay motionless, his head cocked at an odd angle on his neck.

Scott drew rein nearby, and Longarm and Raider weren't far behind him. All three men drew guns before they dismounted to approach the fallen fugitive.

Longarm recognized the man. He was a shootist named Powell, and he was wanted for murder in Texas, Utah, and Wyoming. Since he'd been captured in Texas, the Lone Star State had first claim on him and would have hanged him before authorities in Utah or Wyoming got a chance to do likewise. Now nobody would get to string him up.

Because his neck was already broken. Longarm could tell that by the way his neck was twisted. Powell was alive—his eyes were wide and staring—but he didn't seem to feel the multitude of cactus needles stuck in him anymore.

"Andy Powell," Scott said as he hunkered on his heels next to the man. "So the others left you behind to ambush anybody who tried to follow the main bunch."

Powell licked dry, cracked lips. His eyes and his tongue seemed to be the only things he was capable of moving. "We . . . we drew lots," he gasped out. "I lost and . . . Gaunt wouldn't let me . . . out of it."

Longarm leaned forward. "Gaunt's bossing things?"

"He . . . took over. Nobody wanted to . . . tangle with him."

Longarm could understand that. Even in a group of fast guns, there was a good chance Gaunt was one of the fastest, if not *the* fastest.

"What about the women?" Raider asked. "Are they all right?"

"G-go . . . to hell," Powell rasped. "Why should I . . . talk to you bastards?"

"Because your neck's broke, son," Scott said. "You don't have long to live, so you might as well answer our questions."

Powell's eyes widened even more. "You're . . . a damn liar! I'm just . . . a mite shook up . . ."

"If that's true, then why can't you move your arms and legs? Why can't you feel anything below your neck? You've got a couple hundred cactus needles stuck in you, Andy. Don't they hurt? You yelled loud enough when you rolled through them. But that was before your neck snapped."

Scott's voice was blunt, yet gentle in a way. Longarm figured the Ranger didn't like to see anybody come to a bad end, even an owlhoot.

Powell licked his lips again and asked, "Can I . . . have some water?"

"Sure," Scott said. He glanced around at Longarm, who got the canteen that was on his saddle.

Scott took the canteen and put a hand under Powell's head, lifting it so that he could dribble a little water into the man's mouth. He kept the hand under Powell's head to support it as Powell said, "The women are . . . all right. They weren't hurt . . . when we busted out of there."

"How'd you get out in the first place?" Longarm asked. "Somebody had to have helped you."

"I . . . I don't know. All I know is . . . somebody unlocked the door of that . . . storage building . . . never did see who it was . . . the guards were dead, so . . . Gaunt took some of the men and . . . went in the house . . . while the rest of us saddled some horses . . . They came back with the women . . . and guns . . . and that Eagle statue . . ."

"Are the rest of them heading for any place in particular," Scott asked, "or are they just running?"

"D-don't know," Powell struggled to say. "Gaunt's leadin' the way, but . . . he ain't talkin' . . ."

"He let some of the men strike out on their own," Longarm said.

208

"Y-yeah . . . said we didn't have to . . . stay with him . . . but he was keepin' . . . the women and the Golden Eagle. You reckon I could have . . . a little more water?"

Scott started to lift the canteen to Powell's lips, but before he could give the man another drink, Powell's head jerked a couple of times and his eyes rolled back in his head. His mouth hung open, slack and lifeless.

"He's gone," Scott said, not telling Longarm and Raider anything they didn't already know. He lowered the dead man's head to the ground.

Hoofbeats sounded as Scott pushed himself to his feet. The three men turned to see the rest of the posse riding up. The man who had taken shelter behind the dead horse was now riding double with Doc Weatherbee. He was a small man with thinning dark hair, a sharp nose, and eyes that seemed about to pop out of his head. Longarm recognized him as Benjamin Millard, Corrigan's secretary.

Back at the ranch, Longarm had suspected that Millard might have been the one who helped the prisoners escape, although he couldn't think of any reason for the man to have done so. Now it looked like Millard had actually been the first one to give chase to the fugitives. He had been bushwhacked for his trouble, too.

"Mr. Millard," Scott said, "what are you doing out here?"

"I . . . I was trying to catch up to those men who kidnapped poor Mrs. Corrigan," Millard said. "I was returning to my room from the kitchen in the middle of the night—I have a mild case of dyspepsia, you see, and sometimes a bit of food helps it when I'm having trouble sleeping—when I saw them skulking around like the scoundrels they are. I . . . I wanted to raise the alarm, but I saw that Mrs. Corrigan was a prisoner and I was afraid those men would hurt her. I didn't know what to do."

Raider said, "So you got yourself a gun, saddled a horse, and came after 'em all by your lonesome? That was a mighty foolish thing to do, mister."

"I know," Millard admitted. "I nearly got myself killed, too. But I thought it was my duty to Mr. Corrigan to try to help his wife." He shook his head and said again, "Poor Mrs. Corrigan."

The secretary seemed to be more concerned about Anita than her own husband was, Longarm thought. Corrigan had been a lot more worried about that damned statue. At least he had acted that way.

"Well, what are we going to do with you now?" Scott asked.

"We can't leave Mr. Millard out here on foot," Doc said. "We're too far from the ranch, or anywhere else, for that matter. He'd never be able to walk back to civilization."

"And we don't have an extra horse to give him," Scott said. "Looks like you're coming with us, Millard. We don't seem to have any choice in the matter."

The secretary nodded. "Thank you, sir. I was hoping you'd say that. To be honest, I'd like another crack at those desperadoes. I was just getting the hang of shooting the gun I brought with me."

"You'll likely get your chance," Scott said as he swung up into the saddle. Longarm and Raider did likewise.

Doc nodded toward the dead gunslinger. "What about him?"

Raider answered before Scott could. "There're plenty o' coyotes out here in these parts," the big man from Arkansas said with a savage grin on his face. "Reckon they'll take care o' that little problem."

Scott didn't argue with that verdict, and neither did Longarm. They still had a passel of killers to catch and some women to save, so the Rangers and their companions headed west again, striking out across the Staked Plains toward New Mexico Territory.

# Chapter 28

Scott kept the posse moving until the sun was gone and the last of the light had faded from the sky. As millions of stars glimmered into view in the darkening heavens, the pursuers made camp for the night. It was a cold camp, because a fire would be visible for miles and miles in this flat terrain, and Scott didn't see any point in announcing to the fugitives that they were back there. Let the fleeing gunmen wonder about that. Longarm, Raider, and Doc agreed with that reasoning.

Guards were posted just in case some of the men they were chasing doubled back to try an ambush. Longarm wouldn't put something that tricky past Felix Gaunt. The night passed without any trouble, though, and early the next morning in a chilly dawn, the Rangers were in their saddles again, along with Longarm, Raider, Doc, and Benjamin Millard. So far, Doc's horse had been able to carry both him and Millard without slowing down the rest of the group. Fortunately, the man from Boston was slender and didn't weigh much, and neither did Millard.

Around the middle of the day, Longarm glanced over

his shoulder, checking their back trail out of habit, and he saw dust rising in the distance. He reined in and called Scott's attention to it, saying, "Looks like a good-sized bunch coming up fast behind us."

Millard swallowed nervously and asked, "Could it be Indians?"

"Not likely," Scott said. "It's been four or five years since the Comanches gave much trouble. They never really recovered from the defeat Colonel MacKenzie handed them at the Battle of Palo Duro Canyon. Most of them have gone to the reservations by now."

"Looks like a couple dozen riders," Raider estimated. "Cavalry, maybe? Who else is gonna be gallivantin' around out here in the middle o' the Staked Plains?"

As the riders came closer, it became apparent that they weren't cavalry troopers. They weren't wearing uniforms or carrying a guidon. Instead, they were dressed in all manner of range clothes, and there were even a few town suits and hats among them.

Scott's eyes narrowed. "I don't much like the looks of this," the Ranger said. "I think our posse is about to get some unwanted reinforcements."

The same possibility had occurred to Longarm. "That damn Corrigan went into Big Spring and started running his mouth about a reward," he said.

As the group of riders came closer, Scott nudged his horse out in front of them and held up a hand in a signal for them to stop. The men reined in, but only reluctantly. Longarm did a quick head count and tallied twenty-five of them.

"Who are you men, and what are you doing here?" Scott demanded.

A burly, red-mustachioed man in a derby said, "We ain't breakin' no laws, Ranger, so move aside and let us by. We're after them fellas what stole Mr. Corrigan's Golden Eagle."

"I knew it," Longarm muttered under his breath. He looked over the motley bunch of reward-seekers and spotted a familiar face. "Riley? Riley Hutchins! What're you doing with this bunch?"

The young cowboy nudged his mount forward. "I thought if I was the one who brought that statue back to Mr. Corrigan, he'd give me a job for sure. And I want to do what I can to help those women, especially Miss Weatherbee. I, uh, noticed her back there at the ranch, before all that hell broke loose."

What Riley meant was that he was smitten with Katie, Longarm thought. That would have been just fine—the two of them were more of an age, after all—if not for the fact that Katie was a prisoner in the hands of a bunch of vicious killers.

"You boys should turn around and go back to Big Spring," Scott said.

"Hell, no!" the redhead in the derby exclaimed. "You can't stop us, Ranger. We got as much right to chase those varmints as anybody else."

Scott glanced over at Longarm and said, "Blast it, he's right. They're not breaking any law by trying to earn that reward."

Longarm shrugged. "I reckon we'll have to let them come along. That'll put the odds on our side when we catch up to Gaunt's bunch."

But that numerical advantage was definitely a mixed blessing. The Rangers were all competent, dependable men, seasoned by years of fighting Indians and outlaws. Scott knew that he could count on Longarm, Raider, and Doc as well, since they were all veterans of their own adventures.

These newcomers were an unknown quantity, though. They couldn't be depended upon to follow orders or hold their own in a fight. They might cause more trouble than they were worth or even put the other members of the posse in deadly danger.

But that was a problem they would just have to cope with, since Scott couldn't order them to turn around and go back where they came from. The Ranger gave a weary nod, turned his horse around, and lifted a hand to wave the whole group forward. "Move out," he called.

By nightfall, Longarm was confident that they had crossed the border into New Mexico Territory. Scott hadn't said anything about the Rangers reaching the limit of their jurisdiction, but knowing Texans as he did, Longarm didn't expect them to turn back. If there was no legal, proper way to do something that needed to be done, they would just do it illegal and improper and worry about the niceties later.

In this case, though, they had a hole card. As a federal officer, the boundary between Texas and New Mexico didn't mean a thing to Longarm, and if anybody ever called the Rangers on venturing where they weren't supposed to, he could say that he had deputized them to help him arrest a federal fugitive, namely Felix Gaunt.

Longarm pointed that out to Scott while they were camped that night. The Ranger nodded and said, "I suppose you're right, Marshal. But the border between Texas and New Mexico isn't like the Rio Grande. You can't see it." Scott grinned. "So who's to say we're not still in Texas, after all?"

Longarm chuckled. "Not me."

Raider and Doc came over to join them. "Judging by the freshness of the tracks, I believe we've cut considerably into the lead they had on us," Doc commented.

"Yeah, but how long can we keep pushin' our horses like this?" Raider said. "We're liable to ride 'em right into the ground if we keep up the pace we been hittin'."

"They're not more than a few hours in front of us, and they have to rest their horses, too," Scott pointed out. "I think we'll catch up to them tomorrow."

Late in the day, Longarm had spotted a dark blue line on the western horizon and recognized it as the Sacramento Mountains, which lay on the other side of the Pecos River Valley. The Sacramentos tailed on down into Texas, where they turned into the Guadalupes. Rugged heaps of mostly bare rock, the mountains would offer plenty of places to hide, and he felt sure Gaunt was heading for them with just that in mind. If Longarm and his companions didn't catch up to their quarry before the fugitives reached the mountains, they might just find themselves riding into a real ambush, instead of a delaying tactic like Powell had been.

Leaving Raider, Doc, and Scott talking among themselves, Longarm ambled over to where Benjamin Millard sat cross-legged on the ground and hunkered on his heels beside the secretary. Millard glanced over at him in the gloom and asked, "Did you want something, Marshal?"

Longarm took out a cheroot and clamped it between his teeth, leaving it unlit because he didn't want to strike a match. "I was just wondering," he said. "Were you the one who handled the chore of getting that Eagle statue made?"

"As a matter of fact, I was," Millard replied, and Longarm thought he heard a note of pride in the little man's voice. "Mr. Corrigan entrusted that task to me."

"What's it really worth?"

Millard shook his head. "I couldn't tell you."

"Couldn't . . . or won't?"

"Couldn't. I don't know how many ounces of gold were required to coat it, but I *can* tell you that the coating is more than an inch thick. It's quite valuable, I assure you, but you'd almost have to destroy it to determine its true worth."

"What did Corrigan pay for it?"

Millard hesitated before answering. "I'm not sure I should tell you that." He sighed. "But you *are* a lawman, so I suppose it would be all right. Mr. Corrigan paid fifty thousand dollars to have the statue sculpted and cast and coated in gold. But it's surely worth two or three times as much."

"Why go to the trouble of having the real thing made, when that shooting contest was a fake?"

Millard laughed softly. "You don't know Mr. Corrigan, Marshal. Once the idea of a Golden Eagle occurred to him, he had to have it. Whatever strikes his fancy, he wants, and he'll go to almost any lengths to get what he wants."

"Including that wife of his?"

"I can't discuss my employer's personal affairs, sir." Millard's voice was stiff now. "Not even with a law officer. I'm sure you understand."

Longarm chewed on the cheroot for a moment, then said, "I understand that once Corrigan's got something he went after, he don't care that much about it anymore. I've known fellas like that before. Maybe that's why he was more worried about the Eagle than about his wife. That statue is new to him, and she ain't."

"I'm sure I wouldn't know anything about that, Marshal."

Longarm figured that Millard knew more than he was letting on. Meek little hombres like him tended to blend in to the background. After a while, a man like Corrigan would forget that Millard was even there until he needed the secretary to do something for him.

Longarm changed the subject by asking, "What's under the gold?"

"Excuse me?"

"What's that Eagle made out of? It's not solid gold."

"No, of course not. The base is lead. That makes it quite heavy."

Longarm remembered how Millard had struggled to carry the box containing the eagle out to the party a couple of nights earlier. "Wonder what Gaunt's gonna do with it," he mused. "He can't just melt it down. If he did, the lead would melt, too, and mix with the gold. You could probably separate the gold out, but it'd be a chore. Might take equipment that Gaunt wouldn't have in some mountain hideout, too."

"Perhaps he could chip the gold off the base," Millard suggested. "With a hammer and chisel or something like that."

Longarm nodded. "Maybe. Or maybe he plans to sell it to somebody just like it is."

"I suppose that's possible. It would be worth more in the form it's in now than if it were melted down. It has some artistic value, you know."

"Well, I don't reckon it matters, because we're gonna get it back, along with those women."

"Do you really think so, Marshal?"

Longarm clapped a hand on Millard's shoulder and pushed himself to his feet. "I wouldn't be here if I didn't, Benjamin," he said.

The posse, now swollen to three times its original size, crossed the Pecos River the next morning. So far the men who had come seeking the reward had cooperated with the Rangers. The big redhead with the derby, whose name was Dugan, seemed to have assumed command of that part of the group.

Longarm dropped back a little to ride next to Riley Hutchins for a while. He said, "You know Miss Weatherbee's gonna have to go back to Boston with her uncle after we rescue her, don't you?"

"Well, sure," Riley replied. "What else would I think, Marshal?"

"Oh, I don't know," Longarm said with a smile. "Maybe that you might try to court her?"

Riley's face flushed under his Stetson. "She's mighty pretty, that's for sure. But I don't even know her. Ain't never spoken a word to her, nor her to me."

"That don't always have to mean anything," Longarm pointed out. "More'n one hot-blooded young hombre has decided he was gonna marry a gal the first time he laid eyes on her."

Riley looked away, and Longarm had a hunch those very thoughts had gone through the young cowboy's head at his first sight of Katie.

"Just so you know it ain't liable to work out that way," Longarm told him.

"I don't care about that," Riley said, forcing a gruff tone into his voice. "I just want her to be safe."

"So do I, old son. So do I."

Even though they were out of the Staked Plains now and

crossing the valley of the Pecos, the landscape hadn't changed all that much. There was a little more vegetation, but for the most part the land was still flat and arid. The farther west they rode, though, the more often some little hills and ridges began to crop up. The mountains were plainly visible now, and even though the posse didn't seem to be getting any closer to them, Longarm knew that was an illusion. They would reach the Sacramentos before the day was over.

The fugitives hadn't gone to any trouble to try to cover their trail. Instead, they had just pushed on as hard and fast as they could without ruining their horses. That told Longarm they had a specific destination in mind and wanted to reach it before any pursuit could catch up to them. That thought brought a worried frown to his face. Gaunt knew what he was doing. He wasn't just running away wildly.

That afternoon, an excited buzz went through the members of the posse when they spotted a cloud of dust rising in the distance in front of them. It had to come from the horses of the men they were after. They were closing in now, and everybody knew it.

A few wooded foothills reared up, and the posse was riding past one of them when Longarm spotted a reflection on top of the hill. The lowering sun had glinted off something metal, and that fact screamed a warning to Longarm's brain.

He was about to call out to Scott and warn the Ranger of a possible ambush when the top of the hill suddenly erupted in gunfire. Shots blasted out at an incredibly rapid rate, and a veritable storm of lead scythed into the posse. Men and horses died as bullets thudded into them. Scott wheeled his big black stallion and bellowed, "Back! Get back!"

Unless he was mistaken, Longarm thought as slugs whistled past him, that was a damned Gatling gun that had just opened up on them from the top of the hill!

# Chapter 29

Several members of the posse toppled from their saddles, blood spurting from the wounds ripped in their bodies by the Gatling gun. The devil gun, the weapon was called by some because of its rapid rate of fire and its deadliness.

Longarm whirled his horse and jammed his boot heels into its flanks, sending it leaping into a run back along the trail. As he approached Raider, he saw that the big man from Arkansas had drawn his Colt and was banging away at the bushwhackers with it.

"Come on, damn it!" Longarm bellowed at Raider. "You can't do any good like that!"

Doc rode up alongside Raider's horse and grabbed the reins, which Raider had dropped. He echoed Longarm's warning, shouting, "Let's go, Raider!" as he tried to tug the horse around.

Raider's six-gun fell silent, but only because he had emptied it and the hammer clicked on an empty chamber in the cylinder. He jammed the gun back in its holster, jerked the reins out of Doc's hands, and wheeled his horse around as slugs from the Gatling gun kicked up spurts of dust around the animal's hooves.

The posse was in full retreat now. At least, the men who could still ride were. Half a dozen or more of them had been spilled from their saddles and now lay sprawled on the ground, their life's blood running out onto the dirt. A couple of men had had their horses shot out from under them but were otherwise unharmed. They grabbed the outstretched hands of some of their companions who were galloping past and were hauled up to ride double.

The trail curved around an outcropping of rocks about a hundred yards behind the site of the ambush. That was a long hundred yards as the survivors lit a shuck for the cover provided by the boulders. Horses leaned to the side and almost fell as their riders whipped them around the tight turn.

Longarm, Scott, Raider, and Doc had been in the front of the group, so they were the last ones to reach the shelter of the rocks. Scott grunted and jerked in the saddle as he rounded the turn, and Longarm knew the Ranger was hit. Scott managed to stay mounted, though, so Longarm didn't know how badly he was wounded. As they all retreated from the line of fire, Longarm looked around with grim awareness that their numbers had shrunk.

He made a quick count and saw that two of the Rangers had fallen, as well as five of the men from Big Spring who had ridden out in search of the reward Corrigan had promised. Dugan was there, although one sleeve of his shirt was red with blood where a slug had creased him, and Riley Hutchins was scared but unhurt. Benjamin Millard was even more terrified as he clung to the back of Doc's horse behind the man from Boston.

Longarm rode over to Raider and Doc and asked, "Either of you boys hurt?"

They shook their heads. "We were exceedingly fortunate," Doc said.

"Pure dumb luck, you mean," Raider said. "We should've knowed they'd have some sort o' ambush set up."

"The question is," Walt Scott put in as he pushed his black stallion up to join them, "where did they get a Gatling gun?"

"You recognized the sound of a devil gun, too, eh?" Longarm said.

"Of course. I've encountered them before." Scott glanced down at his left side, where a crimson stain was darkening his blue shirt. "Looks like one of the bullets nicked me."

Had to feel like it, too, Longarm thought. In fact, a bullet furrow like that had to hurt like blazes. Scott suddenly swayed in the saddle, and Longarm reached over to grip his arm and steady him.

"Better get that tended to before you pass out," he advised. He raised his voice and went on, "You men who ain't hurt grab your rifles and find some places to hunker down in case they rush us."

Dugan frowned and said, "Who're you to be givin' orders, mister?"

"I'm a deputy U.S. marshal," Longarm snapped, "and if you don't want to face charges of hindering a federal officer in the performance of his duties, you'll do as you're told!"

That shut Dugan up, and he and the other men dismounted and scrambled to find places among the rocks where they could fight off an attack. Doc and Benjamin Millard helped Scott down from his horse, and Doc set to work patching up the bullet crease in the Ranger's side. When Doc had ripped Scott's shirt open and exposed the wound, Longarm took a look and saw that while the injury was painful and bloody, it wasn't life-threatening.

Raider scratched at his jaw and said, "Where'd those bastards get a Gatlin' gun? It ain't like there's an army supply depot out here in the middle o' nowhere they could rob."

"Maybe it wasn't them who bushwhacked us," Longarm said.

The others looked at him. "What do you mean by that?" Doc asked. "Who else could it have been?"

"Ever since they left the Box C, Gaunt and the others have acted like they were headed *to* some place, instead of

221

just running away from us. Maybe somebody was waiting to meet them, and it was those folks who ambushed us."

Raider shook his head. "That don't make any sense. How could Gaunt or anybody else in that bunch have arranged for somebody to meet 'em, when they didn't have any idea that whole phony contest was nothin' but a damn trap?"

Longarm couldn't answer that, but he again quoted the old hymn, saying, "Further along we'll know more about it."

Raider grunted. "If we ain't dead."

As soon as Doc had tended to Walt Scott's wound, he moved on to the other injured men, doing what he could for them. One man had caught a bullet in the belly, and it was only a matter of time until he died. None of the other men were hurt too badly, just the same sort of scrapes and nicks that Scott and Dugan had picked up.

The Gatling gun had fallen silent as soon as the survivors were out of sight, and there had been no other sign of the bushwhackers atop the hill. Longarm dug a pair of field glasses out of his saddlebags, found a vantage spot where he could see the hill, and studied it through the lenses. As far as he could tell, the hilltop was deserted now. Nothing was moving, and he didn't see the sun gleaming on metal anymore.

That meant the bushwhackers had either withdrawn from the hill, taking their Gatling gun with them, or they were still hidden up there, trying to lure the posse into the open again. Longarm didn't know which was the case, but he knew that some of the men who had been shot out of their saddles might still be alive. They couldn't be left out there to die if it was possible they could be saved.

"You fellas cover me," he said as he lowered the field glasses. "I'm goin' back out there."

"You're liable to get your ass shot off," Raider warned. "I better come with you."

Longarm didn't waste time or energy arguing. He said, "Come on, then."

The two men mounted up and left the cover of the boulders, riding hard along the trail toward the spot where the posse had been ambushed. No one opened fire on them. They reached the men who had fallen, quickly checked on them, and found that none of the men were alive. They'd been shot to pieces by the Gatling gun.

"Damn it," Longarm grated. "I'd like to get my hands on whoever was crankin' that son of a bitch."

"Maybe you'll get your chance," Raider said. "We ain't turnin' back, are we?"

"That's just what they want us to do. They figured to scare us off with superior firepower."

Raider grinned. "Good thing we're too dumb to scare, then, ain't it?"


After taking stock of the situation, Longarm determined that they still had twenty-seven men in fighting shape, although several were wounded and he was also including Benjamin Millard among that number. Five of the more badly injured men would stay behind to wait out the gut-shot man's dying and also to drag the bodies of the men who had died in the ambush to a nearby ravine where one of the sides could be caved in to form a mass grave.

The others would all push on and follow the trail of the fugitives.

Walt Scott discarded his bloody, bullet-torn shirt and pulled on a clean one he took from his saddlebags. As the sun touched the western horizon, he gathered the men together to address them.

"We're going on, but there's a good chance we'll be riding into another ambush. Anybody wants to stay here, or turn back, there'll be no hard feelings."

"Hell with that," Dugan rumbled. "We want that Golden Eagle and the reward Corrigan promised for it."

If they knew how much the statue was worth, they might want to just keep it for themselves, Longarm thought. On the other hand, these men would have a difficult time getting rid of such an item. They would rather have the five grand in cash, and he didn't much blame them for feeling that way.

Since no one was interested in turning back, the group moved out again. They would stay on the trail until dusk settled down too thickly for it to be followed anymore, Scott decreed.

Everyone was even more watchful for trouble now that they had been attacked once. By the time night fell, however, there had been no more ambushes.

Once again, the posse made a cold camp. The term was especially appropriate that night, because a chilly wind swept down out of the mountains that now loomed over them. They had stopped in an arroyo, which would be safe enough as long as it didn't rain higher in the mountains.

The fugitives and their hostages were somewhere up there, Longarm thought as he looked at the dark, brooding peaks. Now it was just a matter of finding them, getting in alive to wherever they were being held, and getting out again.

Yeah, he told himself, that was all.

They posted guards, of course, with the men taking turns standing watch. Longarm was asleep when he felt a touch on his shoulder and came awake instantly. As his hand closed around the butt of his gun, the man who had roused him leaned closer and whispered, "Take it easy, Long. It's me, Raider."

Longarm sat up. When he spoke, his voice was pitched so low that only Raider could hear it. "What's wrong?"

"Somebody's comin'. Sounds like some sort o' caravan."

Longarm listened and heard the same things Raider had: the soft thud of hoofbeats, the jingle of bit chains, the shuffle of feet. Longarm stood up and catfooted with Raider to the edge of the arroyo. They crouched there where they could look out on the faint trail they had been following.

The moon was still only a quarter full, but it and the stars gave enough light for Longarm and Raider to be able to make out the slow-moving forms of a dozen burros being led by Mexican peons. Eight men on horseback flanked the little caravan, four on each side, and another man rode in front. The riders wore steeple-crowned sombreros, short jackets, and tight trousers with silver embroidery down the legs. Each rider carried a rifle. When one of the peons moved too slow to suit the nearest rider, he jabbed the peasant with the barrel of his rifle and ordered him in harsh border Spanish to pick up the pace; the men who were waiting for these guns would be angry if the shipment was late.

Longarm and Raider looked at each other in the shadows of the arroyo. The caravan was headed up into the mountains, and it was a good bet the burros were bound for the same place Gaunt and the other fugitives were holed up, wherever that was.

"We got to find out what this is about," Raider breathed.

Longarm nodded. "Wake up Doc and the others, but tell 'em to keep as quiet as they can. Just follow my lead."

"What are you gonna do?"

Longarm grinned in the darkness. "Go have me a parley with those fancy-dressed hombres and try to find out just what it is they're up to."

# Chapter 30

Longarm hurried to get in front of the caravan. He darted
through some rocks and then stepped out onto the trail,
holding up his left hand for the riders to stop. He was ready
to draw his Colt if he needed to, but he thought it was likely
the *charros* guarding the caravan would be curious enough
to stop and see what he wanted. As far as they knew, they
were being hailed by a lone man, far from anywhere.

The leader reined in and shouted, *"Alto!"* As the other
riders stopped, along with the burros and the peons, the
leader edged his horse forward and snapped, "Who are
you? What do you want of us?"

"I'm glad you boys came along," Longarm said. "Horse
stepped in a hole and busted its leg. I had to shoot it, so I
was set afoot out here. Where are you bound? I'd sure admire to go along with you, wherever it is."

"We are on urgent business, señor, and we have no time
to deal with you. Step aside."

"Say, that ain't too friendly," Longarm said, letting an
aggrieved tone creep into his voice. "Here I am, a poor,
lonesome traveler in need, and you won't even stop to give

me a hand. Must be a mighty important errand you're on. I'd be glad to give you a hand in return for a ride. Shoot, I'd even ride one of them donkeys."

Longarm could see the burros better now, and he could tell that each of the animals had two long, wooden crates lashed to its back. The guards had said something about guns while they were talking among themselves. Longarm had seen enough crates full of rifles to recognize what he was looking at now. He started toward the nearest burro, apparently innocently.

The leader of the Mexican gunmen tensed and put his hand on the butt of his Colt. "Stay back, señor! If you do not let us pass, may the responsibility for what happens be on your head!"

Longarm raised both hands in the air, saying, "Whoa, whoa there! There ain't no need for any trouble, hombre. I just thought maybe you fellas could let me go with you, wherever it is you're headed. I don't much care, as long as it's out of these parts. You see, I, uh, need to vacate this area as quick as I can . . ."

"The law is after you?" The question came sharply from the leader of the pistoleros.

"You might say that."

The man cursed in Spanish. "*Viejo!* You will ruin everything!"

"Ruin what?" Longarm had kept talking, and kept the gunman talking, to cover up any small noises that Raider and the others might make while they were moving into position. He figured he had stalled just about long enough, though.

"There are important men waiting for us, men who will be unhappy if we do not deliver these guns to them on time—" The boss pistolero stopped short, as if realizing that he had said too much. Again he reached for the gun on his hip, evidently intending to shoot Longarm and be done with it.

"I wouldn't do that if I was you, old son," Longarm drawled.

"Why? Because of the lawmen chasing you?"

"Because of the lawmen who are already *here*." Longarm raised his voice. "Cover 'em, Raider!"

The gunman chuckled as if he thought Longarm was trying some sort of trick, but the next second he froze with his gun still undrawn as more than two dozen men stepped out of hiding in the rocks and brush and trained rifles on the caravan. Longarm said to the nearest peasant, "If any shooting starts, you fellas hit the dirt. We ain't interested in you, amigo." He looked at the leader of the guards and added, "But we'll sure shoot you and your pards to doll rags, hombre."

The pistoleros sat stiffly in their saddles, well aware that if they started the ball, they would all die. Their leader snarled at Longarm, "What do you want, gringo?"

"I want to know where you're taking those guns and what's going to happen to them when you get there," Longarm said.

The man spat and cursed. He was going to remain obstinate.

Longarm sighed. "I was afraid of that. All of you throw down your guns."

"What are you going to do? Torture us?"

Before Longarm could answer, one of the peons spoke up. "Señor?"

"What is it, amigo?"

"Disarm them and give them to *us*, señor. We will find out whatever you wish to know."

The leader of the pistoleros drew a sharp breath and stiffened in his saddle. Noting that reaction, Longarm said, "Why, I reckon that's a mighty fine idea. That's exactly what we'll do."

He didn't think the gunmen would want to experience whatever their former slaves had in mind for them. Longarm didn't know for sure that the peons had been treated in brutal fashion by their guards, but it seemed likely that was the case. And the pistoleros didn't want the kind of retribution that was facing them now.

The leader drew his gun from its holster, moving slowly and carefully, and tossed it on the ground. In rapid Spanish, he ordered the others to do likewise. They did so, and once the nine men were disarmed, some of the posse members moved in and hauled them down from their fancy, silver-decorated saddles.

Picking up on what Longarm was trying to do, Raider drew his knife from its sheath on his belt and held it out to one of the peasants. "Here you go, fella," he said. "You can get to work any time you're ready."

"No!" The exclamation came from the leader of the gunmen as the peon eagerly took the knife from Raider. "We will tell you whatever you want to know."

"That's more like it," Longarm said. "Now, let me ask you again: Where were you bound with those guns, and who's waiting there for you?"

The boss pistolero looked at Longarm and said, "Have you heard of an organization known as the Cartel?"

"What is this Cartel?" Doc asked. "I remember hearing something about a group of international criminals who called themselves by that name, but they were broken up a long time ago."

"I know," Longarm said. "I helped break 'em up. But they're back."

As he, Raider, Doc, and Walt Scott watched some of the other members of the posse bind the hands of the pistoleros they had captured, Longarm explained how he and Jessica Starbuck had stumbled onto the fact that the Cartel had re-formed some months earlier. Jessie, owner of the Circle Star Ranch in South Texas and heir to the vast Starbuck business empire founded by her father, had fought the Cartel to a standstill for several years before destroying it with Longarm's help. Unfortunately, the daughter of the mastermind who had founded the criminal alliance was still alive and determined to restore her father's nefarious organization to prominence.

The leader of the pistoleros, who had admitted to being a smuggler and bandit named Horacio Valdez, was to deliver this load of army rifles, stolen from Fort Bliss down in El Paso, to representatives of the Cartel at an old abandoned rancho in the Sacramento Mountains. What the Cartel planned to do with the guns after that, Valdez had no idea, nor did he care. All that mattered to him was the money he had been promised for the weapons.

Walt Scott said, "What connection could this so-called Cartel have with the hombres we're chasing?"

"That beats me, all right," Longarm said with a shake of his head. "But if that bunch of varmints has a hideout here in these mountains, that's *got* to be where Felix Gaunt and the others are heading. There's just nothing else up here."

"I agree," Doc said, "and I have an idea about how we might be able to take advantage of this situation."

Raider grinned. "That idea o' yours have anything to do with switchin' clothes with them Mexicans, Doc?"

"Great minds think alike, they say," Scott said with a smile.

Longarm nodded, satisfied that the others were thinking along the same lines he was. Trailed by Raider, Doc, and Scott, he went over to the rock where Valdez was sitting with his hands tied behind his back.

"Where were you supposed to go once you were up in the mountains?" Longarm asked.

"We were told to follow the trail we were on now, and we would be met," Valdez replied. Now that he was caught, the smuggler was cooperating. Anything was better than being turned over to the bloodthirsty peons who had scores to settle with Valdez and his men.

Longarm nodded. "That's exactly what you're gonna do. The Cartel's expecting you, so you're going to lead this burro train. But instead of your men, we'll be right behind you wearing their clothes. You play the hand out like you would normally until we get to the Cartel's hideout."

Valdez's pride forced him to summon up one more

show of defiance. "And if I do not, gringo? What if I give you away to your enemies?"

"Then I'll make sure you're the first one who gets his brains blown out, old son."

Valdez glared at Longarm for a moment but finally shrugged in acceptance. There was nothing else he could do.

It was nearly dawn by the time Longarm, Raider, Doc, Scott, and four of the other Rangers had donned the *charro* jackets and tight trousers of the pistoleros. Most of the men were too big and tall for the clothes, but Longarm hoped that wouldn't be too obvious while they were on horseback. The rest of the Rangers and some of the men from Big Spring, including Riley Hutchins, swapped clothes with the peons, pulling on the loose-fitting, light-colored shirts and trousers and settling wide-brimmed straw sombreros on their heads.

Dugan was too tall and redheaded to pass for a peon, but he didn't like the idea of being left behind. "This ain't fair," he protested.

"Don't worry, you're not gonna be left out," Longarm assured him. "You and the rest of the boys will follow us. Stay back far enough so you won't be seen, but close enough so you can come a-runnin' if you hear any shooting."

"What about them?" Doc asked, gesturing toward the prisoners.

"We'll have to leave a couple of men to guard them," Scott said. "Otherwise those fellows they were making handle the burros will probably kill them."

Longarm agreed. Even though Valdez and his men were smugglers, *banditos*, and no doubt killers, he didn't want to be responsible for them being mercilessly slaughtered. He picked out a couple of members of the posse and assigned them the job of watching over the prisoners.

To the peons, he said, "I want Valdez and his bunch to still be alive when we get back, *comprende*?"

"*Sí*, señor," one of the men answered. "Although, by the Blessed Virgin, they deserve nothing more than death!"

"Maybe so, but we'll let the law handle that part of it," Longarm insisted. The peons nodded in agreement.

Raider hauled Valdez to his feet and cut his bonds, freeing his hands. "Mount up, hombre," Raider ordered the smuggler. "And remember, if you try anything funny, one of us will put a bullet through your head."

"I remember, señor," Valdez said. "Believe me, I wish to live, even if it is in one of your gringo jails."

To the east, the orange glare over the Staked Plains told of the sun's imminent arrival as the caravan—now manned by the forces of the law—started along the trail that led higher into the mountains. The red rays hit the tips of the peaks above them, making those mountaintops look like jets of flame spearing toward the sky.

Longarm was still a little stunned by the fact that the Cartel was somehow mixed up in this affair. When Katerina von Blöde was released by the government, Longarm suspected that he hadn't heard the last of her or her criminal ring, but he had hoped that she wouldn't turn up again so soon—or at all.

Regardless, though, he still had to find Felix Gaunt and rescue Anita Corrigan, Katie Weatherbee, and Colleen Gallagher. If some of the members of the Cartel got in the way of him accomplishing that mission, Longarm would just have to go right through them.

That thought was in his head as he rode behind Horacio Valdez, following the smuggler into the rugged mountains as the sun peeked over the horizon and flooded the plains with the light of a new day.

# Chapter 31

One of the things that had puzzled Longarm was beginning to make a little more sense. It was unlikely that Felix Gaunt and the other fugitives would have access to a Gatling gun—but members of the Cartel might. If Gaunt and the others had reached the Cartel's hideout and joined forces with them, the Cartel might have sent men along the fugitives' backtrail with that devil gun to discourage any pursuit.

The ambush had wiped out some of the posse members, true, but it hadn't discouraged the survivors. Longarm had only to glance around to see the proof of that. Raider rode across from him, on the other side of the burro train, and Doc was right behind Raider. Longarm didn't have to look around to know that Walt Scott was directly behind him. Even though the Ranger was wounded, he had insisted on continuing with the mission.

Longarm slouched in the saddle to disguise his height. With his darkly tanned skin and sweeping mustache, he figured he could pass for a Mexican at first glance. The same was true of Raider, and to a lesser extent, Scott. And the more fair-skinned men like Doc could tug down the brims of their sombreros to shield their gringo faces. The masquerade just had to work long enough to get them into the Cartel stronghold.

After that, they would play out the hand however it was dealt.

Valdez's gun had been given back to him, unloaded, of course. The smuggler rode at the head of the caravan, as he normally would. Longarm kept a close eye on him, alert for any signs that Valdez might be trying to warn anyone who was watching their progress into the mountains. So far, Valdez seemed to be playing it straight, but Longarm knew they couldn't count on that lasting.

Benjamin Millard had insisted on being one of the men who donned peon garb. He had a revolver hidden under the loose-fitting shirt. Sometimes a mouse turned into a tiger if the situation was right, Longarm thought as he glanced at Millard. The little fella had some fighting spirit, that was for sure.

The trail twisted and turned through the foothills, then climbed steeply. Longarm knew they weren't far from the huge cave that cowboys and other range riders had learned to steer clear of. The cavern's entrance was located in a little bowl at the top of one of these peaks, and Longarm found himself wondering if that might be where the Cartel had its stronghold. He had been there before, and the gaping black hole looked like the mouth of Hades to him and gave him the fantods, especially in the evening, when hordes of bats flew out of it. At least at this time of day all the bats would be asleep.

As Valdez led the way higher, Longarm became even more convinced that the big cavern was their destination. Before they reached it, though, men with rifles in their hands suddenly appeared on rocks overlooking the trail. Valdez raised a hand in greeting and called, *"Hola!"* The sentries must have been expecting the burro train, because they waved the little caravan on.

It was like sticking your foot in a bear trap, Longarm

thought as they rode past the hard-faced riflemen. The trap might not spring right away, but chances were it would snap before you could get your foot back out of it.

He had no inclination to turn back, though. They would free the women and bring Gaunt and the other killers to justice, or die trying.

Longarm spotted what looked at first glance like a large pile of rocks on a rise ahead of them. He realized after a moment that it was a huge stone house instead. That would be the abandoned rancho Valdez had mentioned. As they drew nearer, Longarm saw that the house overlooked the bowl where the cavern entrance was located. The Cartel had chosen well. The stone house would be easy to defend, and if the situation got really desperate, they could retreat into the bowels of the earth, where it would be almost impossible for any posse to root them out.

Their arrival must have been signaled ahead some way, because a group of riders came out of the house to meet them. Longarm kept his head down so that the sombrero he wore would conceal his features, but he stole glances from under the brim of the big hat. He saw Felix Gaunt riding next to a broad-shouldered gent who had an air of command about him. Longarm had thought that the Outlaw Empress herself, Katerina von Blöde, might be there, but it looked like she had conferred this venture to one of her trusted lieutenants instead.

The thing that really made a shock of surprise go through Longarm was the sight of Anita Corrigan riding beside Gaunt. The raven-haired beauty didn't look like a prisoner. She wore tight black whipcord trousers and rode astride like a man. A red silk shirt clung to her body under a black vest, and a flat-crowned black hat hung behind her head from its neck strap. She even had a holstered six-gun strapped around her hips.

Well, that made sense, Longarm realized as he thought about it. *Somebody* had helped Gaunt and the others escape and steal the Golden Eagle. It might as well have been Anita. He knew that she didn't love her husband—probably hated him, in fact. But she knew him well enough to know how badly it would hurt him to have the Golden Eagle stolen.

And she could have gotten close enough to those Rangers who were standing guard to use a knife on them. The more Longarm pondered it, the more he was convinced that Anita Corrigan had been part of the trouble all along.

He exchanged a glance with Raider and saw the frown of disfavor on the former Pinkerton's face. Raider had seen Anita, too, and probably drawn the same conclusions.

What they had to do now was take Gaunt and the other men prisoner and force them to reveal where Katie and Colleen were being held. Sooner or later, things would probably come down to shooting their way out of there. Longarm was almost looking forward to it. This had been a long, frustrating case, and a part of him was ready for some action.

Valdez reined in when he was about twenty feet from the other group of riders. The other members of the caravan stopped behind him. Gesturing at the burros, the smuggler said, "I have delivered the guns stolen from Fort Bliss as promised, Señor Dodd."

The man who sat his horse next to Gaunt and Anita grinned and nodded. "Good job, Valdez," he said. "Take them on to the house and turn them over to my men, and we'll see about your payment."

"I hope that you and the Cartel you work for will consider me for future employment along these lines, señor."

"We'll look at the guns first," Dodd said. "But I'm hopeful we can make future arrangements."

The riders split into two groups and moved aside so that the caravan could continue along the trail toward the stone stronghold. They were tough-looking hombres, and Longarm spotted several men who had been among the fugitives who fled from the Ranger trap at the Box C. Clearly, they and Gaunt had thrown in with the Cartel.

Longarm glanced at Raider and nodded. When they were between the two groups of gunmen, they would make their move. True, they would be in position to be caught in a cross fire, but the outlaws weren't expecting any trouble and could be taken by surprise. Longarm hoped to get the drop on them before they even knew what was happening.

It might have worked that way, too, if Benjamin Millard hadn't suddenly whipped the gun from under his shirt, pointed it at Anita Corrigan, and yelled, "You thought you could double-cross me and get away with it, you bitch!"

She barely had time to gasp, "Benjamin!" before Millard pressed the trigger. The bullet caught her in the chest and drove her out of the saddle. Her lifeless body thudded onto the rocky trail.

"Shit!" Longarm said. The gunmen had snapped their rifles to their shoulders at their first glimpse of Millard's gun, and it looked like the members of the posse were about to be slaughtered in the cross fire Longarm had hoped to avoid.

But before anybody else could pull a trigger, Dodd bellowed, "Hold your fire! Don't shoot, damn it!" He leveled a six-gun at Millard, who still stood there cool and calm with smoke curling from the barrel of his weapon. "Who the hell are you, mister?"

"I'm Benjamin Millard," the little man said with a note of pride and defiance in his voice. "I'm the one who arranged with Miss von Blöde to deliver the Golden Eagle to her representative, which I assume is you."

Dodd nodded. "That's right. I know your name. But Mrs. Corrigan said you were dead."

Millard sneered. "She hoped that I was, I suppose, the treacherous bitch. She was the one who came up with the idea of stealing the statue, but *I* found a suitable buyer for it and was supposed to get a sizable share of the profits. Then *he* came along." Millard nodded at Gaunt, who glared right back at him. "He knew her when she was nothing but a prostitute in New Orleans—"

Well, he'd been right about *that*, anyway, Longarm thought as he tried to keep up with these dizzying revelations.

"—and he knew she had to be up to something under-handed," Millard went on, "so he horned his way in on the deal. But they were both fools. Neither of them had any idea the whole thing was a trap set up by the Rangers."

"You could've warned us, you slimy little polecat," Gaunt snarled.

Millard laughed. "I preferred to wait and see how things played out. I wanted to see if Anita would betray me. And of course, she did. She ran off with you and the Eagle and left me behind with nothing." For a second, his teeth ground together in rage. "I loved her, you know."

Now it was Gaunt's turn to laugh. "Why? Because she let you into her bed a few times to keep you in line? Hell, you shouldn't be surprised she dropped you as soon as she got the chance. She told me you couldn't even do it right—"

"Shut up!" Millard screamed. The gun in his hand bucked and roared twice. "Shut up!"

Gaunt rocked back in the saddle and looked down in shock and horror at the blood welling from the holes in his chest. "You little—" he choked out, but that was as far as he got before he died and slid from the saddle to thump lifelessly on the ground.

"You *are* a trigger-happy little fella, aren't you?" Dodd said to Millard.

"I'm the sort of man you need working with you," Millard said. "An intelligent man, not simply brutal and ruthless like those two." He jerked the pistol barrel toward the bodies of Anita and Gaunt. "You have the Golden Eagle because of me, Dodd. I laid the groundwork for its theft and contacted your mistress in the Cartel to start with. I assume that's enough to buy my way into your operation."

"That decision's not up to me," Dodd said with a shrug. "But from what I've seen so far, I reckon you and the Empress might just get along pretty well."

"If you need anything to prove my worth, there are these guns," Millard said.

"Señor Valdez brought me those," Dodd pointed out.

Millard snorted in contempt. "Señor Valdez is a fool who allowed himself and his men to be captured by lawmen." The little man waved his free hand toward Longarm. "That fellow is a deputy United States marshal. The one behind him is a Texas Ranger, and so are several of the others. Those two"—He pointed at Raider and Doc— "used to work for the Pinkerton Detective Agency, and the rest of these men are after the reward Corrigan put up for the return of the Golden Eagle. There are some other members of the posse a few hundred yards back. You had better prepare a reception for them, too, since those shots will undoubtedly bring them soon."

Dodd still seemed a little amused by the whole thing. "What do you want us to do with all these gents, Millard?"

"I don't care," Millard said with a shake of his head. "You can kill them for all it matters to me. I just want my share, and to work with the Cartel in the future." He smiled. "Although I wouldn't mind being given the chance to make a closer acquaintance with the other two ladies Gaunt brought to you. I've always been partial to both redheads and younger women."

"You son of a bitch!" Riley Hutchins exclaimed as Millard made his lecherous comment about Colleen and Katie. Longarm wanted to warn the young puncher not to lose his head, but it was too late. Riley leaped at Millard, swinging a fist at the little man's head.

Millard twisted toward Riley, bringing the gun around. But rage had given Riley the speed he needed to close the gap between them, and he crashed into Millard just as the gun in Millard's hand roared. Longarm didn't know how bad Riley was hit, but as they fell to the ground from the force of the collision, Riley was still groping for Millard's throat, trying to get his hands around it so he could choke the life out of him.

"Kill the others!" Dodd yelled as he reached for his gun.

Longarm, Raider, Doc, and Walt Scott all slapped leather at the same time.

If hell was going to break loose anyway, might as well set it free all the way and let it run riot, Longarm thought as dozens of guns exploded with a massive roar.

# Chapter 32

Caught in a cross fire they might be, but the posse members outnumbered the Cartel gunmen who flanked them. And they had Longarm, Raider, Doc, and Walt Scott on their side, too, all of whom were good shots and coolheaded under fire.

Scott was riding his big black stallion. He whirled the horse toward the outlaws as twin Colts sprang into his hands. The long barrels spouted smoke and flame as he raked the bad men with lead.

At the same time, Raider and Doc opened up on the Cartel gunmen, and so did the remainder of the Rangers and the reward-seekers from Big Spring. The men who were dressed as peasants jerked weapons from under their loose clothing. Some of them were hit and slumped to the trail, but several of the killers pitched from their saddles, too. A couple of the burros screamed in pain as bullets found them, and that, along with the deafening roar of gunfire, made the rest of the animals stampede. Normally the most placid of creatures, the burros bolted, adding to the confusion.

Longarm drove his horse straight at Dodd, hoping to take the Cartel lieutenant by surprise. Dodd's gun exploded in his hand, going off almost in Longarm's face. Longarm felt the sting of burning powder against his cheek as the slug screamed past his ear. The next instant, his horse slammed into Dodd's, and both animals went down.

Longarm sprang out of the saddle before he could get trapped under his horse. As he scrambled to his feet, he saw that Dodd had done likewise. Dodd slashed at Longarm's head with his revolver, and the big lawman couldn't get out of the way in time. The barrel caught him a glancing blow, raking along the side of his head and leaving a bloody gash behind. Stunned, Longarm slumped to a knee.

Dodd could have killed him then, but instead the man seized the opportunity to vault into the saddle of a riderless horse and race off toward the stone house. Longarm surged to his feet and saw that his own mount was up again and seemed unhurt. He leaped onto the horse's back, ignoring the stray shots that whistled through the air around him, and took off after Dodd.

It made sense that the prisoners would be in the house, and since that was where Dodd was headed anyway, Longarm dogged his trail. A renewed burst of gunfire behind him made him glance over his shoulder. He saw that the posse's reinforcements, led by Dugan, had arrived. They were making short work of finishing off the rest of the gunmen who had accompanied Dodd, Gaunt, and Anita.

It galled Longarm a little that after following Felix Gaunt for as long as he had, somebody else had gunned down the bastard. But justice had at least caught up to Gaunt, even if it had been delivered by a weasel like Benjamin Millard, and in the end, that was all that mattered.

Longarm figured that the Cartel had quite a few men here. Capturing the stronghold wouldn't be easy, even though the posse had already dealt a heavy blow to the outlaws. Dodd had almost reached the house. As Longarm closed in on him, Dodd galloped through a pair of open wooden gates in an adobe wall around the place.

Men ran to close the gates behind Dodd, but Longarm peppered them with gunshots and sent them scurrying back for cover. That delayed the closing of the gates long enough for Longarm to gallop through them.

Dodd had reached the house. He leaped from the saddle and dashed inside, shouting, "We're under attack! We're under attack!"

Longarm heard the sudden stutter of the Gatling gun. Dust spurted from the ground around his horse's hooves as he crossed the courtyard in front of the massive old house. He looked up and saw flame licking from the revolving muzzles of the weapon, which had been placed in a guard tower built onto a corner of the stone pile. The gunners were about to get the range, and Longarm knew he couldn't stop them with a Colt.

But before the rapid-fire rounds could riddle him, one of the gunners cried out and toppled from the tower. The other jerked back, but before the man went out of sight, Longarm saw the crimson spray of blood from his head as a bullet bored through his brain. Longarm looked around and saw Raider sitting on his horse outside the wall, lowering a Winchester. Longarm touched a finger to the brim of his Stetson in thanks, and Raider nodded. The hard feelings that had caused them to pound on each other a few nights earlier had disappeared.

Cartel gunmen opened fire from the windows of the house, and some of them came running from the outbuildings with guns blazing in their hands. Raider, Doc, Scott, and most of the other men galloped toward the stronghold, firing as they came. Since Longarm was already in the courtyard, he swung down from his saddle and ran toward the open front door of the house. He thumbed fresh cartridges into his Colt as he ran. He figured Dodd would head straight for the hostages, and he wanted to find Katie and Colleen.

A slug smacked into the jamb as Longarm went through the door. He spotted Dodd halfway up a broad staircase on the other side of the entrance hall. Longarm snapped a return shot that chipped the stone wall next to the man. Dodd fled up the stairs with Longarm after him.

A couple of gunmen ran into the hall and fired at Longarm as he started up the staircase. He twisted as the bullets whipped past his head and brought his Colt up to trigger a pair of return shots. One of the would-be killers folded up as a slug caught him in the belly. The other one spun off his feet, screaming as he dropped his gun and clutched at his bullet-shattered shoulder. Both of them were out of the fight. Longarm turned and sprinted up the stairs, taking them two or three at a time.

He spotted Dodd ducking through a door about halfway along the second-floor hallway. Longarm went after him, pausing before he stepped into the doorway. "Give it up, Dodd!" he called. "There ain't no way you're getting out of this, and you don't want to die for Katerina von Blöde."

"Go to hell, Marshal!" Dodd shouted back. "My men will take care of yours, and you can't hurt me unless you want both of these women to die!"

Longarm tensed as he heard a female voice cry out in pain. He moved into the doorway, gun leveled, and saw Dodd standing behind a couple of chairs where Katie and Colleen sat, their hands bound behind them. On a table next to the chairs was perched the Golden Eagle, wings still spread as if it were attacking.

Dodd had one hand holding Katie's long blond hair, pulling on it so that her head was tilted to one side. The gunman's other hand held a Colt pressed to Colleen's head. Dodd gave Longarm a cocky grin and said, "I told you, Marshal. You might as well drop your gun, or I'll pull the trigger and this redhead's brains will be splattered all over the room."

Longarm aimed his Colt right between Dodd's eyes and said, "You pull the trigger and you'll be dead yourself about half a second later."

Dodd must have read the ice-cold determination in Longarm's eyes, because he cursed and hauled Katie out of her chair, pulling her up in front of him as he swung his gun away from Colleen and toward Longarm. The big law-man hesitated, not wanting to fire and maybe hit Katie, and Dodd might have killed him if Colleen hadn't suddenly lunged sideway from her chair and barreled into the gun-man. Dodd pulled the trigger, but his shot went wild. Tangled up with the two women, it was all he could do to stay on his feet. He threw his arm up in an attempt to catch his balance, and Longarm took a shot. His bullet tore through the wrist of Dodd's gun hand, breaking bone and causing the Colt to go spinning away.

Dodd shrieked in a combination of pain and rage. He shoved Katie away, then reached out to grab the Golden Eagle from the table. He swung it at Colleen's head. Remembering how heavy the blasted thing was, Longarm knew it would cave in the redhead's skull if it hit her. He snapped a swift shot at Dodd.

The bullet struck the Golden Eagle instead, knocking the statue out of Dodd's hand. Luck was with Longarm, though. The slug glanced off the Eagle and ricocheted right into Dodd's left eye, where it bored on through into his brain. Dodd folded up, dead before he hit the floor next to the statue he had dropped.

Longarm took a couple of steps into the room, heading for Katie and Colleen. Before he could reach them, a door on the far side of the room swung open. Ned Montayne stepped through it. Longarm fired instinctively at the so-called Kid Montana, but the hammer of his Colt clicked on an empty chamber.

An ugly grin spread across Montayne's face as he raised both of his fancy ivory-handled guns. "Looks like I've got you, Parker, or whatever your name really is," he gloated.

"Easy enough to gun a man down when his Colt's empty," Longarm said. "I would have thought you'd want to know which one of us is really faster, Kid. We can settle it. Let me put just one bullet in this gun. I'll holster it, you holster yours, and we'll find out once and for all."

He had hoped to tempt Montayne, but the young killer

just laughed. "Hell with that," he said as his fingers started to tighten on the triggers. "I want to live."

A shot blasted from the doorway behind Longarm. Montayne was thrown backward by the bullet that smashed into his chest. He hit the wall and hung there for a second, then slid down it with the look of horror on his face being slowly replaced by one of slack nothingness as death claimed him.

"And I want you to die," Doc Weatherbee said as he came into the room with a tendril of smoke drifting from the barrel of the gun in his hand.

Longarm nodded at the man from Boston and said, "Much obliged."

"I was glad to do it," Doc replied. "You don't know how glad."

He holstered the gun and went straight to his niece, helping her to her feet and using a clasp knife he took from his pocket to cut her bonds. Katie threw her arms around his neck and hugged him tightly, sobbing with relief.

Raider followed Doc into the room and took care of freeing Colleen, and she hugged him. From the doorway, Walt Scott chuckled and said, "Looks like you and I don't get hugs, Marshal."

"That's all right with me," Longarm said. He became aware that he didn't hear any more shooting. For a while there it had sounded like a full-scale war outside, with the Gatling gun chattering again. "Just tell me you were able to handle all those Cartel hombres."

"They're all either dead or in custody," Scott replied. "Dugan climbed up into that tower, picked up the Gatling gun, and carried it around while one of the other men turned the crank and shot it." Scott shook his head in awe. "I never saw anything like it. But it sure cleaned out those varmints in a hurry. When they saw that devil gun coming, a lot of them tossed down their guns and threw up their hands."

Riley Hutchins limped into the room with a bloodstain on the right thigh of his trousers. He seemed to be moving fairly well, though, so Longarm figured he was just creased.

He grinned at the young cowboy and said, "Good to see you, son. What happened to Millard?"

Riley looked a little sheepish. "Sorry, Marshal. By the time I, uh, let go of his throat, he was pretty much dead."

"Don't worry about it," Longarm assured him. "You saved somebody the time and trouble of a trial, not to mention a hanging."

Riley tried to look past Longarm. "Is, uh, Miss Weatherbee all right?"

Longarm moved aside. "She's fine. Go over there and ask nice, and her uncle might even let you talk to her."

Riley headed past Longarm toward Doc and Katie. Raider and Colleen were kissing by now. The happy reunions were going on despite the presence of a couple of dead bodies in the room.

"Quite a cleanup, eh, Marshal?" Scott said.

Longarm bent and picked up the Golden Eagle, grunting at the effort required to lift it. "Yeah," he said. "It ain't quite over . . . but almost."

Several days later, Longarm hefted the Golden Eagle again, this time to place it on a table in front of Edmund Corrigan. The wealthy rancher's eyes lit up as he saw the statue. "It looks like you have a reward coming to you, Marshal," he said.

Longarm shook his head. "Like I told you, I can't accept it. Give it to Riley Hutchins instead. He killed the man who masterminded the whole deal."

Longarm had already explained Benjamin Millard's role in things to Corrigan, who now shook his head and said, "I still can't believe that Millard would betray me that way." He frowned. "Wasn't this Hutchins fellow the one you wanted me to give a job to?"

"Yeah, but he can use the reward money instead. Him and Miss Weatherbee got pretty close on the trip back here to the Box C. He's going with her to Boston, and as soon as everything gets squared away there, he wants to buy a little spread of his own somewhere. Katie said she'll come back to Texas with him and marry him."

Corrigan's bushy eyebrows rose in surprise. "Really? That's rather fast, isn't it?"

"Those two young folks are lucky. They figured out what they wanted, and they're not gonna waste any time in going after it." Longarm smiled. "They'll have to do some fast talking to convince Katie's father to go along with that plan, I expect, but Doc promised to give 'em a hand with that. He thinks Riley's just about the sort of fella Katie needs to straighten her out."

And thankfully, Doc didn't know about Longarm's own involvement with Katie. Raider had promised to keep that to himself.

Corrigan ran a hand over the sheen of the statue's gold coating. He hadn't said a word about his wife's betrayal of him or her death. Let him deal with that in his own way, Longarm thought. Anyway, Corrigan was about to get a final surprise.

"There's just one more thing I need to tell you about. During that ruckus in the Cartel stronghold, a bullet hit that statue of yours." Longarm pointed to a place low down on the Eagle's side. "Reckon you didn't notice it yet."

"No," Corrigan said with a frown, "but I'm sure it can be repaired—"

"Better take a closer look," Longarm said.

Corrigan bent over the table and did so, and when he straightened up, a look of horrified surprise was on his face. "That layer of gold can't be more than an eighth of an inch thick!"

"I don't think it's even that thick," Longarm said. "Might not even be real gold. I'd have that looked into if I were you, Corrigan."

"But . . . but I paid good money for this statue!"

"Who handled the arrangements for having it made?"

"Why, Millard did, of course." Corrigan's eyes widened even more. "Oh, my God."

Longarm nodded. "Don't reckon you'll ever see *that* dinero again."

Not surprisingly, Corrigan seemed more upset about being rooked on the statue than he did about his wife's death. Since Longarm's business there was concluded, he left the ranch house. The place put a bad taste in his mouth.

Raider was waiting on his horse in front of the house. He nodded toward the place and asked, "How'd he take it all?"

"Not too good," Longarm said. "He was really upset about that damned Golden Eagle being a fake."

Raider grunted. "Fittin', if you ask me. Ain't nothin' real about an hombre like Corrigan except his money. As long as he's got that, he'll get over anything else."

"You're probably right," Longarm said as he swung up onto his own mount. They walked their horses away from the house. Longarm went on, "What are you planning on doing now?"

Raider took a cheroot from his pocket and clamped it between his teeth. "I ain't made any plans past goin' to Big Spring and gettin' a drink. Might be persuaded to hunt up a pretty gal to drink with me."

Longarm took out one of his three-for-a-nickel smokes and put it in his mouth. "That sounds like a pretty good plan to me," he said.

"Now that I think about it, though," Raider mused, "I reckon I ought to figure out what I'm gonna do from here on out. I don't know much about anything except bein' a blacksmith and a detective."

"Maybe what you ought to do is start up your own detective agency," Longarm suggested. "Give ol' Allan Pinkerton a run for his money."

Raider looked over at him. "You really think I could do that?"

"Why the hell not?"

"Yeah," Raider said. "Why the hell not? With that damned Cartel you told me about startin' up again, the frontier's liable to be more lawless than ever!"

"There's a gal down in South Texas you ought to meet. I got a hunch you and Jessie Starbuck'd get along just fine."

"Is she pretty?" Raider asked.

Longarm just grinned and nudged his horse into a run. Raider gave a whoop around his cigar and followed, and soon both big men were lost from sight as they galloped toward Big Spring.

## GIANT-SIZED ADVENTURE FROM AVENGING ANGEL LONGARM.

# BY TABOR EVANS

### 2006 GIANT EDITION

### LONGARM AND THE OUTLAW EMPRESS
978-0-515-14235-8

### 2007 GIANT EDITION

### LONGARM AND THE GOLDEN EAGLE SHOOT-OUT
987-0-515-14358-4

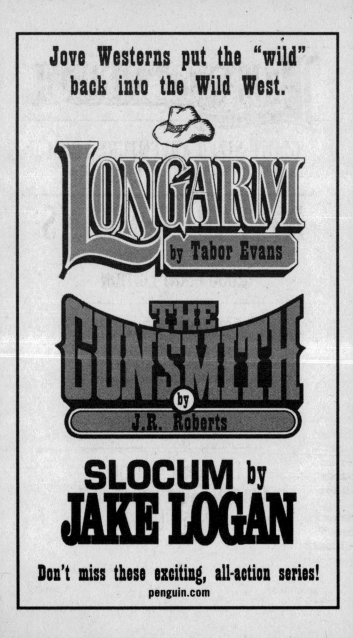